CRY CHAOS

By
DWIGHT V. SWAIN

I0541615

ARMCHAIR FICTION
PO Box 4369, Medford, Oregon 97504

A SWASHBUCKLING OUTER SPACE ADVENTURE!

Gadar, the dark star, had hurled into the solar system and settled into an orbit around the sun over a thousand years ago. It was no longer really a star. It had collapsed upon itself over the eons and had become what was essentially a wondering, dark planet, virtually unseeable to all but the trained astronomical eye. But Gadar and its strange race of silver-haired people held a dread secret that the mighty Gar Shane had to discover before Earth and the rest of the solar system were destroyed. Shane was the leader of the warrior-like people of the asteroid belt, the Chonyas. But when he and his stalwart crew found themselves falling easily into the clutches of a notorious interplanetary drug-dealer, Shane knew that something far more powerful was behind it. Aided by a beautiful slave, he followed the trail from one of Jupiter's satellites all the way to Mars, and finally to Gadar itself, where he was tempted by the beautiful silver-haired Kyrsis, who offered him power and love to betray Earth— and death if he refused!

FOR A COMPLETE SECOND NOVEL, TURN TO PAGE 105

CAST OF CHARACTERS

GAR SHANE

His skill as a warrior was unequaled throughout the asteroid belt, but was his heart vulnerable to the charms of an alien beauty?

TALU

She was a prisoner, a slave with the powers of seduction, but her desire to help Shane didn't guarantee she could be trusted.

QUOS REGGAR

The whole galaxy recognized him for what he was—a vicious, drug-dealing tyrant. Vice after vice after vice were his attributes.

KYRSIS

She was a sly silver-haired woman and an agent of slavery. She was also one of the most beautiful women Shane had ever seen.

DYLAR

He was already an able warrior, but his skills as a technician made him an even greater asset when the going got tough.

THE EARTH DELEGATE

As Earth's representative, he was supposed to be fair and just, but regarding the fate of Shane's people, his mind was a closed book.

CHAPTER ONE

THEY got the great silver ship's hatches pried open, finally, and dragged Shane out by his heels. They dumped him on his face in the gravel and cinders of the ramp like a pole-axed *huecco*.

He wasn't a particularly big man, as men came out here in the spaceways. But there was a spare, hard quality to his close-knit body, and the old scars that marked him told of forgotten battles, bitter fights to the death with no quarter asked or given. Strange suns had burnt him dark as a *Malya*. Mercury's blazing sands, the high deserts of Mars, had dulled the crisp brown of his hair. Faint bluish pockmarks along his left cheek bespoke Pluto and the ice-things that dwelt there.

And the *Chonya* belt still girded his waist; the great iron belt of the asteroids, one link for every chief who'd vowed fealty, eternal symbol of his power as *gar*.

So he lay there in the dirt of the ramp like a dog, while the motley rabble that were his captors gathered round. And because he was the man he was; because of the stories and scars; above all, because of that great iron belt of brotherhood he wore, the token of his might, they hung back just a little, still touched by awe of this fallen great one.

Only then Shane's eyes opened—eyes of that strange, pale blue found only among Earthmen; blank now, unseeing. His fingers scrabbled the dirt. Saliva drooled from the loose mouth and puddled beneath his cheek.

Explosively, a hard faced Venusian *Pervod* laughed. "I claim the belt!" he cried, and sprang forward, reptilian claws gouging Shane's flesh, rolling the Earthman over.

An incoherent, protestful sound rose in Shane's throat. His mouth worked, and his hands batted clumsily at the *Pervod's* claws.

The Venusian's laugh rang out loudly again—harsh, contemptuous. Skillfully, he fended Shane's blows with bony vestigial wings. His claws worked at the boss that clasped the belt.

Shane's blue eyes lost a little of their blankness. The loose mouth drew in a fraction. "No!" he choked, "No!" He clutched at the *Pervod's* wrists; tried to pull them away.

The *Pervod* twisted free. His claws left bloody paths across Shane's palms. Catching the Earthman's shoulders, he lifted him half clear of the ramp, then slammed him down again with stunning force.

Shane lay limp—panting, head lolled to one side.

The *Pervod* unclasped the belt and pulled it free of Shane's body.

Feebly, Shane clutched for the Venusian's ankle, and missed. Shaking, sobbing for breath, he struggled to a sitting position, bracing himself with his arms.

The *Pervod* dangled the belt tantalizingly. "Do you want it, Earthman?" he mocked. "Come get it—quick; while you have the chance!"

Veins stood out at Shane's temples. His fingers dug into the dirt. He brought one leg forward—levered upon it, lurched to his feet, stood swaying.

"The belt of the *Chonyas!*" the *Pervod* shrilled gleefully. "Here it is, *starbo!* The belt of a *gar* for the taking!"

He flicked the belt past Shane's face.

The Earthman lunged for it, staggering wildly. Only collision with the hull of the space ship kept him from pitching to the ground again.

"What? You don't want it?" cried the *Pervod,* sidling closer. "I thought you were *gar* of the asteroids, *yanat*—high chief of the *Chonyas!* Why don't you take your belt?"

Again Shane lunged. But this time the Venusian did not dart away. Instead, he ducked beneath the Earthman's outstretched arms and hurled his weight into Shane's middle.

Shane catapulted backward under the impact and crashed against a heavy-thewed Uranian.

"Not there, *Gar* Shane! Here! This way!" shrilled the Venusian.

The Uranian gave Shane a monstrous shove toward the *Pervod*.

But the Venusian sidestepped swiftly. Shane lurched past him, into the arms of a ghoulishly grinning Martian.

The Martian, in turn, shoved Shane on, sent him caroming off at yet another angle. From one to another they drove him, bouncing him about the ring they had formed like the huge ball in a game of *ha lao*. And all the time the *Pervod* danced and waved the belt and shrieked sadistic laughter.

And then, just once, he came too close.

Like the flash of a meteor, Shane's hand shot out. He caught one end of the belt and let it bring him up short.

His weight jerked the Venusian off balance. Before the *Pervod* could recover, Shane was upon him.

Claws slashing, the reptilian fought to hold the belt.

Only then, at that instant, Shane let go of the precious links of iron. Catching the *Pervod's* wrist, turning as he moved, he ducked between arm and body and levered the arm up behind the Venusian's back.

The brittle reptilian bones snapped with a sound like the crackling of an angry fire. The *Pervod* shrieked in anguish.

The crowd stood frozen in stunned, unbelieving silence.

Shane caught the end of the iron belt and flicked it out in a loop that circled the *Pervod's* scaly throat. Then, one end in each hand, he whipped it tight.

The Venusian's scream cut off in mid-breath. His legs, his unbroken arm, flailed desperately.

But Shane stayed behind him, out of reach of the murderous claws, drawing the belt ever tighter.

The *Pervod* sagged.

The crowd's paralysis broke. The air rang with shouts. Beings from a dozen far-flung planets rushed forward.

The muscles in Shane's arms and shoulders bulged. Belt-ends still tight in his hands, he spun about, dragging the Venusian with him, elbowing the others out of the way. Faster he turned, and faster...faster, till he was whirling like some monstrous gyro-top, the body of the *Pervod* swinging in a giant arc beyond him, clubbing the other raiders down.

They scrambled back as fast as they'd come, the laughter, the mockery, dead within them.

Shane let go one end of the belt. The *Pervod's* body shot out like a stone from a sling, the head half torn from the torso.

Dizzily, the Earthman lurched to the space ship and braced himself against it. Then, very deliberately, he slung the belt about his waist and snapped the clasp. The blue eyes flamed, no longer blank. Knots of muscle stood out at the hinges of his jaws.

"Who *dares* to try and take the iron belt of the asteroids?" he shouted at the rabble ring that hemmed him in.

No one moved. No one spoke. Shane swept them with cold, contemptuous eyes. "Scum!" he spat. "Scum of the spaceways! Carrion, one and all!"

But he swayed as he said it, and his face showed white beneath the tan.

"Scum..." he repeated in a voice gone dead, and pitched forward, unconscious, to the ground.

CHAPTER TWO

THE walls and floor and ceiling and door of Shane's windowless cell had the cold green glitter of pure telonium.

So did the handcuffs and leg-irons that shackled him.

But the bare metal cot hinged to one wall was of steel.

Telonium rated harder than steel, seventeen-point-seven times harder. Its tensile strength figured nine times greater...

Even so, it took Shane most of the night to tear loose one of the cot's cross-straps, using the locking lug of the leg-irons as combination pry-bar and cutter.

The cross-strap measured about two inches wide by two feet long. It had the weight and striking edge to cave in the skull of a Uranian *dau.*

Shane laid it down beside him on the cot, and waited for someone to open the cell door.

After awhile faint whispering sounds of motion drifted in; then a clicking noise.

Shane turned so that shadow half hid his face. He twisted his body in a semblance of restless sleep, and closed his eyes to lash-shuttered slits. His fingers caressed the cross-strap mace.

The door opened. The doorway framed a burly, tentacled Thorian guard.

Then the guard stepped aside and a woman came past him, into Shane's cell, carrying a small, cloth-draped tray. Young and straight and slim, she moved with a *tara's* grace. Her high, firm breasts were bared in the *Malya* fashion, and the dark loveliness of her face was *Malya* also. Glistening blue-black hair hung clear to her waist in softly rippling waves.

Closing the vault-like door behind her, she crossed the cell to Shane's side; paused there for a few moments, looking down at him.

Shane lay very still.

"*Gar* of the asteroids, high chief of the *Chonyas*," the woman said softly, almost to herself. Her voice held a note that might have been weariness, or pain. "You've traveled far, Earthman...so far, to have it all end here."

She moved on to the stand that flanked Shane's cot and busied herself at her tray for a moment. Then, straightening, she held a hypodermic injector up to the light. It contained a colorless liquid. Deftly, she set the screw, adjusted the high-pressure gas ampule that would spray the injection straight into the bloodstream without breaking the skin.

Shane twisted a fraction further around on the cot. His breathing was careful, measured.

Turning, the woman bent over him. She poised the injector, close to his throat.

Shane's manacled hands shot up. He caught the woman's wrist; twisted sharply before she could jerk away.

She gave a sharp little in-drawn cry of shock and pain and came down hard on her knees, lithe body writhing. The injector fell from her twitching fingers.

Shane's heel smashed it into the floor. Already, he was up and off the cot, forcing the woman down onto it.

He said tightly, "The first scream breaks your arm, *Malyalara!*"

"A *Malya* does not scream, *Sha* Shane!" she answered through clenched teeth.

She tossed her head as she said it, proud even through the pain, and for the first time the right side of her face came into full view.

And along that whole right side, someone had cropped the glistening black hair short, square with the temple, in the ugly, outlawed badge of slavery.

For a long moment Shane did not move. Then, slowly, he drew back a fraction and relaxed his grip on the woman's arm.

Some of the tightness left the lovely face. She rose in a single smooth, supple movement. No fear showed in her dark eyes, even now. Rather, they probed boldly—eagerly, almost—as if measuring Shane's metal.

"What do they call you, *Malyalara?*" he asked.

"My name is Talu, *Sha* Shane."

"You wear your hair cropped like a slave's—"

"—Because I am a slave."

"The Federation banned slavery."

BITTERNESS twisted the woman's mouth. The midnight eyes burned with the fierce, blazing anger that had made her people the scourge of the void within the memory of living man. "I tell myself that every day, *Sha* Shane. But it does not free me."

Shane's lips drew thin. "Has it been long?"

"About an Earth year. I was of Hidalgo. First, the slavers sent in *theol*-smugglers. They sought out our leaders—"

"I know," Shane nodded grimly. "*Theol* breaks the will. Not even a *Malya* can fight with the hunger for it in him." He broke off. "And then, *Malyalara...?*"

"Then the slave ships came. What else?" Again Talu's ripe lips took on the bitter twist. "They came by the score— whole fleets of them, blasting and killing and hunting us down. The Federation had taken our proton batteries and our fighting ships away, and *theol* had broken the men who should have led us. So they stripped Hidalgo bare—every man, every woman, every child..."

Shane's fingers dug into the slave girl's arms. "But where did they send you?" he demanded fiercely. "Who wants slaves, in a solar system where power is broadcast free to all planets? What use is there for labor?"

"I do not know."

"My *Chonyas* have been raided, too. But why?" Shane clenched his fists. "Why raid for slaves, when machines can handle any task? Where do they take them? Are they here, in this place?"

Talu shook her head. "No, not here. This is only a

ramping-spot—some small moon the slavers have taken over. But I have seen a woman here, a silver woman—Kyrsis, they name her." A momentary tremor rippled through the *Malyalara*. "She is evil…more evil than words can tell. They say that she is the agent for those who buy. But where she comes from, why her people seek slaves—that I do not know."

"And who serves her? Who is the raider, the *starbo* whose wolf-pack gathers in the slaves?"

"His name is Reggar, Quos Reggar—"

"Quos Reggar!" Shane spat the name as if it were an epithet. "Slaver, smuggler, scum!" He twisted violently against his shackles, blue eyes blazing. "I should have known! I drove him out of the asteroids once—"

"—And he remembers, *Sha* Shane," Talu said softly. "He remembers, and he hates you, and he swears the day will come when you shall pray for death. He has gathered up the scum of the spaceways, the dregs of the void—"

"You mean he captured me only for vengeance?" Shane broke in. "He dragged me here just to kill me…"

TALU shook her head. "No, *Sha* Shane. There is more than vengeance. He has plans for using you, great plans. But that is all I know."

"But how did he capture me? How did he bring me here?" A haunted, haggard shadow flickered across Shane's face. He raised his manacled hands and held his head in them. "I was on a mission, an…important…mission, traveling through space. There was no sign of trouble. And then, all at once, the void went mad. It was a nightmare; I can't remember what happened—" He broke off, shaking his head as if to clear away the fog of memory. Then his hands fell, and his eyes met the girl's once more. "The next thing I knew, I was coming out of it on the ramp, with dirt in my mouth and a *Pervod* at my throat. And I still don't know how I got here."

"It was a projector, they say. A Paulsini projector, focussed on your ship. They captured your minds with it— yours, and all your crews'."

Shane stared at her incredulously. "A Paulsini that can reach out into space and take over a ship...? You're mad as a *ban.*"

"They say it is the strongest Paulsini mind control beam the universe has ever seen, *Sha* Shane," Talu replied. "It was ten Earth years in the building. The power output would send a spaceship beyond the stars."

Shane's eyes narrowed. "The strongest Paulsini beam the universe has ever seen..." he repeated slowly. "It tells something, *Malyalara.* No common slaver ever had the brains or time or money to take on the building of such a machine as that." Thoughtfully, he stared down at his fetters. "And what happens, now that I'm here?"

"I do not know."

"You do not know?" Shane studied the woman's face. "Yet you came here, alone, with an injector, and tried to use it on me."

The other's hands moved in a small, helpless gesture. "The guard was to have done it, *Sha* Shane. But I was there when Reggar gave the order. I had heard of you so many times. I wanted to see you..."

"What was in the injector?"

The girl shook her head. "I do not know. They do not trust me to know too much."

"They do not trust you?" Shane's eyes probed hers while the seconds ticked by. He flicked the shattered remnants of the crushed injector with his toe. "But they let you come to my cell alone." The faintest of edges crept into his voice. "And they kept you here on this moon with them, Talu, and sent the rest of your people on across the void to slavery."

For a long moment Talu stood motionless as some dark statue. Then, all at once, she began to tremble. Her eyes struck sparks. The bare breasts rose and fell too fast.

"Yes, they kept me," she whispered tautly, fiercely. "A woman can often find a place here...for a time."

She swayed forward, and in that instant she seemed suddenly all passion, all temptress. Her body brushed Shane's. The warm, half-parted lips invited him. He stood rigid at the very nearness of her.

Then she drew away once more, and her face had the look of graven stone. "I have made it my business to be kept here, *Sha* Shane," she said icily. "My body is good, and *Malya* blood runs hot, and even slavers can lose their caution. So I stay, and earn what trust I can, and do such work as brought me here. For my grandfather was Toran, the last great *Malya* raider chief. He taught me the old way, the *Malya* way—that blood cries out for blood. I live for the day when my chance will come, and I can let my knife drink deep from the heart of the monster Quos Reggar, who set the slavers on Hildago..."

Grim-faced, Shane studied her. "You say the words, Talu," he clipped, "but will you prove it?"

"Prove it—?"

"The *Chonya* chiefs gave me a belt—the great iron belt of the asteroids, the symbol of my power as *gar.* I swore an oath when I took it...an oath that the *Chonyas'* blood and tears would be my own."

Wordless, the woman watched him, her face a mirror of mixed emotions.

"They have taken my belt away, Talu, these slavers who raid *Malya* and *Chonya* alike. They have locked me here like a berserk *vrong,* and thrown the key away. But my oath still stands. The *Chonyas* made me *gar* because I knew how to fight, and feared no man. So I'll fight here."

The fierce eagerness crept back into Talu's face. Her hands clutched his. "Yes, yes… But what can you do?"

"I'll carve my way, *Malyalara*. I'll give them blood for blood and tears for tears, till the asteroids breath free again!" The ring of steel on steel was in Shane's voice. His face was carved with rocky lines. "You told me that a *Malya* does not scream, Talu. But if you *were* to scream, just once, would that slimy Thorian guard outside pay heed?"

She caught her breath. "And…if he did…?"

Shane smiled a thin, hard, ruthless smile. "Even in leg-irons I can drag myself to the door." He bent over the cot and pulled free the broken cross-strap; slashed with it so it sighed and whispered through the air. "It sings a song of death, Talu…"

The woman's midnight eyes burned murder—bright. Her voice was a breathless whisper, "Strike hard and straight and fast, *Sha* Shane…"

CHAPTER THREE

"NOW…" Shane clipped. The slave girl screamed shrilly, piercingly.

Shane poised, the cross-strap mace drawn back and ready.

A dim whisper of running feet echoed from the corridor outside. The lock clicked sharply. The door burst open.

Light-gun already drawn, the Thorian guard lunged into the cell.

Shane swung the steel.

The Thorian's eyes flicked to the Earthman in the same instant. Desperately, he tried to halt his headlong plunge—to throw himself sidewise, out of the way.

He moved too late. The steel struck home. The end bit in along one side of the Thorian's bulbous head. It made a moist, explosive sound, like the bursting of a melon hurled onto pavement. Vile, gray-green sludge gushed forth.

The Thorian's great body jerked in a tremendous, threshing spasm. The light-pistol, still clutched in one tentacle, needled a wildly-gyrating purple beam close past Shane's shoulder, then cut off again and clattered to the floor. The body went limp and lay still.

Shane dropped to his knees and clawed up the pistol. Twisting, he brought its muzzle close to the hobbling leg-irons. His finger triggered the exciter.

The purple beam lanced forth. The leg-irons' green telonium links took on a weirdly luminous glow.

Somewhere in the distance, a faint, humming sound arose.

Talu said, "Hurry! That noise—it is the guard-car!" Tension echoed in her voice.

Muscles stood out along Shane's neck. But he still crouched motionless, the light-beam rock-steady in his hand.

The humming sound grew louder.

"Hurry…" Talu whispered again in a tight, choked voice.

The telonium links were twisting now—writhing, almost, beneath the pistol's ray.

"Ten seconds more!" Shane clipped.

The leg-irons fell apart.

THE Earthman straightened. His lips were drawn to thin lines. "This guard-car—how does it come?"

"It moves up and down a shaft between the floors; then through the corridors. The Thorian must have rung the alarm as he came—"

"Where will it stop? Here, at this door?"

"No. It is set for the guard-post, down the corridor to the left—"

Shane pivoted. Ignoring the manacles that still held his wrists, he stepped swiftly from the cell.

Here, in the corridor, the humming was like that of a

swarm of angry bees. Far off to the left, red lights winked in the dimness.

Talu caught her breath. "The guard-car!" she cried.

Shane broke into a run—left down the corridor, straight towards the oncoming lights.

"No! No, *Sha* Shane—!"

"The guard-post—where is it?"

"Just ahead. There, to the left—"

The post proved to be a mere niche in the wall, a sort of oversized sentry box with cot and chair and table.

"Under the cot!" Shane snapped.

"But they will trap us here…kill us…"

The red lights were growing ever brighter now. The humming had risen to a low-throated roar. Roughly, Shane forced the *Malya* down and under the cot, then crawled in beside her himself.

"They will trap us…" Talu said again, and the tension in her voice vibrated like a taut-drawn wire. Yet, strangely, her tone held no fear, no panic, only a sort of fierce, throbbing exaltation.

"They'll trap us like lambs trap a lion!" Shane slashed back harshly. His blue eyes burned with a reckless fire. "Would you have us play the sheep—stand back there in the cell and be slaughtered? No! We'll meet them here, where they don't expect us. And if we die, some of them will go along."

Talu's full lips parted. Her laugh came, low and throaty. "You speak like a *Malya*, *Sha* Shane! My grandfather would have been proud to have you raiding with him."

The guard-car braked to a halt abreast them before Shane could reply. A panel in its metal side slid back. Two Martian *falas* and a hairy, heavy-thewed Uranian sprang out.

SHANE triggered his light-pistol's exciter. The purple beam slashed through the dimness, straight to the breast of the first Martian.

A shrill scream of awful anguish burst from the creature's throat-sac. It leaped high in the air, then fell back again, a nerveless, dying heap.

The Uranian and the other *fala* whirled.

Shane lanced out the beam again. It took the top from the second *fala's* misshapen skull.

The Martian was dead before he hit the floor.

But now the Uranian had light-pistols in two of his four huge hands. A beam seared through the cot. Another burned a smoking path along the floor.

Shane surged to his feet, carrying the cot with him like a massive shield. The muscles of his back and arms and shoulders stood out. With a mighty effort, he swung the cot clear of the floor and hurled it broadside at the Uranian.

The hairy behemoth jerked up his two free hands to ward it off. But a tangle of falling covers got in the way. The cot's weight and impact rocked him.

Shane blazed through the cot.

Sagging, the Uranian lurched back against the car. The acrid stench of his burning flesh billowed up in choking waves.

Only then, instead of falling, he lunged forward. Barely in time, Shane leaped aside, lancing in beam after beam.

Blindly, the Uranian charged past him, with no attempt to turn. Straight ahead the creature lunged on, towards the guard-post's rear wall...the vocodor and the row of communication control switches below it.

"The alarm—!" Talu cried shrilly. She darted forward.

Shane caught her wrist and threw her bodily but of the way.

The Uranian crashed against the wall. One great hand swept the whole row of switches down.

An alarm bell jangled deafeningly.

The Uranian half-turned, as if to taunt them. Then his muscles, his joints, seemed to give way. He toppled forward…struck the floor with an echoing thud.

Shane spun about. His eyes sought Talu.

She stood pressed flat to the guard-post's wall now, dark face aglow with an excitement that was mingled with something close akin to panic. "The bell—"

"Forget it! Come on!"

Together, they raced for the glittering metal guardcar.

Shane sprang aboard. "Hurry!" He caught the slave girl's hand and helped her to clamber in after him.

Here, inside, a control panel studded with switches and dials and pushbuttons was set chest-high in one wall. Above it, a narrow, slot-like vision port of transparent silicon extended nearly to the top of the car. A series of charts, displayed beneath sheets of clear plastic cross-hatched with grid lines, flanked the port on either side.

Shane slammed shut the door. He pushed Talu to the instrument board. "Quick! The controls—how do they work?" The very clipped steadiness of his voice rang with urgency.

"It is simple—"

A red spark glinted in the vision port.

Shane froze to the slot. "Another car—coming this way, fast!"

Talu threw a switch. Her fingers flashed over the buttons.

Vibration shook the car.

Talu threw another switch.

With a rumble and roar, the vehicle began to move. Lights streaked past the vision ports, faster and faster.

Shane let out breath. "They're falling back!"

The dark girl pressed more buttons. The car jerked and changed direction, till it had veered from its former course three times. The lights of their pursuer disappeared. The car moved out onto a straightaway once more and picked up speed.

Talu turned. "Where now; *Sha* Shane?"

The Earthman laughed—harshly, without mirth. "The top is always the place to start, *Malyalara*. If you want to kill a snake, cut off its head."

The woman looked at him with a sort of wondering awe. "You mean…Reggar?"

"I mean Reggar!" Shane echoed. His mouth twisted. "They say he cuts a figure when his raider ships come in on a helpless *Chonya* town. We'll see if he looks as bold when someone's hunting him…"

"But by now he knows you have escaped. He will be waiting—"

"He may, or then, he may not. Most men Reggar has captured wanted only to get away."

The girl turned back to the controls. Again, the car veered, and again.

ONCE more, she faced the Earthman. She said, "Give me the light-gun now, *Sha* Shane. We must burn off your shackles while we have this chance."

Shane threw her a bleak smile. "You ride pressure well, *Malyalara*."

The girl's slim shoulders lifted in a shrug. "My grandfather said that pressure proved a man, *Sha* Shane." Already, the light-gun's purple beam was eating at the handcuff links.

"And Reggar…?"

"I have set the controls to take us to him. Five minutes will do it, if we are not cut off by his cars."

"But if we are…?"

"We still may find a way. There are twelve levels here, more corridors than can be counted."

"Yet all on a slavers' moon? All Reggar's?"

"I do not know, *Sha* Shane. But Reggar is here; no other."

The last link holding the handcuffs broke. Talu straightened. "It will not be long—"

With startling suddenness, a bell clanged overhead.

"The crash alarm!" Even as she cried out, the girl punched frantically at the control buttons.

The rear vision slot caught a gleam of red lights—dangerously close already, rushing at them headlong.

Barely in time, their own car veered right at an intersection.

The breath went out of Talu. Her knuckles stood out white beneath her skin.

Overhead, the collision bell clanged again.

This time, the other car hurtled out of a side passageway, cutting them off. Desperately, Talu manipulated the controls. They backed to the nearest cross-hall and fled down it as fast as the car would go.

Talu said, "They are hemming us in, *Sha* Shane. Reggar has guessed your thoughts."

Shane's hand knotted about the light-pistol's butt. "Can we still break clear? Is there a way?"

"If we could get to another level—"

"Try it."

The girl's breath seemed to come a fraction faster. Her eyes caught the same reckless glint as Shane's. Her fingers flicked at the buttons.

Their car swung right. Ahead, a blank wall came rushing to meet them.

"A shaft," said Talu. Her voice shook just a little.

JUST when it seemed that they must surely crash, the car slowed. Then, swiftly, they were dropping straight down, cushioned on a beam of force.

Three levels down, Talu threw a switch. The car swept out of the shaft and down a passageway.

The collision bell clanged.

Talu punched buttons.

Again, the bell.

More buttons.

Red lights, hurtling towards them. "…another level…" Talu whispered.

They climbed a shaft at dizzying speed; rushed off through another corridor.

The bell. Buttons and switches. The bell again.

"They are hemming us in!" Talu choked. A ragged, desperate note had crept into her voice. "The corridors ahead are all dead ends."

"Reggar…?"

"His quarters are not even on this level. Here there is only Kyrsis, the silver woman."

"Kyrsis…"

The bell clanged. The girl pressed a final button.

Weariness, strain, defeat, were in her face. "We are trapped, *Sha* Shane. I am sorry…"

Shane's eyes were hot upon her. He laughed—a wild, fierce laugh that matched the reckless lines that carved his face. "Trapped? Not yet, *Malyalara;* not yet…"

She stared at him in blank bewilderment.

"How do you reverse the car, *Malyalara?*"

The girl pointed to the button.

The bell set up new clamor. Red lights blazed in the rear vision port.

"Jump, Talu!" Shane threw the brake-switch.

She flung back the door; leaped wide.

Shane jammed down the reverse button and sprang after the girl. He sprawled against the corridor wall as the empty car roared back towards their pursuer.

The other car's gears clashed in screaming protest. It shuddered under the braking action.

But too late. Shane's guard-car crashed into the other. The thunder of impact mingled with shrieks, and the scream of rending metal.

"Come on!" Shane cried. Light-gun in hand, he raced towards the wreck.

A third guard-car was already drawing up as they reached it. The panel door opened, and a lone *Pervod* leaped out.

Shane killed him with one slash of the light-beam.

Talu pulled herself up into the car and ran to the control board. The glow of excitement was back on her face once more. "Which way?" she cried.

The reckless glint in Shane's blue eyes was brighter than ever now. "Turn it loose and let it run for a decoy," he said tightly. "Our work just now is here."

For a moment the girl stared at him, confusion written in her face. Then, wordless, she set the controls.

Together, they leaped clear. The car thundered out of sight.

Still unspeaking, Talu turned back to Shane once more, a hundred mute questions in her glance.

Shane chuckled. "We'll visit the woman," he said, "the silver woman, Kyrsis."

The girl's dark eyes went wide. "No! No, *Sha* Shane—!"

"Yes! Reggar's hemmed us in and tied us down. He thinks we're beaten. So now, we strike again, where it will sting and hurt the most. And where better than at his market, this Kyrsis?"

"Please, no—" The girl was pleading now.

"Yes!" the Earthman came back sharply. His voice took on a darkly brooding note, and his face set in rocky lines. "She is the key, *Malyalara*. She is the one who buys slaves in a universe where power is free. I'm going to ask her why."

CHAPTER FOUR

THE DOORS WERE protected by rigid barriers of projected force, and the light-pistol burned out before Shane had quite finished cutting through the wall. But he had taken a long knife from the dead *Pervod* in the third guard-car. With it, he finished the job.

So finally they were inside, crawling through an ever-murkier blackness while the silence hammered at them like a living thing.

And then, suddenly, out of the ebon stillness, a voice said, "Welcome, Earthman…"

A man's voice, this—or at least a voice not of woman—not loud, but harsh and alien; not thunderous, but vibrant with savage power.

"Welcome, Earthman," the voice repeated. *"Welcome to death!"*

Shane flung himself sidewise. He crashed against some piece of furniture. The burned-out light-gun clattered to the floor.

The voice mocked, "Can you not see me, Earthman? And your pistol—why do you not pick it up? Does the darkness get in your way?"

Somewhere—very far away, it seemed—Talu whispered raggedly, *"Sha* Shane…*Sha* Shane…"

Shane said, "Here, *Malyalara*. This way." He groped over the floor as if feeling for the now-useless pistol; slipped and fell flat, and under cover of it, slid the *Pervod's* long knife out of view beneath his jacket.

"Shall I give you light, great *gar?*" the voice taunted. "Shall I let you see me now?"

Shane's moving hand touched the light-pistol. His fingers gripped it—but flat to the floor, not lifting it. Muscles flexed, he poised, eyes probing the darkness. His voice echoed defiance, "Show yourself if you dare, *starbo!*"

"If I dare—!"

Like a quirst striking, Shane hurled the pistol at the voice.

The missile struck home with a meaty thud. A choked oath slashed the blackness.

SHANE lunged forward. But he crashed into more furniture and fell again. Before he could rise, lights blazed.

For the fraction of a second Shane froze. Then—very slowly, very carefully—he turned and pulled himself to his feet.

Talu was already up—breathing too fast, a hand at her throat. Her dark eyes were wide and set, riveted on an open doorway in the opposite wall.

A strange figure loomed hulk-like in the shadows there—a gaunt, rawboned giant in the *vree*-leather garb of the space rovers, with a light-pistol hanging ready in one webbed hand.

Yet this was no ordinary wanderer. The difference stood out in line and stance—a weird note of deviation that caught the eye instantly, even in a universe where bizarre and norm were one.

And about the waist was drawn a great iron belt…Shane's belt, the belt of the asteroids.

Shane sucked in air.

The figure brought up one hand in a peremptory gesture of command.

Weapons poised, a half-dozen guards moved through the doorway. Nondescripts, being drawn from the backwaters of strange planets, they fanned out in a silent, menacing arc before Shane and the slave girl.

Wordless, cold-eyed, Shane stared them down. They halted, hesitating.

Now the giant in the doorway stalked forward, clear of the

shadows.

Numbly, almost, Talu took a dragging step towards the hulking goliath, then another…another…

"Out of the way, *Malya!* Let him see me!" The very repression that echoed in the giant's words was infinitely more fearsome than roars or rantings. A webbed fist lashed out backhanded at the slave girl, and the force of the blow sent her careening almost to Shane's side. "Remember me, Earthman? Remember?"

Shane did not move. He did not speak.

The creature standing there walked on two legs like a human. It's thumbs were opposed. It spoke through its mouth instead of a throat-sac.

BUT the great lobed eyes that saw in the dark were pure *Fantay*, and the scaly roughness of the mottled skin was *Pervod*. The bulge of the skull went with Mars; the peculiar, pad-footed stride with the swamplands of Io. Hybrid, mongrel, the thing was a queer, off-trail mixture of all the races of Mars and Earth and Venus, and the gods of the far stars knew where else.

And there, at its waist, hung the belt of the *Chonyas*.

"I remember," Shane said. "You're Reggar, Quos Reggar—the slaver, the *theol*-peddler." Deliberately, insultingly, he spat on the floor. "Or are you running light-guns to Mimas this time?"

The creature that was Reggar chuckled, but the sound held no mirth. "Your memory's good, you *chitza!* Maybe it even goes back to the days when you passed the word through the spaceports that you'd feed my heart to the *kiavis* if I ever ramped ship in the asteroid belt again."

"I said it; I meant it." Shane's eyes were bleak. He stood unyielding, jaw out thrust, and his words slashed. "When the *Chonya* chiefs came in and struck their banners and picked me, an Earthman, as *gar* of the asteroids to lead them, I swore on the starstone of Hiaroloch that I'd stop scum like you—"

"Only now I'm back," Reggar cut in harshly. "I'm bigger this time, Shane; big enough to make up for all the years I've had to stay away. My fleets are stronger than yours, and my brain is better. Today, when you broke free and fled, I said to myself, where would the Earthman go? What will his first thought be? And I know the way you think so well that I was here in Kyrsis' rooms before you!"

"So?"

"So I've taken your belt, and now I'm going to take your *yodor Chonyas*, too. I'll hit the asteroids, one after another, and clean them out, till there isn't a *Chonya* anywhere left free." The great lobed eyes glittered balefully. The alien voice struck a deeper note. "And you're going to help me, Shane."

"You're mad as a *ban,* Reggar," Shane said tightly.

"Mad? You call me mad?" There was a sort of obscene glee in the other's chuckle. "Is it mad to strive for power, great *gar*—the kind of power you've held these years? Is it mad to hunt slaves for a market that pays triple prices and begs for more? No…that's why I brought you here—"

"Here or a million miles across the void, what makes you think I'd help you?" Shane slashed savagely. Beneath the jacket, his fingers caressed the hilt of the *Pervod* knife. "For that matter, how could I help you? Do you see the *Chonya* chiefs as such fools that they'd follow me into your net, no matter what I said or did?"

THE creature before him grinned hideously. "It won't be as hard as you tell it, Shane. The trick is to split the Federation—and there is where I need you."

"The Federation…?"

"Your acting falls short of your memory, Earthman. Your secret conference on the slave raids—I know about it. You should have been there by now; the meetings start tomorrow. When you don't appear, there'll be talk about the *Chonyas* and *Malyas,* and how they always were slavers till the Federation beat them down."

"You talk nonsense, Reggar," Shane said curtly. But suddenly his mouth seemed a trifle dry.

"Do I?" The alien voice rang with a note of dark triumph. "I have friends, Earthman…friends so respectable, so high-placed, that they would not admit that they even so much as knew my name. But they have their price, and so they still play my game. They will be there, at the conference. They will cry out that the *Chonyas* and *Malyas* are behind these raids as in the days gone by."

"And when we deny it?"

"You'll have no chance to deny it. Reports will come in— confirmed reports that say the Earthman, Shane, great *gar* of the asteroids, has gone the *Chonya* way. That he, himself, is leading raiders, sweeping the lesser moons for slaves."

Bleakly, Shane stared at the creature. His fists clenched spasmodically, and knots of muscle stood out at the hinges of his jaws.

Then that, too, passed.

"A lie is a lie, Reggar," he said tonelessly. "Someplace, sometime, it always breaks down."

"But there will be no lie, great *gar,*" the other mocked. "The reports will speak the truth. For as you say, a lie breaks down, and this is one time I dare not chance a gamble. So you will be out there in the void, in a *Chonya* raider ship. I myself shall supply it. A wild *Chonya* crew will man it, drawn from the dregs that you cast out of the asteroids when the chiefs came in and named you *gar*. Shane the slaver, the worlds will call you."

"And then?" clipped Shane.

THE note of triumph in the mongrel's voice rose higher. A scaly fist came up, in a gesture that spoke of arrogance and power. "Chaos will sweep the void, Earthman—and I shall sweep the asteroids! The fools in the Federation will hang deadlocked for a time, for some still fear war more than they fear raiders. So long as that deadlock lasts, the void is mine! The *Chonyas* have given up their war fleets; they cannot strike back. Yet no matter how they cry of raids and beg for mercy, no one will believe them. My friends will talk of their pleas as stratagems to lure out the Federation fleet. And when at last the deadlock breaks and the warheads roar down on Ceres and Pallas and the rest—why, what will it matter to me? For by then my slavers will have taken the last *Chonya* off and stripped the last rock bare!" The creature paused; hammered the two webbed hands together. "A well-laid plan, is it not, Earthman? Can you find even one small flaw?"

Shane stood motionless for a moment. Then, slowly, his lips twisted into the ghost of a smile. "Yes, Reggar. I find one."

The other eyed him curiously, with an air that might have been a sort of repressed mirth. "And that one, great *gar...?*"

Shane said, "The flaw is me. For your plan to work I must go along. That leaves a decision in my hands—a choice. And I've already made it, no matter what you say or do. I'll have no part of your schemes." His jaw set. "You should have known that without my telling you, Reggar."

The mongrel nodded. Again, the strange note of mirth was in him. "Of course. I did know. As for choices—there are three, not two."

"Three choices—?"

"Three. The first, you may already know. We focussed a Paulsini beam on the ship that was carrying you to the meeting on the slave raids. The frequency of the impulses in your brain was changed. My will became yours. I forced you to come here."

"Yes?"

"It is your first choice. You know the pain when your brain's frequency is forced to change. But if you insist, I shall use it—take control of your body, send you out to raid as I would."

Shane breathed deeply. "And the second?"

"That is even better. You know what happens to a man whose blood has three times tasted *theol?*"

"Yes."

"I sent the woman…" Reggar gestured to Talu. "…to you with an injector. It held *theol…*a special high-potency solution. If you wish, you shall have the three full doses I'd planned for you. After that, I can send you anywhere without fear, for the *theol* will break your will like any other, and you'll do the things you're told to do and always come crawling back for more, and more, and more."

Shane shifted. He flicked a glance to Talu.

SHE had not moved from the spot where she had fallen. Dark eyes unfathomable, face expressionless, she lay there, following Reggar's every gesture.

"Do my choices hit you so hard you cannot speak?" sneered Reggar. "Surely the great Shane would not crawl like an *etavi,* even before he hears my third offer?"

Shane folded his arms and met the creature's glare. His hand clenched on the hilt of the hidden knife. "There's been no groveling yet, Reggar. For my part, there'll be none. Get on with your babblings…"

"I like this third choice best of all," the other said, and his voice now was almost silky. "It is so simple, too. You raid as a slaver under me; of your own free will, you do my bidding—that is all."

"All…?"

"Your word is good across the void, Earthman. I, too, trust it. Pledge me on your soul that you'll serve me as faithfully and well as you know how, take my interests as yours, and you shall leave here as free as any man who ever breathed."

Again the hideous grin split Reggar's face. He rocked with harsh, horrible laughter.

"Do it, Earthman! I beg you, do it! It would be the sweetest revenge of all—you, Shane, *gar* of the asteroids, turning slaver to save your own worthless skin! You, the legend, the man without fear, crushing down your precious *Chonyas* rather than walk the other paths I've offered! Your name linked with mine, your fate in my hands by your choice—"

"One question, Reggar…" Shane broke in. Under cover of his folded arms, he drew the *Pervod* knife half clear. His weight was on the balls of his feet, now; his muscles ready.

"What…?"

"Will your loot buy back your soul from hell when the maggots are eating through your brain?"

"What?"

SHANE'S voice rose to sudden thunder, "Armor your heart, too, Reggar! The *kiavis'* teeth are sharp, and I swear they'll feed on you and the scum that ride with you! I'll see you dead, and your head will rot on a pike at the gates of Ceresta—"

The mottling on the mongrel's face turned livid.

"You want chaos, Reggar? Cry chaos, then! Because if chaos comes, your death comes with it! The *Chonya* war fleet will hunt you down—"

"You *starbo!*" roared Reggar.

He lunged at Shane.

Talu, the slave girl, cried out.

The guards rushed forward.

Shane moved like a leaping tiger. The knife was out, his muscles flexing. A shout of wild triumph rose in his throat.

Again Talu screamed.

Something struck Shane behind the knees—a heavy impact, hard and low.

He lurched—off balance, toppling. His blow went wild.

The next instant Reggar smashed him in the face. The knife flew out of his hand. A guard sledged him from behind.

Shane crashed to the floor. Desperately, he jerked up knees and elbows; twisted, trying to shield himself from Reggar's savage kicks.

His hands slapped another body sprawled against his—the body that had knocked him down. His fingers knotted in silken hair.

Spasmodically, he jerked.

A woman's sharp cry of pain rang out in answer.

It was Talu.

CHAPTER FIVE

THIS ROOM WAS large and luxuriously furnished with the treasures of a score of satellites and planets. Here were rich tapestries from Orlon, a thousand blinding years in the making. Here, a table from Rhea, aglitter with the inlays of the spider men, delicate as the traceries of frost. Great *borvne* crystals from the pits of Neptune had been transformed into lamps, their cold fire blazing like the play of sun on glacial ice. A priceless Grecian vase from Earth, older almost than time itself, created a world of its own in one corner.

But it was the woman who held all eyes...the silver woman.

She came forward now, a strange, shining creature. Her

beauty was a breathless thing—ethereal, almost unreal. The cunningly fashioned toga of silver cloth she wore matched the spun silver of her hair.

Yet her hair's silver could not have been that of age, for her skin still held the fresh glow of youth, though uniquely translucent and silvery itself—nearly as pale and clear as the bodies of Pluto's bloodless ice-things.

As if in studied contrast, her lips gleamed rich purple, more blue than red; and a hundred striking violet tints glinted in her eyes.

Even over the vocodor, her voice had a strange, alien lilt, as if her thoughts, her words, strained the unit's powers, "You...you are the Earthman—the *gar* of the asteroids..."

She came close to Shane as she spoke—very close, until the fragrance of unknown flowers rose in his nostrils. Her pale hands touched his cheeks, and the violet eyes probed his.

They were strange eyes, as strange as the worlds had ever seen—young and clear as a girl's, yet somehow old, too...old as the void itself; and the things that were in them sent queer tremors rippling through Shane like a chill. It was as if the woman were looking beyond the things that others saw— probing deeper, searching for some precious secret element that only she could grasp.

"You are strong, Earthman," she said softly, and now her voice held a throaty urgency, an undertone that might have told of inner tension. "There is life in you...much life. It flows hot in your veins..."

"He is not for you, *Shi* Kyrsis!" Reggar rasped harshly. "Our trap needs bait, and we cannot spare him."

THE hands drew away from Shane's cheeks. The woman turned, and her violet eyes grew big and dangerous, "you cannot—?" she asked, her voice even softer than before. "Who says you cannot, Reggar?"

"*We* cannot, *Shi* Kyrsis," Reggar answered. One webbed hand moved in an angry, incisive gesture. "We, the two of us, you and I. I cannot, because without him to serve as cover, the Federation will sooner or later have my head. And you cannot, because without me there will be no slaves."

The woman's hands cupped, as if the long, purple-nailed fingers held some priceless goblet. "But life is a sacred thing," she whispered. "It runs so strong within him…"

"It runs stronger than you know," Quos Reggar slashed back bitterly. "He is a legend, a madman who has carved his destiny across the void." He slapped the great *Chonya* belt that girded him. "Do you think that weakness won this belt? He is built of blood and iron. Even I confess it, though I hate him. But you cannot let yourself think of that now. For he must live, and he must raid, and he must be seen, if we are to break the power of the Federation and open up the void to slaving. Trust me, I know…"

Shane said, "I once knew a man who trusted Reggar. They were partners together in their dirty business, and as thick as thieves could get. When my blockade—"

"Shut up!" roared Reggar.

"When my blockade drove the slavers out of the asteroids, these two were trapped off Juno…"

Reggar sprang at Shane—webbed hands clutching, great lobed eyes aflame.

But the silver woman, Kyrsis, came between them. Gently, she said, "I'll hear him out, Reggar."

Shane smiled thinly. "When I ordered the pair of them to surrender, Reggar, here, came to me secretly, and offered to send me the partner's head if I'd let him—Reggar—go on a promise that he'd never ramp ship in the asteroid belt again. I agreed, and he brought the head."

"You *chitza!*" screamed Reggar. With agility amazing for his size, he leaped past the woman called Kyrsis.

Shane tried to dodge, but the guards who flanked him seized him.

Reggar struck him across the mouth.

Shane slumped back. He would have fallen but for the guards.

Then the woman's voice came—sharp, ice cold, "I would not do that again, Reggar, if I were you...if I wished to live!" And then, to Shane, "Is there more?"

Blood trickled from Shane's mouth. He swayed, and a crooked grin twisted his swollen lips. "Only one thing, *Shi Kyrsis*," he mumbled. "The partner was Tas Reggar—this creature's brother!"

"He lies..." snarled Reggar. "He lies in his teeth like the *chitza* he is. I have no brother—"

"Perhaps not—now!" Shane baited. "How could you have? You sent me his head in a sack!"

A sound of incoherent fury bubbled in Reggar's throat. The great lobed eyes were flecked with red. Again he sprang at Shane.

But again the silver woman came between them. The violet eyes were probing, thoughtful. "The story has a ring to it, Reggar—a twist that somehow fits you."

The other's mottled face contorted. The webbed hands clenched into fists. "It is a lie," he snarled thickly. And then, in a voice that still trembled with repression, "I have no brother. I had none. But even if the tale were true, what difference would it make? We are here, together..."

Shane said, "What difference? For one thing, it would let her know whose neck would stretch, whose blood would spurt, if the time again came for you to make a choice. You'd cut her throat and save your own—"

"Silence!" roared the giant mongrel. He pivoted to face the woman. "Can you not see this *yodor* Earthman's goal, *Shi Kyrsis*? Is it not plain enough that he seeks to brew distrust between us, in the hope that out of it he can snatch a chance to break us both, and save his hide and his beloved *Chonyas?*"

Slowly, the woman nodded. "Perhaps...yes, probably."

"And is there anyone but me who'll bring you slaves by the thousands?" Reggar pressed on, relentless. "Where else can you find these lives you're seeking?"

The woman made no answer.

"But why?" Shane cut in fiercely. "Where is your home, that you still need slaves? Work is for machines, and power is free. Why throw away living beings upon it?"

The silver woman stared. "You mean—you do not know—?"

"No! Quiet," choked Reggar. "Have you gone mad, *Shi* Kyrsis? This man would destroy us. He must not know."

The silver woman looked from the mongrel to Shane and back again. "Then...how do you plan...?"

QUOS Reggar shrugged. "The *theol* will make him ours. Three injections, spaced one Earth day apart, give the habit." He turned and leered at Shane. "Do you know about *theol,* great *gar?* Have you heard what it does—how it paralyzes the will of even the strongest?"

"I know," Shane answered bleakly. "Call it madness, not habit. It works on the brain a hundred times worse than wormwood—and a thousand times faster."

"You live for it," the, mongrel nodded, chuckling. "Night and day, you dream of it, they say. You'll steal for it, fight for it, kill for it. With every dose, you need it more. And nowhere is there a cure."

Shane said nothing.

Reggar gestured to the guards.

They caught Shane's arms once more and held him rigid.

Reggar drew an injector from inside his tunic, then a bottle. Quickly, he filled the needle and inserted the gas ampule.

Still Shane stood silent, stoney-faced.

Kyrsis said, "Why must you have it this way, Earthman? Give your sworn word that you'll serve us, and Reggar will put away the *theol.*"

"I'd rather take the *theol,*" Shane answered tightly.

"But why, Earthman? Why?"

Shane's laugh was bitter, curt. "It is a thing you would not understand, *Shi* Kyrsis. On Earth, they call it conscience."

A shadow seemed to pass across the silver woman's pale, lovely face. The violet eyes were suddenly uncertain. "I—I do not know…"

"And you never will," Shane answered. Coldly and contemptuously, he met her gaze. "But the time will come, I promise you, when you'll know that I did not lie about Reggar—that no matter what he says, you cannot trust him. Even now—here, today, this very minute—he is planning to betray you."

"But how…?"

"Why bother to tell you more? You would not believe me. But when the day arrives, say to yourself just once, 'I had my chance; the Earthman warned me'."

"Hold him tight," Reggar warned the guards angrily. "The *theol* will put an end to his mumblings…"

He came close to Shane. A webbed hand twitched the Earthman's head. The injector poised close to the suntanned throat.

Shane went completely limp. Dead weight, he sagged loose in the guards' hands.

They swayed under the drag of him; shifted, trying to regain their balance.

Shane writhed in a savage, spasmodic effort to break free. He kicked hard at Reggar.

But the guards' hold held. Reggar twisted out of the way

of the kick. He jerked Shane's head around by the hair.

"It ends here, *chitza!*"

Face contorted in ghoulish triumph, he drove the injector's plunger home.

The *theol* sprayed into Shane's throat...

CHAPTER SIX

THEY were singing in the dungeons—a wild *Chonya* song that had echoed down through the reckless years since that fateful day when the first great raider ship blasted off from the asteroids across the void:

'Oh, they've hunted us for ages. Through the Belt and to the stars;
They have sought advice of sages. And they've set up puppet gars. But
there's Chonya blood within us.
And when Chonyas take their stand,
There'll be blood upon the hatches
And a blight upon the land!"

"My whole crew?" Shane asked tonelessly.

One of the Martian *falas* of the escort nodded.

"Then why bother with me? They can tell you as much about the ship as I."

The *fala* shrugged. But a *Pervod* snarled, "The fools will do nothing without your orders—not even tell us which are the technicians. We broke the captain's back, but still he refused to explain the mechanism."

Shane's blue eyes grew cold as the pits of Neptune. "He's dead, then?"

"Yes, and so will the rest of them be, unless you tell them to obey."

"I'll give them their orders," Shane answered curtly. The muscles were standing out along his jaws.

They moved on, into the dungeon's outer room, where crowding *Chonyas* shouted their hate and shook the bars…

A crewman with a bloody bandage about his head leaped onto a bench and, pointing, cried out, *"Gar Shane!"*

The singing died away.

"Your first trick is your last!" the guard in charge snarled in Shane's ear. Roughly, he shoved the Earthman forward.

Shane strode through the settling silence. Wordless, he looked about him—at the glittering, unbreachable, green telonium walls; at the lean, tough horde of *Chonya* crewmen, pressing hot-eyed and intense against the bars; at the guards who flanked and backed him, light-guns out and lance-prods ready.

HE swung back till again he faced the *Chonyas*—took a step or two with a reckless swagger. His back was stiff, his head unbowed.

In a hard flat voice he said, "These slavers who hold us here want full technical data on the Abaquist meteor repellers on our ship. Already, they have broken your captain's back because he would not give it to them."

The silence echoed.

"We were brought here with our minds locked in the control of a Paulsini beam. Through it, these *starbos* can drag out our innermost thoughts—force us to do their will. They would use it on us now, if they could. But they have insulated this whole satellite against it, so. It is useless so long as we are here."

Still there was no sound, save for the restless scrape of feet, the rustle of heavy breathing.

"We are their prisoners, utterly and completely. They have even taken away the belt your chieftains gave me…" Shane ran his hands along his waist. "…the *Chonya* belt, the great iron belt of the asteroids."

The scraping and rustling grew louder. A low, guttural rumble ran through the crowd.

"They say they'll cut us down if we do not obey them, and they've smeared their hands in your captain's blood to prove it!"

From somewhere in the back of the crowd, a *Chonya* shouted, "Where do you stand, *Gar* Shane? What would you have us do?

"I?" Shane swept them with his gaze. "I? What would you have me say? We are their prisoners, are we not? They have conquered us, even if by a trick. We have no choice but to do their will...for now." He paused; laughed harshly, cynically. "Were I to tell you otherwise, I, too, would die within the moment—and we all know it."

The captive crew flung back his bitter laughter. The first flush of hate was washed from the fierce faces, replaced by narrowed eyes and calculating glances.

Shane called, "Repeller crew—forward!" And then, quickly, "Orshawn...Dylar...Hebza...Tisban...Korch..."

MEN pressed through to the bars. Without waiting, Shane wheeled to the guards. "Here are your men...the repeller crew itself. They will give you everything."

A *fala* shoved him aside, against the bars of the cage. A Mercurian threw the lever that controlled the lock.

Barely audible, one of the *Chonyas* whispered, "*Gar* Shane! You know—?"

"—that the repeller is fully automatic? That there is no crew?" Shane bared his teeth in the caricature of a smile. His eyes were very hard and bright. "Yes, *Chonya*; I know."

Now the crewmen that Shane had named were out. The door of bars clanged shut again.

A Thorian caught the Earthman by the arm. "Get on! And if these dogs of the asteroids do not tell us and Quos

Reggar wants to know, both you and they will die by inches!"
He cuffed Shane towards the dungeon's entrance.

Shane reeled ahead, half falling, and the guards laughed at
the sight of him; and one booted him from behind so that he
nearly sprawled on the glistening green telonium floor. But
he clutched the outer door and recovered, hanging by the
edge of it as it swung on its hinges till he was almost into the
corridor beyond.

Only two guards remained there, both *Pervods*.

The fire in Shane's cold blue eyes burst into wild, singing
flame. Suddenly the laxness left his face. The awkwardness
fell from his stance.

"Now, Chonyas!" he shouted.

In the same instant he whirled and shoved the great door
open with all his might.

The edge caught the first of the guards behind him, a *fala*,
full in the face.

Shane leaped upon the creature as it staggered. He caught
the barrel of the thing's light-pistol and wrested it away.

With a hoarse cry the guard sprang after him, clawing for
the weapon.

Rock-steady, Shane triggered the exciter. The pistol's
purple beam struck the *fala* full in the face. Still clawing—
clawing in the agonies of death now—the creature lurched
backward.

Beyond it boiled a scene of strange, wild carnage. The
Chonyas of Shane's mythical "repeller crew" had leaped upon
the other guards—tearing away weapons, beating them down.

Now one wrenched the ray-key that activated the locking
lever from the Mercurian and slammed it home. The bolt
that held the door of bars lifted.

With a wild roar, the *Chonyas* inside the cage burst forth.

The *Pervods* in the corridor beyond the dungeons rushed to
bar the great outer door.

Shane blasted the first before he had even crossed the threshold.

The second turned to flee.

The Earthman's light beam caught him in the middle of his first step.

A *Chonya* came running, a bloody lance-prod in his hands, eyes blazing with excitement. "*Gar* Shane! What now? The ship…?

"You know where it is?"

"Yes. Close by here—"

"No matter. Get the men aboard and man the guns. Blast all the corridors but one. I'll need that to get back to you."

"But where…?"

"There's a job to do before we leave, if we're not to be dragged back here as we were before."

"The Paulsini…!"

"Right!" Shane laughed harshly. The sheer joy of battle shone in his face. "They'll expect us to blast off the instant the crew's aboard."

The *Chonya*'s eyes gleamed fiercely. "You'll need help…"

"Three men, and a guard to guide us…"

The *Chonya* laughed aloud. "Two others and a guard, *Gar* Shane! I am the first!" he cried, exulting.

Commands crackled, then, and other crewmen crowded forward; and in brief seconds Shane and the *Chonyas* and a bloody-headed, bewildered Uranian were roaring down the echoing dimness of the corridor in a guard-car.

Then, on the Uranian's order, they changed direction, and now they were hurtling through vast, high-ceilinged chambers where giant machines stood row on row in countless thousands. No living being was anywhere evident…only the machines, churning endlessly at their task with cold efficiency.

"Converters!" Shane muttered, half beneath his breath.

"Power converters… A different kind, one I've never seen before."

"Nor I," a *Chonya* technician at his side echoed grimly. "Who needs such power today, *Gar* Shane? And the source—where is it? It would take whole seas of energy to feed these monsters. There are too many!"

"Too many," Shane nodded. For a long moment he peered through the vision slot in silence, then backed away again. "A slaver is a slaver, Dylar. Some are small, and some are big. But this is too big for any slaver. The whole surface of this moon is covered with a rabbit-warren such as this, twelve levels deep. We find power converters by the million—more than a major planet could use, even in the days before the Federation began to broadcast free power to all."

Another of the *Chonyas* broke in now. "The Uranian says the Paulsini lies just beyond the next stop, *Gar* Shane—and his fear runs too high for him to lie."

Shane studied the great, hairy beast through narrowed eyes. "Is there a guard?" he clipped.

The Uranian shook his head jerkily.

"Get ready, then!" the Earthman rapped. Again his eyes sought out the Uranian, and after a moment he gestured towards him. "Shove him off first, and then land running."

The guard-car slowed.

Shane shaded his eyes and studied the dim spaces ahead through the vision port, the light-pistol ready in his hand.

Then the car was swaying, grinding to a stop. Two of the *Chonyas* pushed the Uranian towards the door.

But before they reached it their prisoner suddenly sprang aside. He caught one of the crewmen and hurled him bodily through the doorway by brute strength.

OUTSIDE, the corridor was suddenly laced with lances of

purple light. A scream of anguish choked off in the *Chonya*'s throat.

" A trap!" the technician, Dylar, cried. He jerked back levers on the control panel, and the car lurched forward again.

The Uranian lunged for him.

But Shane was already pivoting. He fired as he moved, and the great beast slammed to the floor, its four mighty arms flailing in a death-spasm.

"Stop the car!" Shane shouted.

Dylar threw a switch. The vehicle's mechanism shuddered and went dead.

"This way!" the Earthman snapped. He leaped to the corridor and ran back towards the Paulsini station. The *Chonyas* followed, close on his heels.

More of Reggar's men were there, clustered about the body of the fallen crewman. Then the sound of running feet reached them. They whirled.

Not even breaking stride, Shane blasted at them. Hastily, they fell back into a doorway, the same doorway from which they had loosed their barrage at the guard-car.

The Earthman moved in close to the left wall, out of their range of vision, and crept closer.

Abruptly, a purple beam lanced past his head, so close he could feel the searing heat of it. He jerked back against the crewman behind him.

"It's a stalemate till we can think of something," he clipped savagely. "They can't move, but neither can we."

The *Chonya* laughed. "Dylar will take care of that!" he chortled gleefully.

Like an echo, the now distant guard-car roared to life again. The next instant it was racing towards them.

Shane and the *Chonya* pressed back against the wall.

The car hurtled past them. A light-beam slashed from it

as it came abreast the doorway where the guards were huddled.

There was a flurry of motion and hoarse shouts of panic.

Shane and the other *Chonya* moved in.

The last of Reggar's men sought to flee. But the technician, Dylar, cut them down.

Then Shane was bursting into the place where the great Paulsini mind-control projector was housed.

IT was an awesome sight, a shaft that seemed to stretch away to infinity overhead. And in its center stood the incredible Paulsini tube, that infinitely delicate electronic unit that was the heart of the projector, core of the whole weird device that so deftly changed the frequencies of the waves within men's brains. A gigantic tube, almost unbelievable, so large that it staggered the imagination.

Even Shane stood half-incredulous as he stared up at it.

"It must be a hundred feet tall," he said numbly. "No wonder they can reach out into space…"

Dylar nodded. "Yes. The whole center floor of the shaft is a huge lift, a hydratomic elevator to push the tube up into the air above this structure that covers the surface." He pointed a quivering finger. "See! There is a great lid capping off the shaft! No doubt it is linked to the lift mechanism so that it opens as the tube rises…"

Behind them, the other *Chonya* suddenly slammed shut the corridor door. "Guard-cars!" he called tensely. "A whole line of them, headed this way!"

It broke the spell of Shane's fascination.

"Our only hope for getting away from this moon alive is to smash this projector," he quipped tightly.

"And that means—smash this tube," Dylar answered. "Any other thing that we might do could be repaired."

Shane strode to the tube; hammered savagely at the

transparent silicon with his light-gun's butt.

"It is no use," the *Chonya* technician told him grimly, "a tube as incredibly huge as this one will stand up against anything smaller than a proton cannon. It has been designed for strength—to handle power...temperature changes... shock and impact...the sheer weight of its own structure." He shook his head. "I fear we've come here for nothing, *Gar* Shane. No efforts of ours can hope to smash this."

Bleakly, Shane stared at the monster tube...at the glittering metal of the lift on which it stood...at the great shaft, rising high above them to the cap of the dome.

The *Chonya* at the door said, "They're unloading here by hundreds, and they've brought enough equipment for a siege! When they start moving in, there'll be no stopping them."

Dylar's eyes flicked swiftly about the shaft. "There may be another way but—"

"No!" Shane snapped. His jaw was hard. He brought up a clenched fist; shook it grimly. "We came here to smash this thing. We're going to do it." He turned on his heel and ran to the nearest door. "Come on...we've got to find the control room!"

"The control room—?"

"Here! This is the place..." It was a windowless cubicle, but with a second door set opposite the one by which Shane stood. He scanned the massive control panels, the complicated dials and instruments. "Quick...how do you start the lift?"

Outside, the other *Chonya* called, "They're coming! I'll try to hold them." His voice was a trifle ragged.

"The lift?" Dylar stared at the Earthman. "But why...?"

"Forget 'why'!" Shane slashed fiercely. "Quick! Show me..."

The technician scanned the maze of instruments. "This must be it! See...here is the linking mechanism that couples it to the shaft cap, so that the top opens as the tube rises."

Out beyond the shaft, something crashed. "They're trying to smash in the door!" the crewman there shouted, "There—! I got him!

Shane whipped up his light-pistol. Face etched with strain, he focussed the beam on the linking mechanism. Wires gave way.

Dylar stared.

Gears twisted under the heat of the beam. A shaft snapped.

"Start the lift!" Shane clipped between clenched teeth.

"Of course!" cried Dylar. He threw switches.

"Here they come!" the *Chonya* outside shouted.

The next instant, his voice bubbled off in a scream. Shane leaped to the doorway, lanced a beam of light as a tentacled Thorian came into view. The creature slid back out of range.

The Earthman shot a glance at the Paulsini tube.

Smoothly, silently, it was rising, climbing swiftly towards the top of the shaft.

A *FALA* hurled a lance-prod at Shane. It grazed his ribs. The sting of it hurt. Cursing, he dropped to one knee and triggered a beam at the Martian.

"It's almost there!" Dylar cried. Shane risked another glance.

Even as he looked, the end of the tube reached the dome. For an instant it seemed to hesitate there. Then, with a faint groaning as of machinery under strain, it thrust on again...harder...harder...harder...

The machinery of the lift groaned louder.

"Watch out!" shouted Dylar.

Shane leaped back in the same fraction of a second that the great tube burst. The noise was like a thunderclap. It was as if the tube had exploded in mid-air. Shane glimpsed a

Uranian racing towards him, and knew that he had waited too long, that he could never bring his pistol up in time; then saw the hairy thing reduced to a bloody pulp by a great shard of blast-driven silicon.

It broke the paralysis that gripped him. He caught Dylar's arm. "Come on! Quick! To the ship!"

"Through that horde in the corridor?" The technician shook his head. "No, *Gar* Shane. You have performed a miracle—but not even you can travel that road."

A woman's voice said, "Then come this way."

Shane and the *Chonya* whirled.

She stood in the shadows of the control room's second doorway—a slim, shining figure in a toga of silver cloth.

Shane said, "Kyrsis—!"

"Yes. Shane." Her voice still had its strange, alien lilt. The rich purple lips parted in a smile, and she reached for his hand. "Come quickly. I shall take you to your ship."

"To the ship?" Shane stared at her blankly. "But why—?"

"Why?" She laughed softly, and now there was mockery in the violet eyes. "Why not, Shane? It is the only way you can hope to escape this moon of madness. And the reason I help you to escape is—I want you to take me with you…"

CHAPTER SEVEN

Now they were hurtling through the utter blackness that was space, away from the bleak moon that had been their prison. To port, Jupiter loomed monstrous, overwhelming, its great Red Spot weirdly aglow with seas of flaming hydrogen that seethed and boiled amid gigantic ice-cliffs carved from frozen gases. On the other side, Ganymede and Callisto swung slowly in their orbits; and beyond them, dwarfed by them, tiny Jupiter IX raced through the sky in the counter direction.

A navigator said, "The place they held us is Jupiter V—the satellite closest to the planet. The manuals say it is abandoned now. But it was built up as a power station by the Jupiterian entente in the days before the Federation began to broadcast energy."

"And now Quos Reggar holds it," the mate echoed. "What is your command, *Gar* Shane? Shall we ramp at Europa and report it?"

Bleakly, Shane stared into the visiscreen. Gadar, the dark star, hurled across the void into the solar system a thousand years ago, was coming into view now, the faint silver gleam of its profile barely visible.

"Or we could try Callisto," the mate went on. "They would notify the Federation unit stationed at Europa—send out patrols—"

"No," Shane said, "No. We'll go on to Federation headquarters, the Martian meeting. The things we have to tell will mean more there."

Abruptly, he turned and left the pilot room, and made his way to Kyrsis' quarters.

She came to his knock, and a glow of pleasure suffused her pale, silvery face at the sight of him. "Enter Shane…" The cool fingers touched his hand, drew him in. The violet eyes clung to his, as if in the sharing of some precious secret.

He closed the door behind him; breathed in deeply. "Why did you choose to come with me, Kyrsis?"

The rich purple lips curved and parted. As always, her eyes seemed to mock him. "How many times have you asked me, Shane?"

"How many times…?" he echoed, and now his voice had a bitter ring. "I wish I knew. But I still have no answer." He strode to the visiscreen across the room and snapped it on with an angry flick. Stared broodingly into it.

Gadar was almost to the screen's center now.

SHANE said, "You're like that dark star, Kyrsis. What men can see is beautiful—but beneath the surface you're both all mystery. Where did you come from? Where are you going? And why? I always come back to that one question: why, why, why?"

She came very close to him then, and what might have been sorrow was in her face, her eyes. "I've told you, Shane. To me, life is a sacred thing...more sacred than you can ever dream. To see it wasted as yours would have been is the sin above all sin. And there was Reggar. After you'd told me the things you did, how could I believe him? How could I trust him? I had to get away from him, and quickly. If I could do it and save you, too, would I not have been a fool to throw away the chance?"

He turned on her. "But where is your home—your moon, your planet? Why do your people need...slaves?"

She shook her head sadly. "I am sorry, Shane...truly sorry. But those secrets are not mine to tell...unless..."

"Unless what?"

"Unless you are willing to travel with me...to take the road Quos Reggar took." Again her hand was on his arm, her silvery body close to his. A note of tension crept into her voice. "Because we need slaves, Shane! You cannot know how desperately we need them. Nor is it hard. They do not suffer..."

For a moment the Earthman stood there with her, and her hand left his arm and came up to caress his cheek. "If you would but learn to understand us...there is so much to learn."

Shane swayed a little. His blue eyes dulled, and his breathing was shallow, uneven.

The woman's eyes mirrored indefinable things, things old beyond all measure.

Shane stood rigid. Then, jerkily, he pulled away.

"I don't care why you need slaves," he said thickly. "It doesn't matter how you treat them."

The silver woman spread her hands. "You see?"

"But your people could work out a better way—"

"No." The word rang final. "For us there is—can be—no better way."

Shane's lips twisted. The dullness was gone from his eyes now. "Then, Kyrsis, we can never meet. You have picked your people's road, and I have taken the *Chonya* way."

"But then—"

"There can be nothing more. But you saved my life, and I must buy it back. So I'll land you at Horla, on Mars, and set you free, and you can go your way."

He turned to go.

Then the woman said, "Your throat, *Gar* Shane!"

The Earthman pivoted, face hard. "Yes?"

"There are flecks of green beneath the jaw—a slight eruption of the skin."

"I saw it in a mirror a while ago," Shane answered tightly. "It goes with *theol.*"

"The first injection," the silver woman nodded, and now her smile was lazy, taunting. "With the second, the welts grow darker. After the third there are…more obvious symptoms."

"You saved my life," Shane said, thin-lipped. "I'll see you safe to Mars."

He wheeled and left the room.

THE committee on the interterrestrial slave trade was listening to a speaker from Titan when Shane reached the Federation chambers.

"Slavers? I can give you two names for slavers!" the Titanian cried out in a frenzy. "One is *Chonya* and the other is *Malya*... And those are the names for 'pirate,' too, and 'cutthroat' and 'thief' and 'hypocrite'!"

Grim-faced, Shane started forward.

A basilisk-eyed Mercurian with a sly and smirking air barred his way. "Your credentials, please. You cannot enter the chamber without credentials."

"I left my credentials with a mongrel outlaw named Quos Reggar," Shane clipped tightly. "He ambushed my ship on the way. The chairman, the delegates—any of them can identify me."

"My deepest regrets, but identification is not enough." The Mercurian was openly grinning now. "My orders are specific: regardless of excuse, there will be no admission without credentials."

"The *Chonyas* and *Malyas* have made the asteroid belt a spaceship graveyard!" the Titanian ranted shrilly.

"Get me the chairman," Shane rapped.

"My orders are specific," the Mercurian repeated, smirking. "The issue of your attendance has already been discussed, Earthman, and you are barred—"

Shane raised his hand, tried to flag attention.

The chairman looked quickly away. Committee members turned till their backs were to him, or else openly ignored him.

"They have looted the void for a thousand years!" the Titanian screamed. "When we finally put that down, they grew clever, and now they wail of raids, even while they re-energize their proton cannon and hose the blood from their hatches.

A sudden, mirthless grin twisted Shane's face.

"You lie in your teeth!" he shouted. Slamming the Mercurian to one side, he strode forward.

THE Titanian cut off in mid-breath, great blue-green

wattles shaking. Committee members spun about.

"Order!" bellowed the chairman, hammering on his desk. "Order in the chamber!"

"To hell with your order!" Shane shouted back, eyes blazing. "I said he lied. I'll back it…"

"The *Chonya* delegate must wait his turn. He must clear his credentials—"

"Let someone wait who has yet to count his dead. I'm here to see that the *Chonyas* get justice and an end to slavery, not words. I'll stay till action's taken!"

A rubbery, flat-faced European leaped up. "And why were you not here before? Where have you been? What have you been doing?"

"Yes!" roared a delegate from Ganymede. "Eye-witnesses already have told us that the *Chonyas* are raiding for slaves again—and there are those who say that you, *gar* of the *Chonyas*, raid with them—that a raid is what kept you absent here—"

"My crew will tell you—"

"Your crew?" rasped a Venusian *Vansta*. "Your *Chonya* crew? Who ever heard of a *Chonya* with a mote of truth within him?"

A wave of raucous laughter swept through the chamber.

Then the delegate from Earth was on his feet, a tall, heavy man with thinning hair. "Silence!" he thundered. "Silence!"

The laughter, the shouts, died away.

The Earth delegate addressed Shane, "There is a woman called Kyrsis, of an unknown race, who is known to have been buying slaves. Do you know her?"

"Yes, but—"

"And is it true that when you landed at the Horla spaceport, less than an hour ago, this woman was with you?"

"Yes—"

"That you knew her to have been buying slaves, yet you let

her go free, instead of turning her over to the constituted authorities?"

"But she—"

"Answer yes or no—is it true?"

"Yes, but—"

" 'Buts' have no place in this committee, Shane." The Earth delegate swung about. "My fellow members. I am ashamed to confess that this renegade came from Earth. Now, as Earth delegate, the least I can do to atone is to demand, in the name of Earth, that he be placed under arrest as a slaver; and that the *Chonyas* whom he leads be expelled from the Federation, placed outside the protection of its laws, and subjected to an immediate punitive campaign by the Federation fleet to destroy their sovereignty and reduce them to the status of wards of the Federation…"

FOR the fraction of a second, silence echoed. Then the great room exploded into a cacophony of hate, a tumult of affirmation: "Yes, yes—!" "Seize him!" "Jail him!" "Burn him down!"

Two uniformed *Fantays* and the Mercurian from the door rushed towards Shane.

The Earthman stood as if frozen in his tracks. Then, explosively, he leaped backward, twisting, and suddenly the light-pistol that had swung at his hip was in his hand.

"Who dares to seize me?"

The *Fantays,* the Mercurian, stopped short.

Blue eyes contemptuous, cold as death, Shane looked from them to the delegates…the chairman. "I'm going out now," he said.

No answer came…no comment or sound save that of the crowd's loud, nervous breathing.

"I'm going," he repeated savagely. "I'm going—because the Federation holds knaves and fools enough that decent men no longer dare feel safe within it. The truth finds a graveyard here, and justice hangs in chains. Better to fight you and the slavers both than count on your weak-kneed aid. From this moment on, the *Chonyas* will carve their own way."

Not one of them would meet his eyes.

"No comments, no arguments?" The Earthman laughed sourly; he brought up the light-gun in a gesture that held at once both menace and defiance. "Then I'll leave you now. You may follow me—if you dare!"

Boldly, not even glancing back, he strode out of the room.

CHAPTER EIGHT

"THIS is the place," the *Chonya* said. "This is where the silver woman came."

Shane studied the structure. It was a house—a sort of fortress-dwelling in the ancient *Fantay* style, set a hundred feet from its nearest neighbor. Even in the semidarkness of the early Martian night it looked old, moldering old. Light from Phobos and Deimos, the tiny moons that raced across the sky overhead, glinted on the bosses that studded the great iridium-alloy door, and the weathered walls of *lyndyse* stone rose sheer and blank and forbidding to the second floor. Even there, the windows showed as narrow streaks of yellow light, crisscrossed with heavy bars.

"We are not the only ones drawn by this place, *Gar* Shane," the *Chonya* went on. "There was a *Malya*, a tough young buck with the walk of a fighting man. He stayed in the shadows, surveying the house from every angle, but not going near. After awhile, he went away. Then, later, a Europan came, a flat-faced *chitza* who looked this way and that, as if he was afraid he would be seen. He knocked at the door, and after they'd checked him through a peephole, they let him in. Later, there were three others, all shrouded in *fala* capes so I could not tell their race. They, too, went in."

"And none came out?"

"Only the Europan. He skulked away again in but a few moments."

"A *Malya*, a Europan, and three in *fala* cloaks," Shane repeated, half to himself. And then, speaking to the *Chonya*, "It's time we found out what black brew is cooking there, Nettar. Where are the hook and rope?"

"Here, *Gar* Shane," the other answered. He drew a coiled line and grappling iron from beneath his coat. "Which side shall it be?"

"To the left are fewer windows," said Shane. "Wait here for me, Nettar."

"No, *Gar* Shane. It is madness to go alone into such a deathtrap—"

Shane's mirthless laugh rang through the darkness. "Worse madness for two. There'd be three times the noise."

"But *Gar*—"

"My mission holds less peril than you might think. But should trouble come—should I not return—I want you here, outside, to carry the word."

SILENTLY, then, Shane ran to the building and left along it. He swung the grapnel in a tight arc…sent it flying high into the air in an expert throw, over the roof of the house.

The hook landed with a flat thunk…

Shane hugged the shadows, listening tensely. But no sound came from within.

He tugged experimentally on the line.

The hook held.

Bracing his feet against the wall, leaning out from it, supported by the rope, the Earthman climbed swiftly upward. In half a minute he was over the coping and lying flat on his belly on the roof, drawing up the line.

The round dome of a typical *Fantay* solarium, glowing dimly with yellowish light from some point within but below Shane's line of vision, rose in the middle of the flat roof. Cat-like, the Earthman came to his feet and crossed to it, there to peer cautiously down through the crystal into the room below.

The solarium was empty, illuminated by only one dim lamp.

Quickly, Shane pried loose a crystal panel. Squeezing through the opening, he dropped to the floor.

A door stood half-open across the room. Noiselessly, Shane moved to it, paused and listened.

No sound came. The Earthman stepped outside, and found himself in a narrow hallway. Following it, he came to a stairway, descended cautiously.

Below, the lights were brighter, the air faintly redolent of age and cooking *palorsch*.

And somewhere a woman was singing softly.

Shane eased out his light-gun. Silently, he left the stairs and moved down another hallway. To the right, a door loomed. From the other side came a muffled mumble of voices.

But not the song. Cat-footed, Shane passed the portal.

The song came clearer now—a haunting, taunting melody in a tongue the Earthman did not know. The singer's voice held an alien lilt, a thread of silvery tone.

Kyrsis' voice.

It came from behind another door, and this one was open a crack.

Again Shane paused and listened. But there was no sound except the singing.

THE Earthman stepped to the door's hinge side; threw a quick glance up and down the hall—it was still empty.

Staying back of the jamb, out of sight from the room, he pressed his left hand against the door ever so gently and pushed it open—slowly, as if it were moving with a draft.

Still there was no sound but Kyrsis' voice. But after a moment it swelled a fraction, and the whisper of her footsteps crept through.

Then, suddenly, her profile was framed between half-open door and jamb.

In two swift steps, Shane was inside—pushing her back, heeling shut the door.

The silver woman's great violet eyes went wide. She opened her mouth to scream. But before the sound could come, Shane's arm was about her. His hand clamped over her open mouth.

For an instant her body writhed against him. Her fists beat at his chest, her feet at his ankles.

He said, "If I break you, Kyrsis, the choice will be yours, not mine."

For a long moment her eyes probed his, her body still rigid, straining against him. Then, slowly, she relaxed.

Shane let her go.

Her pale, beautiful face held no expression now. With one last enigmatic glance, she turned from him and moved with perfect poise to a mirror that hung upon another door across the room. Her slender fingers smoothed her hair, rearranged her rumpled gown.

After a moment Shane followed her, stood close behind her, so that their eyes met in the mirror. Gently, he gripped her shoulders. "I came for a reason, Kyrsis," he said.

"A reason, Shane...? She said it almost absently, her fingers still busy with her hair. "What reason?"

Shane's jaw was hard. "Perhaps you've heard that the Federation cast me out."

"Of course. It was expected." The rich purple lips curved

in the faintest of mocking smiles. "Why else do you think I came to Horla with you, except to lay the ground?"

THE lines in Shane's face deepened. "I don't know. That's why I took this chance to see you now."

"What, Shane? I don't understand…"

"Once, on our way here, you asked me to try to understand you and your people. You said our paths might run together if I were to take the slavers' road."

"Shane!" Suddenly her body again was rigid. She twisted, stared up into Shane's eyes. "You mean—you would give up the *Chonya* way? You would raid for slaves as Quos Reggar raids?"

The Earthman's lips twisted. "I'd raid—on my own terms," he answered.

"On your terms…?"

"You might not care to meet them, Kyrsis."

"At least, tell me what they are."

"When the *Chonya* chieftains called me in, I took their way for mine. If I raid now, it will be because their ships are with me."

"But how…?"

Shane laughed harshly. "The Federation has turned us out, with the slaver brand upon us. If we must wear it, we'll earn it. Why should we stand by, helpless and hopeless, while both Reggar and the Federation fleet bleed us white? Better that we raid ourselves. At least then we'll get booty." His blue eyes gleamed. "We'll bring slaves to your people, Kyrsis—smug, fat slaves from the planets of the Federation. We'll drag them out by the thousands…"

A strange excitement seemed to seize the silver woman. "Yes, Shane, yes… We'll take your *Chonyas*—"

"There's more," Shane said.

"Yes…?"

"If you take us, you let Quos Reggar go."

She stared at him. "Are you mad, Shane?"

"No, Kyrsis—far from mad." He clenched his fist, and his face grew dark with anger. "Reggar is the dog who took away my belt. If he had his way, he'd see me with my brain rotted out with *theol*. So he is part of my price—the part that counts the most—"

"—The part that proves you are not so different from other men after all, *Gar* Shane." Kyrsis laughed softly. The things that showed in the violet eyes were very old. "For awhile I almost saw you as separate from the rest—a man apart, so hard and strong that nothing could sway you from what you saw as duty. But now..." She shrugged. "...you seek to save your *Chonyas*, yes. But Reggar hurt your pride when he took your belt, so now, above all, you seek for vengeance."

"And if I do?" Shane replied somewhat hotly, "does it matter to you? I bring you the *Chonyas*-born raiders, a race that has carved its name in blood across the void. Beside them, what is Reggar? —A mongrel, a cross-bred *chitza* served by the scum of the spaceways." He broke off. "But you are the one who must decide. What is your answer?"

The smile left the silver woman's face. Turning, she walked thoughtfully across the room, not speaking.

After a moment, Shane followed.

AGAIN Kyrsis turned, looked up at him. Her expression was unfathomable. "You are a bold and clever man, Shane," she said. "It is a pity you can never hope to be quite clever enough."

"You mean...?"

"She means you've failed again, you *chitza!*" cut in a harsh familiar voice from the mirrored door behind Shane.

The Earthman spun about.

His great carcass draped in a *fala* cloak, Quos Reggar stood in the doorway, light-gun in hand.

Shane froze. His mouth took on a bitter twist. "I should have known you'd follow her here. But the *fala* cape—"

"It fooled you?" Reggar laughed harshly. "I thought it would. And Kyrsis did well, too, leading you over to my door, where I was sure to hear you."

Shane said nothing.

"There's someone else here for you to see," leered Reggar. He raised his voice, "Talu!"

"Here, *Sha* Reggar."

Shane caught his breath at the sound of her voice. But that was all, for then she was coming through the doorway, slim and graceful, her waist-long blue-black hair a-ripple in the light, her dark *Malya* face as proudly lovely as before.

And as before, she bore a tray in her hand.

"*Sha* Shane…" Her voice, her face, told nothing; nor could Shane interpret the message that flickered, just for an instant, in her eyes.

Reggar said, "Once before I sent Talu to you with an injector, Earthman, and you nearly broke her arm. This time, it will be different."

Shane made no attempt to answer.

"The injector, Talu…"

Face wooden, the *Malyalara* stripped back the cloth and picked up the hypodermic from the tray. "It is ready, *Sha* Reggar."

"*Theol* was in that other injector, *starbo*, and this one holds *theol*—now. It will be your second dose. Madness is just one more away."

SHANE stood very still. He looked from Kyrsis, with her pale ethereal beauty and silver hair and translucent skin, to Talu, the slave girl—dark, tempestuous, all *Malya*; then back to Reggar again. Instinctively his muscles tensed.

The mongrel said, "You'll take the dose, Earthman—because if you so much as move a hair, I'll burn your arms off." The light-gun in his webbed hand was rock-steady.

"Talu…"

"Yes, *Sha* Reggar." Quickly, efficiently, she stepped to the Earthman's side. "Twist your neck, *Sha* Shane."

"Twist it!" echoed Reggar. His huge lobed eyes were flocked with red.

Teeth clenched, eyes hot with hate, Shane obeyed.

The *Malyalara* pressed the plunger.

Reggar let out a breath, stepped back. "Tomorrow, great *gar*, you get the last," he gloated. "Then, after that, you'll serve with my fleet…serve gladly, happy to help us in every way, just for the sake of another shot of *theol.*" He chuckled ghoulishly. "It will be a fitting fate—the more so after the way you've tried so many schemes to split *Shi* Kyrsis from me, so that you could dispose of each of us alone. In fact…"

Somewhere, some living creature screamed. There was horror in the sound—a hideous note, as if soul were being torn from body.

Reggar froze. "What…?"

From the hallway came the faintest whisper of footsteps.

The mongrel's light-gun prodded Shane. "You, *chitza*—open the door!"

Wordless, Shane crossed the room. He gripped the handle, pulled back the door. Outside, the hall had gone black, lights out.

Instantly, before he could so much as draw a breath, dark hands came out of nowhere; seized him and jerked him half into the hall. A knifepoint pricked his belly.

"Move and die, Earthman!" a voice breathed in his ear…a man's voice, cold, and hard, and heavy with a *Malya* accent.

Shane stood as if carved from stone. From the room

behind him, now, came another fierce *Malya* voice, "The light-gun, Reggar!"

For an instant silence echoed. Then Reggar cursed, and there was the thud of the pistol hitting the floor.

NOW the *Malyas* holding Shane shoved him back into the room. There, another *Malya*—a hard-bitten, swaggering little man—already had Reggar pressed back against the wall, penned there by a knife like the one digging into Shane's belly. Other dark, cold-eyed fighting men stood by the mirrored door to the huge hybrid's quarters.

Talu was with them, her face aglow with fierce joy. "*Malya*s, *Malya*s—!"

The silver woman, Kyrsis, stood silent and apart. But shadows of strain showed in the lines and hollows of her face.

"We have done our work well," the leader of the dark men said. "We have the Earthman, Shane. We have Reggar, the mongrel. We have the silver woman. There'll be joy and feasting at Amara when we ramp our ships."

"You are of Amara, *Malya?*" Shane asked.

The other's dark eyes gleamed. "We are of Amara, Earthman—and before you die, you'll wish you'd never heard of us or our asteroid! Other races may let the slavers raid and not strike back. But we claim blood for blood…"

Shane said, "I am *gar* of the *Chonyas*, not a slaver. Ask Talu, the slave girl. She is of your people—"

"Who takes the word of a captive woman?" The *Malya* laughed thinly. "We *Malya*s have raided for slaves ourselves, in our day. A woman's heart goes with her man, not her race."

"Check with others, then—"

"We have checked already. The word is out—you raid with Reggar. You came to Horla with the woman, Kyrsis. It is enough!" Fierce lights gleamed in the *Malya's* eyes. He grinned—a savage, death's-head grimace. "We've tracked you down across the void, you three, and now we'll see you pay for the *Malya* blood you've spilled—battling the *zanths* for your lives in Amara's great arena…"

CHAPTER NINE

THIS was Amara's great arena. The oval pit was a full twenty feet deep and floored with sand…sand that here and there was churned and trodden, stained dark brown with men's life blood.

Above the pit, seats rose into the star-flecked night in steep-banked tiers.

Those seats were full, now—packed from pit to rim with the savage, dark-faced *Malya* breed, a blood-lusting horde whose cries for slaughter rose in great, swelling waves like the screams of primeval beasts.

In the forefront, ringing the rim of the pit, sat the *Malya* chieftain and his court—the old raiders, the men of power, the warriors and their women.

And there, too, sat another woman, a slim, lovely *Malyalara*, placed close beside the chief himself.

Talu.

Slave girl no longer, she now wore a gown of richest *kalor*. Jeweled clips held the rippling, blue-black hair, and a jewel-studded harness accented her shoulders' softness, her throat's clean curve, and the bare breasts' proud, firm swell.

Ankle-deep in the sand of the pit, Shane surveyed them, one and all.

Now the *Malya* chief leaned forward across the rim, a long fighting knife in his hand. His deep-set eyes gleamed anticipation. "You are the first, Earthman…you and this knife against a *zanth!*"

Boldly, Shane met the chieftain's stare. "And if I win...?"

For the fraction of a second a sort of dull, throbbing silence seemed to fall over the crowd. Then it broke in a gale of wild, tumultuous laughter, echoing and re-echoing upward to the stars.

"If you win...?" the *Malya* chieftain choked. "Have you stayed too long in the sun of Mercury, *chitza?* No man has ever come out of the pit over a *zanth.*"

"What holds for other men is not for me. I asked...what if I win?"

ADMIRATION showed in the *Malya's* dark face. "If you fight as boldly as you talk—small wonder that the *Chonyas* made you *gar!*" And then, "If you win, you'll live—but here, on Amara, forever a slave."

"I ask no more," Shane came back coldly. Again his blue eyes swept the crowd, the sparkling night of a thousand stars. For a moment his gaze lingered on Talu, catching the fever in her eyes, the tension carved in every line. The noise of the shouting horde above beat down upon him. The fetid stench of the *zanth* came to his nostrils from the tunnel-chute.

"Your weapon, Earthman!" cried the *Malya* chief, and threw it down. "Keeper, prepare to loose the *zanth!*"

In one swift motion, Shane swept up the knife. Then, quickly, he moved to the shadows along the wall of the pit, out of the smoky torches' flickering glare.

In the tunnel, the *zanth* roared thunderously. Shane caught a glimpse of the panic on Kyrsis' pale face, where she sat in the prisoners' cage; of the fear that crawled in Quos Reggar's great lobed eyes.

Overhead, the *Malya* chieftain cried, "Turn loose the *zanth!*"

The heavy-grilled gate at the tunnel mouth swung up. In the blackness beyond the *zanth's* eyes burned like coals of fire.

Again it roared, and then again. Then, slowly, it came forward, out into the pit, there to stand for a moment, blinking against the glare.

Shane sucked in air. This *zanth* was big, bigger than any he had ever seen…well over twenty feet. The murderous, serrated tail alone measured at least seven feet, and the great jaws were of a size to snap a man in two in a single bite. Its scales were big as dinner plates and just as thick—rough with age. Spurs and claws gleamed in the torchlight like curved knives.

Then the great, ringed nostrils flared as the creature scented Shane. The spiked diamond head came round, twisting and turning on the monstrous, snake-like neck; darting and probing to the full five feet of its length. The stink of its breath swept over the Earthman in a nauseous wave.

Shane stood very still.

But already the *zanth* was turning. The bulging eyes gleamed redly, searching for him.

The knife-haft was slippery in Shane's hand. A rill of sweat crept down his spine.

The *zanth* paused now, the spiked head moving sinuously to and fro. The tail flicked the bloodstained sand. Its powerful, armor-scaled body seemed to draw together.

Shane forgot to breathe.

The *zanth* lunged.

SHANE dived as the great spiked head lanced forward. The jaws snapped shut where he had been with a clacking like the sound of monstrous castanets.

After that, there was no time for anything but action.

For even before the Earthman hit the ground, the thing was whirling. The claws of its eight feet sprayed the sand like a windstorm. Again, it lunged.

Desperately, Shane rolled out of the way.

But now the serrated, seven-foot tail lashed out at him, with a force that would have smashed through a solid brick wall.

Again Shane rolled-in, towards the *zanth's* body.

One of the feet clawed for him. A six-inch talon raked a bloody path along his side.

Panting, the Earthman scrambled away—back to the shadows, the wall of the pit.

The *zanth* whirled; charged.

Taut-muscled, Shane waited till the diamond head hammered forward. Then, in the last instant, he leaped aside.

The *zanth's* head smashed against the wall of the pit. Savagely, Shane stabbed for the crevice where the jaw-plates met, trying for the creature's tiny brain.

But the tough cartilage turned away the blade. With a roar, the *zanth* struck at him.

Shane leaped high into the air, and the awful head passed beneath him. Twisting, he landed on the writhing, tree-thick neck; balanced there for a precarious moment.

The *zanth* reared back, clawing for him, and Shane sprang clear. Again he took up his stand against the wall.

This time, the *zanth* broke off its charge to flail at him with its tail. Barely in time, the Earthman got out of the way. He was breathing hard, now—his whole body shaking under the strain.

The *zanth* lunged.

Desperately, Shane snatched up a handful of sand, hurled it straight into the oncoming monster's glaring eyes.

The creature came up short, shaking its head.

Shane moved like a striking quirst. Again he snatched sand, hurled it.

THE *zanth* raised its head high, to the full length of the

five-foot neck. Clawing, it leaped at the Earthman. The awful talons shredded his clothes, tore at his flesh.

Shane threw himself sideways.

The head lanced towards him.

He slashed at the eyes with his knife and felt the steel blade bite in.

A wild roar burst from the creature's throat. It threw itself at Shane in a frenzy, clawing and snapping and threshing.

Once more, Shane sprang aside—then darted back before the creature could make the double turn. Leaping to its neck, he threw himself flat upon it, clinging to it with legs and one arm as to a writhing log, while with the other hand, the knife hand, he stabbed again and again at the bulging eyes.

The *zanth* roared its agony. Twisting and jerking, it struggled to unseat the Earthman. One clawed foot reached his leg and laid it open. But still Shane clung to his place, slashing and stabbing.

Blindly, the monster crashed against the pit's wall. It reared, then surged forward, clawing its way up the sheer face. The great spiked head rocked and swayed; beat against the stonework in a spasm of pain, less than three feet below the rim.

A fierce light flamed in Shane's eyes. Clutching the base of the spike, he suddenly let go the *zanth's* neck with his legs. His toes dug into the overlap between the scales, and all at once he was running upward—up the snake-neck, onto the diamond head itself.

And then, before the *Malyas* realized what was happening, he leaped from the head to the rim of the pit. The fighting knife flashed in a savage arc. A warrior's shout choked off in a rush of blood. The others about him scrambled back from the slashing blade.

Behind Shane, back in the pit, the *zanth* screamed and hurled itself upward. Its head came over the rim. With a mighty, surging leap, its forefeet followed. A terrible roar burst from its throat as it caught the scent of the *Malya* warrior's blood, and it clawed its way onward, upward, out of the pit and into the rising tiers of seats.

IT was a nightmare, a world gone mad. Wildly, the screaming *Malya*s fled. But the *zanth's* great tail lashed out and a score of them fell, crushed or smashed into the pit. The knife-claws tore; the great jaws ran ruby-red with blood.

Forgotten, Shane followed the panicked mob.

Only then, somehow, a voice slashed through to him through the tumult, "Shane—*Shane!*"

He whirled.

Talu was running towards him, across the seats. "This way!"

For an instant he hesitated, then changed his course to meet hers.

She caught his hand. "This way!"

Together, they raced back towards the chief's box at the rim of the pit, and now Shane saw that a trap door in the floor had been lifted.

"Hurry!" cried the *Malyalara*. "In a moment the warriors will bring in a proton cannon to kill the *zanth,* and someone will think of you, too. You must be gone before then!"

Shane shot one look at the pitch-black shaft. "Where does it go?"

"To a passage below the arena that leads to the chief's castle and the ramps. We can steal a flyer there. But hurry!"

Shane shot one quick look back.

The *zanth* still raged and ravened through the crowd, but already the warriors had rallied to hem it in.

Tightly, he said to Talu, "You first, then."

"First?"

"Do you think I'd let you get behind me?" he clipped

bitterly. "Fool that I am, I'll go with you, because I have no choice. But my knife will be in your back every step of the way, ready for your next betrayal."

" 'Betrayal'?" she repeated, and now the heat of anger was in her voice, her eyes. "Did you say betrayal, Earthman?"

"What would you call it?" He made no effort to keep the fury from his tone. "Who tripped me when I would have stabbed Quos Reggar? Who shot a second dose of *theol* into my veins?"

She drew away from him, then, and the look she threw stung like a whip. "Come, *Sha* Shane. If that is your belief, then I must indeed go first." Lithely, she lowered herself over the edge of the shaft and disappeared down a metal ladder set in one wall.

Knife still in hand, Shane followed. The effort made him shake, and under the strain of climbing, the claw-wound in his side began to bleed again.

Then, at last, they were in the murky passageway below, and Talu was leading him swiftly through the darkness. Once Shane staggered and would have fallen had not the *Malyalara* caught him; and once he dropped the knife. But she picked it up again, and her groping hand strayed into the blood as she sought to return the weapon. So she made him sit down while she tore up some garment and bandaged his wounds, and her fingers were very gentle.

They went on again, then, for what seemed endless miles, till at last they came to a huge, dim-lighted ramping-spot where dull black *Malya* flyers stood in ordered rows, their bubbles pointed up into the starlit sky. And finally they even found one with its lower hatches open, and the girl helped Shane to climb aboard. She strapped him in the pilot's seat and herself in the other seat beside him.

For a long time, it seemed, he worked at the controls with clumsy fingers, till at last, somehow, they were blasting off, roaring up and up and up into the gaudy heavens. And Talu talked to him, and braced him and helped him hold the jet-globe steady, while seconds, or maybe hours, ticked by.

Only then, suddenly, the sky about them was full of ships, great black-hulled ships that were built for ranging clear across the void. They came in hundreds—thousands, maybe—blazing in thunderous silence through the blackness of spatial night. And one of the ships swerved and came alongside the little *Malya* flyer, and a great hatch opened in its side and sucked them in.

Then the hatch slid closed again and the darkness about them was complete. Even their jets were blacked out, killed by the great ship's pickup neutralizers.

Still Shane sat in silence, staring stupidly, straight ahead.

But the body of the girl, Talu, came warm against him in the ebon murk, her voice a fierce, husky whisper in his ear, "You must believe me, Shane! I didn't betray you—not ever! The things I did, I had to do, in order to live to pay back the blood debt of my people. You could never have killed Quos Reggar with one thrust, no matter where, for he is a cross-bred mongrel, and his body doesn't work as ours do."

Shane forced out words, "Why tell me now? Why care about it?"

"Why? Why?" The girl's voice held a tremor now, a fear not even the black could hide. "I tell you so that you will know, and not die hating me to your last breath. That I could not stand! For die we will, and soon—because this ship is one of Reggar's slavers!"

CHAPTER TEN

"HERE IS LIFE!" the vendor cried. "Fresh life from new planets! Young slaves, with the hot blood surging through their veins! And all yours—yours for the asking, going for the price you set yourselves!" He struck a note on a silver gong. "Look at this next wench—a warm and vibrant thing, my friends, throbbing with life and spirit! What am I offered for her?"

The woman on the block was Venusian, a weary, fading creature with the sucking tube and ear-stalks of the *Transmi*. Her eyes were veined with weeping, her sagging face shadowed with fear and fatigue.

"Come! Make the first bid!" cried the vendor. "Who'll start it? Do I hear five hundred?"

"Fifty," called a voice from the rear of the crowd.

"Fifty! Do you seek to insult me? She's worth five hundred if she is a *xi*—"

"You mean, you insult us, vendor," the bidder retorted caustically. "A fool can see that the life runs low within her. She would not last the night."

"Fifty!" cried the vendor. "I'm offered fifty, friends. Who'll raise it to sixty?"

No one spoke. After a moment, the vendor struck the silver gong again. "Sold to Callan at fifty!" He pushed the Venusian down the steps. "Get on with you, woman…"

An attendant pushed Shane forward, heavy with irons. "An Earthman, vendor…"

The vendor struck the gong. "An Earthman, my friends; a fighting man—powerful, surging with life in spite of his wounds. Who'll start it?"

Coldly, Shane swept the auction room with his glance.

Here in front on one side were the slaves—a motley assortment dragged to this final degradation from a dozen far-flung planets. One by one, they were thrust upon the block, exposed to the ghoulish appraisal of the crowd that filled the room.

The crowd. A crowd of silver men and women, with gleaming hair and violet eyes and pale, translucent skins. A hundred hungry-eyed, avid brothers and sisters of *Shi* Kyrsis.

Even the room itself was strange. The materials resembled nothing known anywhere in all the void. The lush decor followed an alien theme.

"This man is good for longtime use!" exhorted the vendor. "See the strength of him—the fire and vigor! You cannot pass him by…"

A door to Shane's right opened.

A woman came in, a silver woman.

The woman.

Kyrsis.

An old man close to the block called eagerly, "I'll give a hundred, vendor!" in a thin, cracking voice.

"A hundred I'm offered! Now who'll make it a hundred and fifty? No one can afford to let this strong man go at a mere hundred—"

"Hundred and ten!" someone shouted.

Kyrsis turned. For the first time, her eyes met Shane's, and she stopped suddenly, staring as if paralyzed.

"Hundred twenty!"

"Hundred thirty!"

"Do I hear a hundred forty? Surely no fine, strapping, fighting man can go for less—"

"Two hundred," Kyrsis said. "Two hundred! The Lady Kyrsis bids two hundred—"

"Two fifty, vendor!" cried the old man by the block.

"Three hundred," came back Kyrsis.

"Do I hear three fifty—?"

"With his wounds, he is worth no more than three," the old man mumbled.

"Three twenty-five then! Do I hear three twenty-five?"

"Three ten—"

"Three fifty," echoed Kyrsis. The vendor paused and looked about. "Three fifty is bid…" He struck the gong.

"Sold to the Lady Kyrsis for three fifty."

Shane left the block, strode to the silver woman's side; and for a moment they stood there in vibrant silence, alone in the crowd, dueling with their eyes.

Then Kyrsis asked, "What dark fate brought you here, *Gar* Shane? When I last saw you, you were hewing a path through the *Malya* horde at the arena…"

"And you were in the prisoners' cage." The Earthman ignored the strange tremor in the silver woman's voice. His words were clipped. "Talu and I escaped and fled Amara in a flyer. But one of Quos Reggar's slavers sucked us in and brought us here."

"The slavers came to rescue Reggar," Kyrsis said. "They swept Amara clean." She looked down, breathing deep as if to still some inner tension. And then, "Talu was with you? They brought her here—?"

"—and put here aside. Her hair was cropped, so they knew she already had a master." Shane laughed harshly. "Me—I'd worn no yoke, so they sent me to the block."

"Then…let us go. I have already done my other buying." The tremor in Kyrsis' voice was stronger, now—a sort of undercurrent of strange excitement.

"Your 'other buying'—?"

"A few young slaves to…to train for household use." The silver woman's fingers trembled, cold as ice, upon Shane's arm. "Come! Let us go now, quickly…"

SHE LED Shane out through other rooms, where other vendors hawked their wares, and other slaves stood shamed or sobbing, bared to the eager, weirdly-lusting eyes of the silver people.

Then they reached a sort of transit station, and an attendant brought a car of a type Shane had never seen before, and they got in.

Three frightened children, a *Malya* boy of perhaps twelve and two *Chonya* girls even younger, huddled at the back, their dark eyes big with panic.

"Your slaves, Lady Kyrsis?" Shane asked coldly. The barb in his voice would have slashed through the scales of a *zanth*.

The silver woman kept her eyes on the controls. The car hurtled off through a tube-like passage. She did not answer.

Then the car halted. They got out—Shane, Kyrsis, children—and entered rooms, rooms luxuriously furnished in the alien style of the silver people.

"And now?" Shane inquired thinly.

Kyrsis' breathing was fast and shallow, her face even more pale than before. She spoke too rapidly, in a ragged, uneven voice. "You are weary, Shane…so weary. You must rest now. Here…let me take off your shackles. There is a room here you will like—a quiet room…"

She unlocked the cuffs on his wrists and tossed them aside, then led him swiftly to an adjoining sleep chamber. Foam-soft cushioning a foot thick blanketed a dais along one wall, big enough for a dozen men. A lingering perfume filled the air. Soft lights cast a silvery glow. From somewhere came faint strains of elfin musk.

"Rest here, Earthman," the silver woman said softly, "Rest until I call you…"

For a moment her icy fingers touched his cheek. Then she left the room, closing the door behind her.

Shane stared after her, a frown furrowing his brow. After a moment, he stepped to the door and tried the handle.

It was locked.

SHANE'S frown deepened. He rubbed a grimy hand across his cheek where the cold of Kyrsis' fingers still lingered. He finally turned to a more thorough inspection of his quarters.

As he pivoted, light glinted on the glass-like surface of the wall that flanked the door—caught a vague flicker of movement.

Shane moved on across the chamber with no sign that he had seen it.

An alcove held a radiation bath. The Earthman stepped into the cubicle and flipped the switch, luxuriating under the warm tingle of the molecular bombardment. Slowly, the sweat and dirt and grime faded from his body, the dried blood washed away. The worst of the weariness left his muscles. His bones almost stopped aching.

Refreshed, he snapped off the radiation and, leaving the cubicle, drank greedily from a crystal bubbler set beside it.

Now he went back to the sleeping chamber. His eyes flickered over the spot in the wall beside the door.

The surface showed blank and dead as the rest.

Shane grinned sourly to himself; crossed the room and tried the door once more.

It was still locked.

The Earthman hesitated. Then, grimly, he braced one foot on the casing beside the lock, gripped the handle, and threw his full weight on it.

Inside the lock, something snapped. The handle twisted askew.

Again Shane tugged, his muscles swelling with the strain.

The broken handle pulled from its socket. Inserting a forefinger in the hole, Shane manipulated the lock, pulled back the bolt.

The door swung open.

Shane stepped outside. He glanced at the wall behind the spot where he had seen the movement.

A PICTURE hung there. Lifting it aside, he found a small, hinged panel. Opening it, he discovered that a lens set behind the shiny coating of the inner wall enabled him to survey the entire sleep-chamber.

Again, the sour grin twisted Shane's lips. Swiftly, he strode through the silence, checking the other rooms. He found them empty—all but one. Its door was locked.

The Earthman drew back a moment.

A picture hung a few feet to one side of the locked door.

Shane stepped over to it and lifted it from the wall.

It concealed another peephole. Shading his eyes, the Earthman peered through the lens.

Kyrsis was within…Kyrsis and one of the captive *Chonya* girls.

The silver woman held the child upon her lap. She was talking to her—smiling, squeezing the chubby hands. Her manner was gentle, tender.

Yet under it all, somehow, hung a weird, unholy note— grotesque, obscene.

Some of the fear had left the child's eyes now. She smiled wanly…nestled, not quite so tense, in the silver woman's arms.

Kyrsis' eyes closed. Her lips parted, and Shane knew that she was singing as she rocked the child.

The child's lips drooped. Trustingly, the small arms half-embraced the silver woman. The tired head rested on Kyrsis' breast.

The child slept.

Now new emotions came to Kyrsis' lovely face…strange passion—a horrid anticipatory glow. Her nostrils flared. Her violet eyes grew large, gleamed with fires older than time itself. She cradled the child. Ever so tenderly, yet with a terrible air of strain, her parted lips sought the girl's.

Shane stood frozen, tight in indecision's grip.

The child moved languidly in Kyrsis' arms—restless, not struggling, and for a moment the silver woman straightened, sucked in air. Then, again, she pressed her lips against the girl's.

Shane cursed beneath his breath and turned towards the door.

But even as he did so, Kyrsis rose, the child still in her arms. The silver woman's face was serene now, ethereally beautiful, unmarred by any trace of strain. Gently, she laid down the still form of the child. Then, coming erect again, she moved towards the door.

Shane slid the picture back into place and stepped out of sight in the adjoining room.

The door to the room in which Kyrsis had been, opened and closed. The silver woman passed down the hall, out of sight.

Tense, silent, Shane made for the room from which she'd come.

The door was unlocked now. Swiftly, he slipped inside and stepped to the couch where the *Chonya* child still lay, so very still. He touched the soft hand. Lifted it with trembling fingers.

Behind him, the door-latch clicked.

Shane turned.

Kyrsis stood watching him. "You come unannounced, Earthman," she murmured coolly.

"I came in as you left," Shane said, and suddenly his hands, his voice, his whole body, were shaking uncontrollably, gripped in a paroxysm of surging fury. "I saw you here, with the child. Do you hear me? I saw you—!"

"So...?" Kyrsis' face was still calm, the violet eyes unfathomable.

The veins at Shane's temples stood out, throbbing. With a tremendous effort, he brought his voice under a semblance of control.

He said, "This child is dead..."

CHAPTER ELEVEN

THEY stood there thus for a long, taut, echoing moment.

Then Kyrsis said, "You leave me no choice, Earthman. I see I must tell you Gadar's secret."

"*Gadar—?*"

Her lips twitched. "Yes, Earthman. Gadar, the dark star—the star hurled into your solar system from across the void—cold, bleak, barren, uninhabited Gadar."

"You mean that you—your people—are of Gadar?"

The silver woman nodded. "Yes. When our star cooled, in the course of that endless voyage across the void, we had no choice but to burrow deeper and deeper, like animals—cutting ourselves away from the awful cold of outer space, hunting desperately for the last dim vestiges of warmth at our planet's core. Then, when at last we had come into the family of your sun, we saw no reason to let it be known that we existed. For we knew the thing we had to do if we were still to live, and we knew that if you knew it, Gadar would be doomed."

"Then…this is Gadar? We are inside it now…deep down below the surface?"

"So deep that even the echographs of your Federation's exploration parties did not find us. Here, for a million years, we have built our civilization." A new glint came to the woman's violet eyes, a note of excitement to her voice. "The things we have done, Shanc! The incredible things! You will never believe them until you see them. We have conquered time and space and matter—"

"And the child is dead," Shane said.

"The child—" Kyrsis broke off, and a shadow crossed her face. "Yes, the child is dead."

UNSPEAKING, the Earthman waited. His temple veins no longer throbbed, but his jaw was hewn of granite.

Kyrsis said, "There are so many things your childish science knows that are not true…and one of them is the nature of life."

Shane studied her, narrow-eyed. "So? In what way?"

"You think that life comes into being when certain conditions are correct. But we know otherwise."

"I hear only words, not meaning," Shane clipped coldly.

"Of course. Because the whole pattern of your thinking is based on false assumptions." The silver woman groped for words. "The thing I seek to say, too simply, is that life is not a creature of conditions. It is an entity, a basic element, a product of the whole great cosmic process of creation. Either it exists in a place, or it does not." She shrugged. "Your solar system has it."

"And Gadar…?"

"Gadar had it once, ten million years ago. But life is like any other resource. You use it up. It dissipates and scatters, transmuted into useless forms by a process that not even our science can reverse." Her voice fell. "Then, Shane, your planet dies."

Shane stared at her. "So you bought slaves—"

"Of course we bought slaves!" A note of hysteria crept into the silver woman's laugh. "Power, you talked about power just a score of days ago. Why would anyone buy slaves in a universe where power is free? What we sought was life—life in a form we could drink up, before our bodies finally died…" She came close to Shane, her pale face smooth and glowing, the violet eyes afire. "Look at me, Earthman. Look closely. How old would you guess me? How many of your Earth years?"

Shane did not speak.

"A hundred years, Earthman? A thousand? Ten

thousand? A hundred thousand?" She laughed—softly at first and then wildly, up and down the scale. And then, steadying herself once more she said, "Shane, I first drew breath a million years ago! Our science has kept me as I am—young in body and mind and heart. But without new life—without the living slaves we buy—I would wither and die in months. This child…" And she gestured to the limp, dead body of the *Chonya* girl. "…what did she know of life? What did she care? I played with her, and comforted her, and she was happy; and then I sucked the life out of her body, and you hate me for it. But was it so wicked, really? Was it not better that I should live, I who have learned to love life through a million endless year, than she, who would have wasted that life and thrown it away in some dull corner of the asteroid belt?"

SHANE shifted; stared down at the dead child for a long, long moment, then back at the woman again.

"I am sure you must be thinking, 'is there no other way?'" Kyrsis whispered. Her pale hand touched the Earthman's arm. "I tell you, Shane, there is none, how many years have our scientists sought it? How many eons of spatial time? But always, the answer is no. We must have life itself—humanoid life, like that of this girl here. No other can be transmuted to our bodies."

"If life is an element, as you say, a thing that wells up with creation, out of the birth of a planet, then you could have moved to another planet," Shane said in a dull, flat voice. "If life is gone from Gadar, then you could have migrated, picked a new home."

"It sounds so easy, does it not?" the silver woman taunted. "But where life exists, there life forms evolve. We could have taken such a planet only by conquest. Would your worlds have liked that, Shane? Would they have been willing to see us come in and seize their homelands? You fought out of pride, for the belt the *Chonya* chieftains gave you. Would the worlds of your system do less if we tried to invade them?"

Shane stood mute.

Kyrsis' arm slipped about him. The rich purple lips came close to his. "Come with us, Shane! Join us!" she whispered. "For a million aching years I have sought a man like you. Do not leave me, now that I've found you…"

A weakness crept through Shane's body.

With a tremendous, savage effort, he hurled the silver woman from him.

"You'd steal my life as Quos Reggar stole my belt," he nearly shouted. Stark murder was in his eyes.

"No, Shane. No…!"

"Words…" the Earthman lashed fiercely. "Words, to lull me as you lulled that *Chonya* child." He caught Kyrsis' arm, dragged her up from the place where she had fallen. "You talk of life as if you, your people, were the only ones who knew the way to live it. But life belongs to each man, alone…his precious own, to waste or hoard as he sees fit…"

The woman asked, "And what will you do, now that you have decided?"

"Decided…?"

THE look she threw him was a study in contempt. "I can see it in your eyes, Earthman. For a moment you hung, unsure, caught up by the vision of the wealth and power that might be yours; of me at your side, and endless years for us together. But then it dawned upon you that I might suck your life out, as we suck those of the other slaves we take, though such was not my plan. The thought brought fear, and in the same instant you became the great *Gar* Shane, who would strike down Gadar and save your solar system." She laughed, and the sound was chill as outer space. "You are as much a child as that dead lump there beside you. Do you think to pit yourself against my people—scientists who could plot your every thought ten million years before your birth? You are but a fool, and you will die as all the others have died, and Quos Reggar will wear your belt and serve us!"

"There comes a time for every man to die," Shane said. "If this is mine, I'll face it." He picked a heavy, club-like, metal ornament from a table, and his face had the rugged lines of carven stone. "We go now, Kyrsis. And if I can die—remember, so can you!"

"But where?"

Shane bared his teeth in a death's-head grin. "To your ramps, *Shi* Kyrsis. Even slavers carry a fleet alarm."

"A fleet alarm?"

"When a space ship wallows through the void, out of control, a crewman throws the switch on the fleet alarm box. It sends out a distress call on a Federation beam—a call so strong that it can reach to the farthest star."

"And then…?"

"The fleet command sends aid." The Earthman laughed thinly. "They send a patrol most often, or even a single ship. But when they get a call straight out of the core of Gadar, they'll waste no time on mere patrols or squadrons. There'll be a fleet, the whole great Federation fleet, sweeping down upon your planet."

"Indeed?" the woman mocked. "So your Federation's fleet will come. What can they do to us, burrowed here deep within the solid rock of Gadar? And we have weapons, Earthman—weapons the like of which you've never seen."

"Then roll them out," Shane said. "This will be your chance to use them." He pushed her through the doorway—on past the other rooms and out into the car.

She asked, "What can you do if I will not aid you?"

Shane shrugged. "I'd have no choice but to go my way

alone, I suppose…" And then, sinking in the barb with a savage twist, he said, "…after I'd beaten your brains out, killed you so dead that not even your people's science could ever put you back together…"

THEY traveled through endless miles of tube-like passage, after that, but always climbing ever upward—the silver woman sitting at the controls, Shane watching, hawk-like, alert in every nerve and fiber, the heavy club gripped ready in his hand.

Then, finally, they reached a place where great volcanic pipes led upward, and slaver space ships towered base-down, ramped and ready.

There was a guard, a silver guard, who said, "It is forbidden to go farther."

"Of course," Shane said—and smiled and struck him down.

"Must I go further?" Kyrsis asked. Panic was in her voice.

"Much further," Shane replied. Again he threw her a death's-head grin. "Life is a sacred thing, you've said, and I am a fool—fool enough, at least, to think it should be true for my *Chonyas*, as well as your people. So drive on—out along the ramp to where Quos Reggar's own great ship is waiting."

"Not Reggar's own ship—!" The silver woman's lips were trembling. "Earthman, he may be on board now. He brought me back to Gadar with him, and—"

"—And if he's here, so much the better!" The recklessness was back in Shane's stance now. The blue eyes gleamed a chill excitement. "Why do you think I seek his ship, except to find him? He is the key to this bath of blood; were it not for him and his kind, your people might have been hard-put to implement their plans for slaughter. Fool that I am, lacking your skill and science, I've a feeling that if I can cut

Quos Reggar's throat, I'll have traveled far towards choking off this madness!" He lifted his club. "Drive on, *Shi* Kyrsis! Quickly, before the vision of that dead *Chonya* child again seeps through me."

Trembling, the silver woman worked at the controls. The car went racing down the ramp to where Quos Reggar's ship stood waiting.

"Inside," Shane said. "Keep close before me…"

They clambered aboard the slaver, tight with tension. But there was no sign of life. Reggar's own quarters lay deserted.

"The control room, then," the Earthman said tightly.

In silence, they climbed the long steel ladder.

A lone *Pervod* sat in the control room, rewiring a panel. He looked up, saw Kyrsis already in the doorway. Lust touched his sly reptilian face. "Ho, woman—!"

Shane smashed his skull.

And there was the black metal cube that was the fleet alarm box.

"You spoke of weapons, Kyrsis?" Shane said bleakly. "Now is the time, then. Roll them out!"

He threw the switch.

CHAPTER TWELVE

THEY were coming now—a horde of great silver ships that lanced through the void like streaks of light, hurtling down on Gadar. The slim, sleek *Chonya* craft were with them, too…the dull black *Malyu* flyers; and Shane knew that his other calls had gotten through—that the worlds and the asteroids were uniting against slavery and death and chaos.

A siren blasted a shrill alarm. Quos Reggar's renegades swarmed onto the ramp, racing for their ships to take up the challenge.

The light of battle shone in Shane's blue eyes. The

reckless laugh rose in his throat. With a jerk, he levered the slaver flagship's great hatches shut. His thumb rammed home the contact button for the interlacing belts of proton cannon that girded the craft.

The exploding flame of pronic blasts erupted across the short-range visiscreen's whole viewer—searing the outlaws from the ramp, smashing the slaver ships off their bases, turning the great volcanic pits to a holocaust of flaming ruin.

And Shane the Earthman, *gar* of the *Chonyas*, high lord of the asteroids, laughed his wild, bold, reckless laugh and jammed the contact button home again…again…again…

But now a voice came through the amplifier—Quos Reggar's voice, shaking with rage and hate and fury, "Though it costs me my own ship, I'll blast you, *chitza!* You'll sear as my men have seared—"

Shane flicked the switch. "Blast, then, Reggar. Blast—but you'll blast the Lady Kyrsis with me!"

Beside him, Kyrsis screamed, "No, Reggar! Not that—not that! The meteors—"

Shane snapped the switch. "The meteors—"

The silver woman's poise was gone. She shook her fist, and the glittering metallic hair came tumbling down about her shoulders. "You'll see, Earthman! You'll see! We have weapons such as you've never dreamed of…"

SHANE'S eyes flicked back to the long-range visiscreen—to the silver fleet that raced towards Gadar. It was closer now…so close he could see the fore-jets opening for the landing.

Only then, abruptly, the fleet was swerving—swinging wide in wild, irregular maneuver.

And then the meteors came—bright halls of flame in swirling clouds and clusters, with cores of stone and molten iron; flashing across the screen in the path of the Federation fleet…hurtling through space in a murderous barrage.

And one ship swerved too late, and a great orange-and-purple monster crashed into it with a burst of fire and sparking shards.

"You talk of power, Earthman?" Kyrsis raged shrilly. "You brag of your Federation's broadcast system? Then look at this, and know what power really means! We have tapped a source of energy so great it makes all others puny—a source your science left untouched, though it lies within your own solar system! But we have harnessed that force. We have concentrated it into great controlled magnetic fields that we can shift at will, so strong they pull the very meteors from their courses and hurl them to the place that we desire them to strike…"

Shane rocked, and shock was suddenly written on his lean, hard face. Wordless, he stared into the screen.

"And there is more, *Gar* Shane—much more," the woman cried. Swiftly, she stepped to the screen and twirled the dials. "There was a plan we drew for such a time as this—a plan to smash barbarian worlds to dust and ashes. We'll hurl the meteor swarms down on their cities, clouds of them so huge they'll cut through any atmospheric layer." She whirled. "Here, see your homeland, Earth! It will be the first to go! Already, the field is concentrating, forming—drawing in the meteor clouds out of the void…"

The viewer on the long-range screen was clearing. And there was Earth, Shane's native planet, a great, green-glowing arc in the lower corner. A lone spaceship was rising in the foreground, speeding out into the void. But already, about it, were meteor clusters…gathering swarms that grew with every passing minute.

"You see, *Gar* Shane? The people of your Earth are doomed!" the silver woman jeered in paranoiac frenzy. "There is no hope, no way to save them. The other planets, too, will go, till at last there is no one left but we of Gadar. Then we shall migrate out of this dark star, into your worlds, where life is not yet spent and faded. My people's strength will rise anew…"

BLEAKLY, Shane stared into the screen, through a moment that lasted all eternity.

Then, in one explosive motion, he snatched the space-phones from their rack. His voice crackled out into the void, *"Chonyas…Chonyas…*Shane, your *gar,* is calling…"

And taut-drawn *Chonya* words came back: "We stand by for your orders."

"I want a ship," Shane answered tightly, "a single fast *Chonya* ship, equipped with Abaquist repellers, to try to break through the meteor swarm and come down to Gadar to me on the fleet alarm beam."

"We come, *Gar* Shane…"

Even with the words, a slim, sleek craft was breaking from the milling fleet, swerving through the sky in a monstrous arc.

Then it was coming round again—striking its course, plunging down on Gadar. Straight into the blazing meteor swarm it sped, and even on the screen Shane could see it tossing, careening, staggering, lurching with shock.

And then it was through the swarm and out again. Its hull was ripped, its hatches battered, but still it plummeted down towards Gadar.

Kyrsis cried: "Now I know you are truly mad, not just a fool, if you think you can fight both my people and Quos Reggar here on Gadar with the crew of a single ship!"

Shane said, "We're leaving now," and levered back the hatches. Again he fired a burst from the proton cannon to clear the way…saw the shaft's walls vibrate with its violence.

The *Chonya* ship hurtled down the huge volcanic pipe like a Shooting star. Barely in time, it braked and based upon the landing ramp.

Before she could read his thoughts, Shane snatched up Kyrsis bodily and raced through the smoldering pronic rubble to the *Chonya* craft.

"Blast!" he shouted, and swung aboard; and almost before the hatches were shut, the ship was in the air again, lancing up into the sky.

The commander said, "Where now, *Gar* Shane? What are your orders?"

THE Earthman said harshly. "Send out the word to break the Federation fleet into squadrons, each to stay far from the others, and all to strike at Gadar. We'll see how many meteor swarms our friends down there can muster."

"And the rest of us…the *Malya*s, *Chonya*s…?"

"You'll follow me," Shane said. He took the jet-globe. "I'll set the course."

Kyrsis' eyes were like great violet flames. "Pay him no heed, *Chonya!*" she cried hoarsely. "Kill him! Lock him away! He is of Earth, and he has gone mad with fear for his homeland! He takes you there to try to battle another, greater meteor-swarm! It will be the death of all of you!"

The *Chonya* glanced curiously at her in her disarray, then looked into the visiscreen, the jet-globe. "A *Chonya* holds no fear of death, Silver One," he observed, iron-steady. "Besides, our course is set for Jupiter, not Earth."

"Jupiter?" the woman cried, and now a note of underlying panic was in her voice. She clutched Shane's arm. "Why Jupiter, Earthman—why?"

"Not Jupiter, Kyrsis, but one of Jupiter's moons," Shane answered thinly. "You see? There it lies in the visiscreen."

"Jupiter V…" the silver woman whispered excitedly. "No, Shane! No…"

"Yes, Kyrsis," the Earthman came back coldly. "Jupiter

V, the place where Reggar held me prisoner. And the satellite closest to the planet, a satellite heaped twelve levels deep with power converters."

"No, no—"

Relentlessly, Shane hammered on. "Who was it that wanted all that power? Who built that great Paulsini unit? Not any slaver, surely… No, that took skill and science and years of work. And when it was done, your people had more power than the world had ever known—power drawn from the endless seas of energy of Jupiter's great Red Spot, the heat of oceans of flaming hydrogen, the force that lies congealed in gases held under such pressures that they turn to solids, all turned somehow to your use by those new converters that I saw there."

The silver woman looked at him. A little of the wildness left her eyes, replaced by something that might have been cunning. Her voice came down to its former liquid murmur. "And what will you do when you get to this moon, Earthman? Will it bring back the cities of your native planet?"

"Say what you mean," Shane came back tightly.

"Perhaps Earth could be spared—for your aid against the other worlds of the Federation."

Shane's eyes blazed. "You *do* think me a fool, *Shi* Kyrsis. After all that has gone, can you believe I would trust you?"

"It is a chance you must take, if you would save Earth's cities."

STRAIN showed in Shane's voice, his face. But his jaw stayed hard, his blue eyes steady. "If Earth must go, then go it will, *Shi* Kyrsis. For all I know, the meteors may this moment be hurtling down. But even if they are, and though it costs me my life and my homeland, I'll still take the chance in order to break your life-sucking people's power."

"But you cannot destroy that power—"

The *Chonya* commander broke in, "More meteors, *Gar!* They gather between us and the satellite!"

And Kyrsis jeered. "You see, Earthman? You have lost already!"

Shane said to the *Chonya,* "We're going through."

"Through the swarm?" The commander's face lost a little of its color, but his voice stayed firm. He picked up his space-phones. "I shall give the order."

"We're going through," Shane repeated grimly, "and some of us...those who have repellers...may get there. There will not be many, but only a handful of workers can be on that moon, with Reggar's crew withdrawn, so even a few ships will be enough."

"Yes, *Gar,*" the *Chonya* nodded coolly. He spoke into the space-phones and gave the order.

The ship lanced into the swarm.

There was a nightmare quality to those endless moments. Space was suddenly ablaze about them with a thousand screaming lights that slashed at them from all directions. Off to the right, a great ball of fire appeared from nowhere and blotted out a ship. A streak of flame speared through another, and it exploded in mid-flight.

And still they drove on through the tempest, tossed and jostled, beaten, butchered.

An alarm bell clanged fiercely.

"A rip in the hull, upper port," the *Chonya* reported grimly.

Jupiter V was very large in the screens now. It loomed like a monstrous metal ball, glistening with the hood of structure that encased it.

"The swarm is following us now," the commander said. "It moves with us, traveling even faster than are we." His lips twisted wryly. "Their control is getting better all the time."

Shane stared into the visiscreen. It was as if the satellite were hurtling up to meet them. The exploding speed of it made the screen seem almost to whirl.

And still the meteors swarmed and blazed around them.

"Thirty seconds more," the *Chonya* said. "We must brake by then, or crash instead of ramp."

JUPITER V now extended past the edges of the screen. They could see but a segment of it—a segment that raced ever upward, ever towards them, dividing into a thousand finer details every second.

"Twenty seconds," the *Chonya* reported.

The meteor swarm seemed to close in about them—tighter, tighter.

"Fifteen seconds."

The meteors' light was stunning, blinding.

Shane's teeth were clenched, his lips parted, his eyes glued tight to the viewer of the visiscreen. The muscles stood out along his neck. The tension about him was a living thing.

"Ten seconds."

A sort of paralysis seemed to grip the Earthman. He stood frozen, still staring like one in a trance.

The ribs in the satellite's casing stood out, now—the ports, the vents.

The meteors seemed to have grown to blazing suns.

"Five seconds."

Shane's paralysis broke. He snatched the phones, and suddenly his eyes were blazing like the nightmare scene beyond their hull. "Veer off!" he shouted. "Don't land! Veer—!"

The *Chonya* commander's hand struck the jet-globe with a crack like a whip. It spun till it sang, racing round and round.

The ship swung out in a wild gyration. Reeling, slashing crazily across the moon's perimeter, it hurtled off through space.

Behind them, the other ships, too, were peeling clear.

But not the meteor swarm. Down it plunged, down, in the course the ships had followed, straight at the hundred-mile ball that was Jupiter V.

"They'll crash—!" the *Chonya* cried, and jubilation was in his voice, "They did not know we were so close! Now it's too late to turn them!"

The explosive flash of the meteors bursting through the satellite's casing came like an exclamation point. Great cracks appeared—monstrous fissures, spewing flame.

And still more meteors hurtled down—the whole, vast, captive swarm. The planetoid's casing glowed red-hot, then white, till the moon was a fiery, radiant sphere.

Then suddenly, it seemed to shiver. A gigantic explosion ripped one side, sent the planetoid spinning over. A huge, wedge-shaped chunk tore loose and blasted off through space; then another...another.

WITHOUT a word, the Commander of the *Chonya* craft picked up the manual on interspatial navigation, riffled through to the page on Jupiter V. Tore it out, crumpled it, dropped it to the floor.

Shane threw him a grim, tight grin and said, "There's still work, back on Gadar."

The *Chonya* spun the jet-globe; focussed the visiscreen on the dark star.

Even as the image drew sharp and clear, a ship shot out of one of the great volcanic pipes that served as the planet's ramping spots.

Shane's face went dark again. "That's Reggar's ship. Where is he going?"

And then, beside him, Kyrsis said, "Oh, no—!"

Shane turned at the sheer, stark panic in her voice.

Her face showed even more.

The Earthman looked back to the visiscreen again; and this time he, too, rocked under the impact of the thing that was happening.

Gadar was moving from its orbit!

Faster it went, and faster, slashing a course towards outer space. The ships of the Federation fleet raced madly from its path.

"No!" *Shi* Kyrsis cried again. "No, they must not leave me!" Her face was working now, contorted. The silvery tones seemed duller, more like lead.

In an awe-struck voice Shane said, "This is the way they must have come. It was no cosmic accident. They hurled their own planet across the void…"

"No, no!" the silver woman shrieked, and the wild hysteria in her tones was giving way to madness. "They can't, they can't! I must go with them…" Her twitching face was no longer human.

Then, before anyone could stop her, she turned and ran— out of the door, away from the control room.

But outside the room there was no place to run…only an echoing, well-like shaft that dropped away a hundred feet through the vitals of the ship, its depths linked only by a steel-runged ladder.

Unseeing, unheeding, the silver woman plunged over the brink and plummeted downward. Her scream rose and fell in the banshee wail of a soul in torment.

It ended with a sound like the bursting of an air-filled paper bag a room or two away.

The *Chonya* sucked in air. He let it out with a sound that might have been pity.

White-lipped, Shane said, "There was a *Chonya* child, a little girl…" Abruptly, he turned away and spun the jet-globe.

The ship's commander frowned. "I do not understand, *Gar* Shane."

The Earthman's eyes stayed on the visiscreen. He said, "My road still lies before me. It leads to Quos Reggar, and my great iron belt, and Talu, the *Malyalara.*"

CHAPTER THIRTEEN

THEY picked up the trail in the asteroid belt, in the wreckage of a gutted town. It led to Horla, then, and from there to the burning sands of Mercury's barren wastes, and then back out to the moons of Saturn. But always Reggar was a jump ahead, and always there was blood and death and pillage.

Once, on Juno, Shane thought he had cornered him. But Reggar blasted off as the Earthman ramped in, and they lost the trail in the outer asteroids.

And then one night Shane came to Titan.

As always, there was desolation. As always, the great slave ship was gone. And a weeping *bartok* woman shook her fist at Shane and cried, "So now you come! But they have killed my man. My children starve, and I am left to care for Reggar's cursed, dying *Malyalara…*"

Shane turned on her. "A *Malyalara…*? Quos Reggar's *Malyalara?*"

An emotion that might have been fear flickered in the woman's eyes, and she would have fled had Shane not caught her arm. "Please, Earthman…" she pleaded piteously. "My man is still warm in his grave. I say strange things— senseless, without meaning. Please let me go—" And when Shane released her, she scurried off through the rubble like a frightened mouse and disappeared in the ruins of a broken building.

But Shane followed her—cautious, cat-footed, through alleys and shadows and tumbled wreckage until finally she went into one of the ancient, conical, loaf-like hovels in the oldest part of the native city.

For ten long minutes the Earthman watched and waited. Then, half-angrily, he rose from the place where he lay hidden, and slapped the gun slung at his hip, and strode to the door through which the woman had gone. His knock echoed.

After a moment the woman opened the door a crack. When she saw who it was, her eyes went wide, and she tried to force the door back shut.

But Shane put his weight against it and held it open, and said, "I want to see your house, *bartok.*"

"No, no…" the woman panted.

"I must," Shane said. As gently as he could, he pushed her aside, and stepped into the room.

And there was Quos Reggar.

THE giant mongrel stood in the corner, behind the door through which Shane had entered. A light-pistol gleamed in one webbed hand, and the great lobed eyes were hot with hate.

And about the creature's waist still was drawn the iron-linked belt—Shane's *Chonya* belt, the belt of the asteroids.

"Welcome, Earthman," the mongrel rasped, just as on the other night that now seemed so far away, so long ago. "Welcome to death…"

Shane froze in his tracks—statue-like, taut-muscled. His eyes alone moved…gauging Quos Reggar, measuring the distance, weighing the light-gun against his own draw.

And the mongrel saw the things in the cold blue eyes—the death, the decision; and he snapped sharply, "No, *chitza!* Wait…!"

"Why?" clipped the Earthman. "Why put it off?" And there was recklessness in his voice—a fierce exaltation.

"Because it may be you need not die!" the mongrel came

back swiftly. "Because there are things you do not know…things that still may save your life and make it worth living."

Shane still stood taut, motionless, waiting. He did not answer.

"I thought you would come to Talu's name," the hybrid told him, and now the creature's tone held a gloating note. "I planned it well—and you, fool that you are, came to the trap as on wings of fire."

"Get on with it—say what you have to say!" Shane slashed harshly. "We both know what is between us. Why waste this time?"

"The time is not wasted," Reggar answered. "Your coming here as you did proves something…a fine point on which much may hang, for you as well as me."

Shane bared his teeth. His left hand moved in a savage, contemptuous gesture. "Get on with it!" he slashed again. "What is it you seek to say?"

A sly smile of sorts came to Reggar's lips. He called, "Talu…"

"Here, *Sha* Reggar." She stepped through the doorway, lithely graceful as always, garbed in a *bandong* of scarlet and gold. A gold clip held the midnight hair, and a gleaming fire-ruby of Neptune hung by a golden chain in the hollow of her throat.

Her eyes met the Earthman's, poised and calm. "*Sha* Shane."

A TOUCH of color came to Shane's lean face. Quickly, he looked away, back to Quos Reggar.

But a ghoulish grin twisted the mongrel's lips. "Why stare at me, Earthman? Look at her, look at her… Is she not lovely?"

Shane's eyes did not waver. "I'm listening, Reggar," he

97

answered tightly.

The hybrid chuckled. "You came quickly, Earthman...so quickly, when you heard mention of this woman. You threw caution to the winds and came alone, in spite of all sense and judgment."

"So—?"

"So I knew there was a feeling between you and this *Malyalara*—a thing without logic, beyond your judgment, perhaps what you humanoids call love."

The color heightened in the Earthman's face. "You're mad as a *ban*, Reggar," he challenged angrily.

"I think not," leered the mongrel. "And it is good. Because you shall have—the woman—untouched, too, Earthman. For I am not as your race, and she could never catch my fancy, save as a pretty toy."

"And the price, Reggar?" Shane queried tightly. "What must I do to earn such favor?"

The creature before him shrugged. "I need not feign you have not hurt me. For you have. You and your *Chonyas* have harried me through the void, and up and down among the planets. You've tracked me down as the *zanth* tracks down its prey. But now, I tire of being hunted. My crew is weary and sick, and the hull of my ship is worn to cracking. So I have stayed behind this time to strike a bargain with you, if I can."

"A bargain?" The Earthman laughed harshly. "When was your word ever worth a *xi* that I should take it now?" His eyes narrowed, and he studied the other. "Besides, what bargain could I make? The Federation hunts you also."

"The Federation?" Reggar sneered. "Loot will always buy someone in the Federation. But you—you fight from hate; and that is different."

"Then why haggle with me? Why not kill me now, if indeed you fear me?"

"Why does anyone bargain?" Again the mongrel shrugged.

"Because you have something I want and need—something I cannot get without your aid."

"Well? What is it?"

Thoughtfully, the great lobed eyes surveyed the Earthman. The rasping voice sank lower, "It is sanctuary, *Gar* Shane. That is what I seek…a place in the asteroids to hide—away from the eyes of the Federation. As for you, you need not even call off your war against me. Not openly; you will merely manage to never quite find me."

THE Earthman frowned. He looked away—to Talu, still standing in the open doorway; to the woman who'd lured him here, mousy and frightened in the farthest corner; to the tawdry room and its tawdrier trimmings.

Then, at last, his eyes moved back to Reggar. In a tone of wonderment, he asked, "Did you really think that I might agree to this? That I might break the oath I swore; betray the trust the *Chonyas* gave me with their great iron belt?"

Almost silkily, Reggar murmured, "Before you refuse, there are things you should consider."

The cloak of control fell away from Shane. His blue eyes blazed. His jaw was hard. "I swore my oath on the star-stone of Hiaroloch, Reggar," he said harshly. "There's nothing in this world or any other that will make me break it." And then, with great force, "Get on with your killing, butcher—and make sure your first beam hits me true, for it will be your last…"

The mottlings stood out on Reggar's scaly face. The light-gun thrust forward, and muscles stood out along the webbed hand's bones. "Perhaps there is a thing you have forgotten, *chitza!*" he snarled. "Perhaps you do not recall—the *theol!*"

"The *theol?*" And though the words came out as a question, already the color was draining from the Earthman's face.

"Yes, the *theol, starbo*—and you know what I mean, for the fear is crawling through your eyes like the worms of Thora! Two doses you've had. A third will make you my slave forever…"

The muscles in Shane's neck knotted. His head came forward just a fraction. "Wrong, Reggar!" he clipped. "To make me stand and take the *theol,* the fear of death must be in me even stronger. And that dread I do not have. I'll fight— here, now! So the choice is yours, not mine! You must kill me, or die yourself—"

"Wait, Shane—!" cried the mongrel. "There is more! There is the woman—the *Malyalara!*"

Shane went rigid.

"I can kill you," rasped Reggar. "Have no doubt about it. My gun is out, and yours is still holstered. But let me tell you this…if I do, Talu is the one who shall suffer. I'll sell her in the brothels of Uranus. The great, hairy beasts there shall have this woman of yours—and she will be a long time dying…"

SHANE'S lips drained white. His face grew gray. Suddenly his hands were shaking.

"Is it not a pretty picture, Shane?" the creature before him gloated. "You dead—the *Malyalara* sold for the sport of the beasts there on Uranus—and all because you would not stretch your oath even a little—?"

"Damn you, Reggar," the Earthman whispered. "Damn you…"

"Then it is agreed?" the mongrel cried, in a voice alive with hideous glee. "You will promise me sanctuary, somewhere in the asteroids? You'll pledge your sworn word to hide me and shield me and give me aid?"

"Reggar…" The veins were throbbing in the Earthman's temples.

Only then Talu cried out, "No, Shane! No—!" She rushed forward, hurled her lithe body straight at Quos Reggar. "I would rather die than see you yield! You know the things this monster has done to the *Malya*s, the *Chonyas!* Kill him, kill him—!"

A roar of rage burst from the mongrel. His clubbed light-gun slashed down at the woman's bare breasts, trying to drive her off. Shane leaped like a tiger. He clawed at the hybrid's pistol; wrenched it back—away from Talu's supple body, hard against his own.

Twisting and snarling, Reggar crushed down the exciter.

A faint, misty spray spurted from the muzzle, straight into Shane's throat.

But now Shane's own gun was out. Purple light slashed like a sword at the mongrel's belly.

Reggar reeled back. He smashed a wild blow to Shane's head, sent the Earthman crashing to the floor. Again Shane fired.

Reggar's mottled face went black under the beam. An awful scream rose in his throat. He tottered…lurched…fell.

Talu was with Shane, then—clutching him to her, the dark face all anguish. "Shane, Shane…"

DAZEDLY, the Earthman muttered, "The light-gun…what happened to his light-gun? He triggered it straight into my throat…"

With an effort, he rolled to the weapon and broke it open.

The ray mechanism was gone. A hypodermic injector had been inserted in its place.

Shane's hand clutched his throat.

There was still a trace of moisture there…clear, colorless moisture.

Talu whispered, "Shane, let me hold you…"

Shaking, he forced her away. His voice quaked, "No,

Malyalara. No! Get away from me—now, while you have the chance—"

"Shane, what is it?"

Numbly, he showed her the gun. "An injector—with *theol.* It makes three doses. In the end, Reggar wins. The madness will come upon me—"

"No, Shane…" She would have embraced him.

"Get away!" he shouted fiercely. "Don't you understand? This was the third dose—the dose that brings madness. And there is no cure—"

His face was a mask—all despair, and all fury.

She laughed, gently, then—warm, comprehending. There was no panic in her face, her voice. "No, Shane," she told him. "There will be no madness."

He stared at her blankly. "It is *theol…*"

"Yes, it is *theol.* But not the third dose."

"Not the third—?" His tongue stumbled.

"No, Shane. Because before the third, there must be a second, and I gave you what Reggar thought was the second that night back at Horla. But he left me alone for a moment with the injector, and I replaced the *theol* with another solution—without color, but harmless."

A choking sound rose in the Earthman's throat. His trembling hands touched her—smoothed her hair, brushed her shoulder.

She came to him—smiling, lips warm with welcome. And suddenly their bodies were together, tight-welded, and he was whispering feverishly, "Talu…Talu…"

And when at last they parted, she said, "I am yours, Earthman…yours now and forever. But you still have a role to play, your oath to uphold. You are *gar* of the *Chonyas.*"

"And you will rule with me," he answered her fiercely.

"Your belt, Earthman…"

"My belt…the belt of the asteroids." Bending, he stripped

the iron links from the corpse of Quos Reggar and girded it tight about his own waist once mere. His eyes met Talu's. "Come, *Malyalara…*"

Together, they crossed the threshold into the night and the stars.

THE END

If you've enjoyed this book, you will not want to miss these terrific titles…

ARMCHAIR SCI-FI & HORROR DOUBLE NOVELS, $12.95 each

D-121 **THE GENIUS BEASTS** by Frederik Pohl
THIS WORLD IS TABOO by Murray Leinster

D-122 **THE COSMIC LOOTERS** by Edmond Hamilton
WANDL THE INVADER by Ray Cummings

D-123 **ROBOT MEN OF BUBBLE CITY** by Rog Phillips
DRAGON ARMY by William Morrison

D-124 **LAND BEYOND THE LENS** by S. J. Byrne
DIPLOMAT-AT-ARMS by Keith Laumer

D-125 **VOYAGE OF THE ASTEROID, THE** by Laurence Manning
REVOLT OF THE OUTWORLDS by Milton Lesser

D-126 **OUTLAW IN THE SKY** by Chester S. Geier
LEGACY FROM MARS by Raymond Z. Gallun

D-127 **THE GREAT FLYING SAUCER INVASION** by Geoff St. Reynard
THE BIG TIME by Fritz Leiber

D-128 **MIRAGE FOR PLANET X** by Stanley Mullen
POLICE YOUR PLANET by Lester del Rey

D-129 **THE BRAIN SINNERS** by Alan E. Nourse
DEATH FROM THE SKIES by A. Hyatt Verrill

D-139 **CRY CHAOS** by Dwight V. Swain
THE DOOR THROUGH SPACE By Marion Zimmer Bradley

ARMCHAIR SCIENCE FICTION CLASSICS, $12.95 each

C-55 **UNDER THE TRIPLE SUNS**
by Stanton A. Coblentz

C-56 **STONE FROM THE GREEN STAR**
by Jack Williamson

C-57 **ALIEN MINDS**
by E. Everett Evans

ARMCHAIR MASTERS OF SCIENCE FICTION SERIES, $16.95 each

G-13 **SCIENCE FICTION GEMS, Vol. Seven**
Jack Vance and others

G-14 **HORROR GEMS, Vol. Seven**
Robert Bloch and others

ACROSS HALF THE GALAXY...

...the Terran Empire maintained its sovereignty with the consent of the governed. It was a peaceful reign, held by compact and not by conquest. Again and again, when rebellion threatened the Terran Peace, the natives of the rebellious world turned against their own people and sided with the men of Terra; not from fear, but from a sense of dedication.

There had never been open war. The battle for these worlds was fought in the minds of a few men who stood between worlds; bound to one world by interest, loyalties and allegiance; bound to the other by love.

Such a world was Wolf. Such a man was Race Cargill of the Terran Secret Service.

AUTHOR'S NOTE...

I've always wanted to write. But not until I discovered the old pulp science-fantasy magazines, at the age of sixteen, did this general desire become a specific urge to write science-fantasy adventures.

I took a lot of detours on the way. I discovered s-f in its golden age: the age of Kuttner, C. L. Moore, Leigh Brackett, Ed Hamilton and Jack Vance. But while I was still collecting rejection slips for my early efforts, the fashion changed. Adventures on faraway worlds and strange dimensions went out of fashion, and the new look in science-fiction—emphasis on the *science*—came in.

So my first stories were straight science-fiction, and I'm not trying to put down that kind of story. It has its place. By and large, the kind of science-fiction which makes tomorrow's headlines as near as this morning's coffee, has enlarged popular awareness of the modern, miraculous world of science we live in. It has helped generations of young people feel at ease with a rapidly changing world.

But fashions change, old loves return, and now that Sputniks clutter up the sky with new and unfamiliar moons, the readers of science-fiction are willing to wait for tomorrow to read tomorrow's headlines. Once again, I think, there is a place, a wish, a need and hunger for the wonder and color of the world way out. The world beyond the stars. The world we *won't* live to see. That is why I wrote THE DOOR THROUGH SPACE.

—*Marion Zimmer Bradley*

THE DOOR
THROUGH SPACE

By
MARION ZIMMER BRADLEY

ARMCHAIR FICTION
PO Box 4369, Medford, Oregon 97501-0168

*For more information about Armchair Books and products, visit our
website at…*

www.armchairfiction.com

Or email us at…

armchairfiction@yahoo.com

CHAPTER ONE

Beyond the spaceport gates, the men of the Kharsa were hunting down a thief. I heard the shrill cries, the pad-padding of feet in strides just a little too long and loping to be human, raising echoes all down the dark and dusty streets leading up to the main square.

But the square itself lay empty in the crimson noon of Wolf. Overhead the dim red ember of Phi Coronis, Wolf's old and dying sun, gave out a pale and heatless light. The pair of Spaceforce guards at the gates, wearing the black leathers of the Terran Empire, shockers holstered at their belts, were drowsing under the arched gateway where the star-and-rocket emblem proclaimed the domain of Terra. One of them, a snub-nosed youngster only a few weeks out from Earth, cocked an inquisitive ear at the cries and scuffling feet, then jerked his head at me.

"Hey, Cargill, you can talk their lingo. What's going on out there?"

I stepped out past the gateway to listen. There was still no one to be seen in the square. It lay white and windswept, a barricade of emptiness; to one side the spaceport and the white skyscraper of the Terran Headquarters, and at the other side, the clutter of low buildings, the street-shrine, the little spaceport cafe smelling of coffee and *jaco*, and the dark opening mouths of streets that rambled down into the Kharsa—the old town, the native quarter. But I was alone in the square with the shrill cries—closer now, raising echoes from the enclosing walls—and the loping of many feet down one of the dirty streets.

Then I saw him running, dodging, a hail of stones flying round his head; someone or something small and cloaked and agile. Behind him the still-faceless mob howled and threw stones. I could not yet understand the cries; but they were out for blood, and I knew it.

I said briefly, "Trouble coming," just before the mob spilled out into the square. The fleeing dwarf stared about wildly for an instant, his head jerking from side to side so rapidly that it was impossible to get even a fleeting impression of his face—human or nonhuman, familiar or bizarre. Then, like a pellet loosed from its sling, he made straight for the gateway and safety.

And behind him the loping mob yelled and howled and came pouring over half the square. Just half. Then by that sudden intuition which permeates even the most crazed mob with some semblance of reason, they came to a ragged halt, heads turning from side to side.

I stepped up on the lower step of the Headquarters building, and looked them over.

Most of them were *chaks*, the furred man-tall nonhumans of the Kharsa, and not the better class. Their fur was unkempt, their tails naked with filth and disease. Their leather aprons hung in tatters. One or two in the crowd were humans, the dregs of the Kharsa. But the star-and-rocket emblem blazoned across the spaceport gates sobered even the wildest blood-lust somewhat; they milled and shifted uneasily in their half of the square.

For a moment I did not see where their quarry had gone. Then I saw him crouched, not four feet from me, in a patch of shadow. Simultaneously the mob saw him, huddled just beyond the gateway, and a howl of frustration and rage went ringing round the square. Someone threw a stone. It zipped over my head, narrowly missing me, and landed at the feet of the black-leathered guard. He jerked his head up and gestured with the shocker which had suddenly come unholstered.

The gesture should have been enough. On Wolf, Terran law has been written in blood and fire and exploding atoms; and the line is drawn firm and clear. The men of Spaceforce do not interfere in the old town, or in any of the native cities. But when violence steps over the threshold, passing the blazon of the star and rocket, punishment is swift and terrible. The threat should have been enough.

Instead a howl of abuse went up from the crowd.

"*Terranan!*"

"Son of the Ape!"

The Spaceforce guards were shoulder to shoulder behind me now. The snub-nosed kid, looking slightly pale, called out. "Get inside the gates, Cargill! If I have to shoot—"

The older man motioned him to silence. "Wait. Cargill," he called.

I nodded to show that I heard.

"You talk their lingo. Tell them to haul off! Damned if I want to shoot!"

I stepped down and walked into the open square, across the crumbled white stones, toward the ragged mob. Even with two armed Spaceforce men at my back, it made my skin crawl, but I flung up my empty hand in token of peace.

"Take your mob out of the square," I shouted in the jargon of the Kharsa. "This territory is held in compact of peace! Settle your quarrels elsewhere!"

There was a little stirring in the crowd. The shock of being addressed in their own tongue, instead of the Terran Standard which the Empire has forced on Wolf, held them silent for a minute. I had learned that long ago: that speaking in any of the languages of Wolf would give me a minute's advantage.

But only a minute. Then one of the mob yelled, "We'll go if you give'm to us! He's no right to Terran sanctuary!"

I walked over to the huddled dwarf, miserably trying to make himself smaller against the wall. I nudged him with my foot.

"Get up. Who are you?"

The hood fell away from his face as he twitched to his feet. He was trembling violently. In the shadow of the hood I saw a furred face, a quivering velvety muzzle, and great soft golden eyes which held intelligence and terror.

"What have you done? Can't you talk?"

He held out the tray which he had shielded under his cloak, an ordinary peddler's tray. "Toys. Sell toys. Children. You got'm?"

I shook my head and pushed the creature away, with only a glance at the array of delicately crafted manikins, tiny animals, prisms and crystal whirligigs. "You'd better get out of here. Scram. Down that street." I pointed.

A voice from the crowd shouted again, and it had a very ugly sound. "He is a spy of Nebran!"

"*Nebran*—" The dwarfish nonhuman gabbled something then doubled behind me. I saw him dodge, feint in the direction of the gates, then, as the crowd surged that way, run for the street-shrine across the square, slipping from recess to recess of the wall. A hail of stones went flying in that direction. The little toy-seller dodged into the street-shrine.

Then there was a hoarse "Ah, aaah!" of terror, and the crowd edged away, surged backward. The next minute it had begun to melt away, its entity dissolving into separate creatures, slipping into the side alleys and the dark streets that disgorged into the square. Within three minutes the square lay empty again in the pale-crimson noon.

The kid in black leather let his breath go and swore, slipping his shocker into its holster. He stared and demanded profanely, "Where'd the little fellow go?"

"Who knows?" the other shrugged. "Probably sneaked into one of the alleys. Did you see where he went, Cargill?"

I came slowly back to the gateway. To me, it had seemed that he ducked into the street-shrine and vanished into thin air, but I've lived on Wolf long enough to know you can't trust your eyes here. I said so, and the kid swore again, gulping, more upset than he wanted to admit. "Does this kind of thing happen often?"

"All the time," his companion assured him soberly, with a sidewise wink at me. I didn't return the wink.

The kid wouldn't let it drop. "Where did you learn their lingo, Mr. Cargill?"

"I've been on Wolf a long time," I said, spun on my heel and walked toward Headquarters. I tried not to hear, but their voices followed me anyhow, discreetly lowered, but not lowered enough.

"Kid, don't you know who he is? That's Cargill of the Secret Service! Six years ago he was the best man in Intelligence, before—" The voice lowered another decibel, and then there was the kid's voice asking, shaken, "But what the hell happened to his face?"

I should have been used to it by now. I'd been hearing it, more or less behind my back, for six years. Well, if my luck held, I'd never hear it again. I strode up the white steps of the skyscraper, to finish the arrangements that would take me away from Wolf forever. To the other end of the Empire, to the other end of the galaxy—anywhere, so long as I need not wear my past like a medallion around my neck, or blazoned and branded on what was left of my ruined face

CHAPTER TWO

The Terran Empire has set its blazon on four hundred planets circling more than three hundred suns. But no matter what the color of the sun, the number of moons overhead, or the geography of the planet, once you step inside a Headquarters building, you are on Earth. And Earth would be alien to many who called themselves Earthmen, judging by the strangeness I always felt when I stepped into that marble-and-glass world inside the skyscraper. I heard the sound of my steps ringing into thin resonance along the marble corridor, and squinted my eyes, readjusting them painfully to the cold yellowness of the lights.

The Traffic Division was efficiency made insolent, in glass and chrome and polished steel, mirrors and windows and looming electronic clerical machines. Most of one wall was taken up by a TV monitor which gave a view of the spaceport; a vast open space lighted with blue-white mercury vapor lamps, and a chained-down skyscraper of a starship, littered over with swarming ants. The process crew was getting the big ship ready for skylift tomorrow morning. I gave it a second and then a third look. I'd be on it when it lifted.

Turning away from the monitored spaceport, I watched myself stride forward in the mirrored surfaces that were everywhere; a tall man, a lean man, bleached out by years under a red sun, and deeply scarred on both cheeks and around the mouth. Even after six years behind a desk, my neat business clothes—suitable for an Earthman with a desk job—didn't fit quite right, and I still rose unconsciously on the balls of my feet, approximating the lean stooping walk of a Dry-towner from the Coronis plains.

The clerk behind the sign marked TRANSPORTATION was a little rabbit of a man with a sunlamp tan, barricaded by a small-sized spaceport of desk, and looking as if he liked being shut up there. He looked up in civil inquiry.

"Can I do something for you?"

"My name's Cargill. Have you a pass for me?"

He stared. A free pass aboard a starship is rare except for professional spacemen, which I obviously wasn't. "Let me check my records," he hedged, and punched scanning buttons on the glassy surface. Shadows came and went, and I saw myself half-reflected, a tipsy shadow in a flurry of racing colors. The pattern finally stabilized and the clerk read off names.

"Brill, Cameron…ah, yes. Cargill, Race Andrew, Department 38, transfer transportation. Is that you?"

I admitted it and he started punching more buttons when the sound of the name made connection in whatever desk-clerks use for a brain. He stopped with his hand halfway to the button.

"Are you Race Cargill of the Secret Service, sir? *The* Race Cargill?"

"It's right there," I said, gesturing wearily at the projected pattern under the glassy surface.

"Why, I thought—I mean, everybody took it for granted—that is, I heard—"

"You thought Cargill had been killed a long time ago because his name never turned up in news dispatches any more?" I grinned sourly, seeing my image dissolve in blurring shadows, and feeling the long-healed scar on my mouth draw up to make the grin hideous. "I'm Cargill, all right. I've been up on Floor 38 for six years, holding down a desk any clerk could handle. You for instance."

He gaped. He was a rabbit of a man who had never stepped out of the safe familiar boundaries of the Terran Trade City. "You mean *you're* the man who went to Charin in disguise, and routed out The Lisse? The man who scouted the Black Ridge and Shainsa? And you've been working at a desk upstairs all these years? It's—hard to believe, sir."

My mouth twitched. It had been hard for me to believe while I was doing it. "The pass?"

"Right away, sir." He punched buttons and a printed chip of plastic extruded from a slot on the desk top. "Your fingerprint, please?" He pressed my finger into the still-soft surface of the plastic, indelibly recording the print; waited a moment for it to harden, then laid the chip in the slot of a pneumatic tube. I heard it whoosh away.

"They'll check your fingerprint against that when you board the ship. Skylift isn't till dawn, but you can go aboard as soon as the process crew finishes with her." He glanced at the monitor screen, where the swarming crew were still doing inexplicable things to the immobile spacecraft. "It will be another hour or two. Where are you going, Mr. Cargill?"

"Some planet in the Hyades Cluster. Vainwal, I think, something like that."

"What's it like there?"

"How should I know?" I'd never been there either. I only knew that Vainwal had a red sun, and that the Terran Legate could use a trained Intelligence officer. And *not* pin him down to a desk.

There was respect, and even envy in the little man's voice. "Could I—buy you a drink before you go aboard, Mr. Cargill?"

"Thanks, but I have a few loose ends to tie up." I didn't, but I was damned if I'd spend my last hour on Wolf under the eyes of a deskbound rabbit who preferred his adventure safely secondhand.

But after I'd left the office and the building, I almost wished I'd taken him up on it. It would be at least an hour before I could board the starship, with nothing to do but hash over old memories, better forgotten.

The sun was lower now. Phi Coronis is a dim star, a dying star, and once past the crimson zenith of noon, its light slants into a long pale-reddish twilight. Four of Wolf's five moons were clustered in a pale bouquet overhead, mingling thin violet moonlight into the crimson dusk.

The shadows were blue and purple in the empty square as I walked across the stones and stood looking down one of the side streets.

A few steps, and I was in an untidy slum which might have been on another world from the neat bright Trade City which lay west of the spaceport. The Kharsa was alive and reeking with the sounds and smells of human and half-human life. A naked child, diminutive and golden-furred, darted between two of the chinked pebble-houses, and disappeared, spilling fragile laughter like breaking glass.

A little beast, half snake and half cat, crawled across a roof, spread leathery wings, and flapped to the ground. The sour pungent reek of incense from the open street-shrine made my nostrils twitch, and a hulked form inside, not human, cast me a surly green glare as I passed.

I turned, retracing my steps. There was no danger, of course, so close to the Trade City. Even on such planets as Wolf, Terra's laws are respected within earshot of their gates. But there had been rioting here and in Charin during the last month. After the display of mob violence this afternoon, a lone Terran, unarmed, might turn up as a solitary corpse flung on the steps of the HQ building.

There had been a time when I had walked alone from Shainsa to the Polar Colony. I had known how to melt into this kind of night, shabby and inconspicuous, a worn shirtcloak hunched round my shoulders, weaponless except for the razor-sharp skean in the clasp of the cloak; walking on the balls of my feet like a Dry-towner, not looking or sounding or smelling like an Earthman.

That rabbit in the Traffic office had stirred up things I'd be wiser to forget. It had been six years; six years of slow death behind a desk, since the day when Rakhal Sensar had left me a marked man; death-warrant written on my scarred face anywhere outside the narrow confines of the Terran law on Wolf.

Rakhal Sensar—my fists clenched with the old impotent hate. *If I could get my hands on him!*

It had been Rakhal who first led me through the byways of the Kharsa, teaching me the jargon of a dozen tribes, the chirping call of the Ya-men, the way of the catmen of the rain-forests, the argot of thieves markets, the walk and step of the Dry-towners from Shainsa and Daillon and Ardcarran—the parched cities of dusty, salt stone which spread out in the bottoms of Wolf's vanished oceans. Rakhal was from Shainsa, human, tall as an Earthman, weathered by salt and sun, and he had worked for Terran Intelligence since we were boys. We had traveled all over our world together, and found it good.

And then, for some reason I had never known, it had come to an end. Even now I was not wholly sure why he had erupted, that day, into violence and a final explosion. Then he had disappeared, leaving me a marked man. And a lonely one: Juli had gone with him.

I strode the streets of the slum unseeing, my thoughts running a familiar channel. Juli, my kid sister, clinging around Rakhal's neck, her gray eyes hating me. I had never seen her again.

That had been six years ago. One more adventure had shown me that my usefulness to the Secret Service was over.

Rakhal had vanished, but he had left me a legacy: my name, written on the sure scrolls of death anywhere outside the safe boundaries of Terran law. A marked man, I had gone back to slow stagnation behind a desk. I'd stood it as long as I could.

When it finally got too bad, Magnusson had been sympathetic. He was the Chief of Terran Intelligence on Wolf, and I was next in line for his job, but he understood when I quit. He'd arranged the transfer and the pass, and I was leaving tonight.

I was nearly back to the spaceport by now, across from the street-shrine at the edge of the square. It was here that the little toy-seller had vanished. But it was exactly like a thousand, a hundred thousand other such street-shrines on Wolf, a smudge of incense reeking and stinking before the squatting image of Nebran, the Toad God whose face and symbol are everywhere on Wolf. I stared for a moment at the ugly idol, then slowly moved away.

The lighted curtains of the spaceport cafe attracted my attention and I went inside. A few spaceport personnel in storm gear were drinking coffee at the counter, a pair of furred *chaks*, lounging beneath the mirrors at the far end, and a trio of Dry-towners, rangy, weathered men in crimson and blue shirt cloaks, were standing at a wall shelf, eating Terran food with aloof dignity.

In my business clothes I felt more conspicuous than the *chaks*. What place had a civilian here, between the uniforms of the spacemen and the colorful brilliance of the Dry-towners?

A snub-nosed girl with alabaster hair came to take my order. I asked for *jaco* and bunlets, and carried the food to a wall shelf near the Dry-towners. Their dialect fell soft and familiar on my ears. One of them, without altering the expression on his face or the easy tone of his voice, began to make elaborate comments on my entrance, my appearance, my ancestry and probably personal habits, all defined in the colorfully obscene dialect of Shainsa.

That had happened before. The Wolfan sense of humor is only half-human. The finest joke is to criticize and insult a stranger, preferably an Earthman, to his very face, in an unknown language, perfectly deadpan. In my civilian clothes I was obviously fair game.

A look or gesture of resentment would have lost face and dignity—what the Dry-towners call their *kihar*—permanently. I leaned over and remarked in their own dialect that I would, at some future and unspecified time, appreciate the opportunity to return their compliments.

By rights they should have laughed, made some barbed remark about my command of language and crossed their hands in symbol of a jest decently reversed on themselves. Then we would have bought each other a drink, and that would be that.

But it didn't happen that way. Not this time. The tallest of the three whirled, upsetting his drink in the process. I heard its thin shatter through the squeal of the alabaster-haired girl, as a chair crashed over. They faced me three abreast, and one of them fumbled in the clasp of his shirtcloak.

I edged backward, my own hand racing up for a skean I hadn't carried in six years, and fronted them squarely, hoping I could face down the prospect of a roughhouse. They wouldn't kill me, this close to the HQ, but at least I was in for an unpleasant mauling. I couldn't handle three men; and if nerves were this taut in the Kharsa, I might get knifed. Quite by accident, of course.

The *chaks* moaned and gibbered. The Dry-towners glared at me and I tensed for the moment when their steady stare would explode into violence.

Then I became aware that they were gazing, not at me, but at something or someone behind me. The skeans snicked back into the clasps of their cloaks.

Then they broke rank, turned and ran. They *ran*, blundering into stools, leaving havoc of upset benches and broken crockery in their wake. One man barged into the counter, swore and ran on, limping. I let my breath go. Something had put the fear of

God into those brutes, and it wasn't my own ugly mug. I turned and saw the girl.

She was slight, with waving hair like spun black glass, circled with faint tracery of stars. A black glass belt bound her narrow waist like clasped hands, and her robe, stark white, bore an ugly embroidery across the breasts, the flat sprawl of a conventionalized Toad God, Nebran. Her features were delicate, chiseled, pale; a Dry-town face, all human, all woman, but set in an alien and unearthly repose. The great eyes gleamed red. They were fixed, almost unseeing, but the crimson lips were curved with inhuman malice.

She stood motionless, looking at me as if wondering why I had not run with the others. In half a second, the smile flickered off and was replaced by a startled look of— recognition?

Whoever and whatever she was, she had saved me a mauling. I started to phrase formal thanks, then broke off in astonishment. The cafe had emptied and we were entirely alone. Even the *chaks* had leaped through an open window—I saw the whisk of a disappearing tail.

We stood frozen, looking at one another while the Toad God sprawled across her breasts rose and fell for half a dozen breaths.

Then I took one step forward, and she took one step backward, at the same instant. In one swift movement she was outside in the dark street. It took me only an instant to get into the street after her, but as I stepped across the door there was a little stirring in the air, like the rising of heat waves across the salt flats at noon. Then the street-shrine was empty, and nowhere was there any sign of the girl. She had vanished. She simply was not there.

I gaped at the empty shrine. She had stepped inside and vanished, like a wraith of smoke, like—

—Like the little toy-seller they had hunted out of the Kharsa.

There were eyes in the street again and, becoming aware of where I was, I moved away. The shrines of Nebran are on every corner of Wolf, but this is one instance when familiarity does not breed contempt. The street was dark and seemed empty, but it was packed with all the little noises of living. I was not unobserved. And meddling with a street-shrine would be just as dangerous as the skeans of my three loud-mouthed Dry-town roughnecks.

I turned and crossed the square for the last time, turning toward the loom of the spaceship, filing the girl away as just another riddle of Wolf I'd never solve.

How wrong I was!

CHAPTER THREE

From the spaceport gates, exchanging brief greetings with the guards, I took a last look at the Kharsa. For a minute I toyed with the notion of just disappearing down one of those streets. It's not hard to disappear on Wolf, if you know how. And I knew, or had known once. Loyalty to Terra? What had Terra given me except a taste of color and adventure, out there in the Dry-towns, and then taken it away again?

If an Earthman is very lucky and very careful, he lasts about ten years in Intelligence. I had had two years more than my share. I still knew enough to leave my Terran identity behind like a worn-out jacket. I could seek out Rakhal, settle our blood-feud, see Juli again…

How could I see Juli again? As her husband's murderer? No other way. Blood-feud on Wolf is a terrible and elaborate ritual of the code duello. And once I stepped outside the borders of Terran law, sooner or later Rakhal and I would meet. And one of us would die.

I looked back, just once, at the dark rambling streets away from the square. Then I turned toward the blue-white lights that hurt my eyes, and the starship that loomed, huge and hateful, before me.

A steward in white took my fingerprint and led me to a coffin-sized chamber. He brought me coffee and sandwiches—

I hadn't, after all, eaten in the spaceport cafe—then got me into the skyhook and strapped me, deftly and firmly, into the acceleration cushions, tugging at the Garensen belts until I ached all over. A long needle went into my arm—the narcotic that would keep me safely drowsy all through the terrible tug of interstellar acceleration.

Doors clanged, buzzers vibrated lower down in the ship, men tramped the corridors calling to one another in the language of the spaceports. I understood one word in four. I shut my eyes, not caring. At the end of the trip there would be another star, another world, another language. Another life.

I had spent all my adult life on Wolf. Juli had been a child under the red star. But it was a pair of wide crimson eyes and black hair combed into ringlets like spun black glass that went down with me into the bottomless pit of sleep...

Someone was shaking me.

"Ah, come on, Cargill. Wake up, man. Shake your boots!"

My mouth, foul-tasting and stiff, fumbled at the shapes of words. "Wha' happened? Wha' y' want?" My eyes throbbed. When I got them open I saw two men in black leathers bending over me. We were still inside gravity.

"Get out of the skyhook. You're coming with us."

"Wha'—" Even through the layers of the sedative, that got to me. Only a criminal, under interstellar law, can be removed from a passage-paid starship once he has formally checked in on board. I was legally, at this moment, on my "planet of destination."

"I haven't been charged—"

"Did I say you had?" snapped one man.

"Shut up, he's doped," the other said hurriedly. "Look," he continued, pronouncing every word loudly and distinctly, "get up now, and come with us. The co-ordinator will hold up blastoff if we don't get off in three minutes, and Operations will scream. Come on, please."

Then I was stumbling along the lighted, empty corridor, swaying between the two men, foggily realizing the crew must think me a fugitive caught trying to leave the planet.

The locks dilated. A uniformed spaceman watched us, fussily regarding a chronometer. He fretted. "The dispatcher's office—"

"We're doing the best we can," the Spaceforce man said. "Can you walk, Cargill?"

I could, though my feet were a little shaky on the ladders. The violet moonlight had deepened to mauve, and gusty winds spun tendrils of grit across my face. The Spaceforce men shepherded me, one on either side, to the gateway.

"What the hell is all this? Is something wrong with my pass?"

The guard shook his head. "How would I know? Magnusson put out the order, take it up with him."

"Believe me," I muttered, "I will."

They looked at each other. "Hell," said one, "he's not under arrest, we don't have to haul him around like a convict. Can you walk all right now, Cargill? You know where the Secret Service office is, don't you? Floor 38. The Chief wants you, and make it fast."

I knew it made no sense to ask questions, they obviously knew no more than I did. I asked anyhow.

"Are they holding the ship for me? I'm supposed to be leaving on it."

"Not that one," the guard answered, jerking his head toward the spaceport. I looked back just in time to see the dust-dimmed ship leap upward, briefly whitened in the field searchlights, and vanish into the surging clouds above.

My head was clearing fast, and anger speeded up the process. The HQ building was empty in the chill silence of just before dawn. I had to rout out a dozing elevator operator, and as the lift swooped upward my anger rose with it. I wasn't working for Magnusson any more. What right had he, or anybody, to grab me off an outbound starship like a criminal? By the time I barged into his office, I was spoiling for a fight.

The Secret Service office was full of grayish-pink morning and yellow lights left on from the night before. Magnusson, at his desk, looked as if he'd slept in his rumpled uniform. He was a big bull of a man, and his littered desk looked, as always, like the track of a typhoon in the salt flats.

The clutter was weighted down, here and there, with solidopic cubes of the five Magnusson youngsters, and as usual, Magnusson was fiddling with one of the cubes. He said, not looking up, "Sorry to pull this at the last minute, Race. There was just time to put out a pull order and get you off the ship, but no time to explain."

I glared at him. "Seems I can't even get off the planet without trouble! You raised hell all the time I was here, but when I try to leave—what is this, anyhow? I'm sick of being shoved around!"

Magnusson made a conciliating gesture. "Wait until you hear—" he began, and broke off, looking at someone who was sitting in the chair in front of his desk, somebody whose back was turned to me. Then the person twisted and I stopped cold, blinking and wondering if this were a hallucination and I'd wake up in the starship's skyhook, far out in space.

Then the woman cried, "Race, *Race*! Don't you know me?"

I took one dazed step and another. Then she flew across the space between us, her thin arms tangling around my neck, and I caught her up, still disbelieving.

"*Juli!*"

"Oh, Race, I thought I'd die when Mack told me you were leaving tonight. It's been the only thing that's kept me alive, knowing—knowing I'd see you." She sobbed and laughed, her face buried in my shoulder.

I let her cry for a minute, then held my sister at arm's length. For a moment I had forgotten the six years that lay between us. Now I saw them, all of them, printed plain on her face. Juli had been a pretty girl. Six years had fined her face into beauty, but there was tension in the set of her shoulders, and her gray eyes had looked on horrors.

She looked tiny and thin and unbearably frail under the scanty folds of her fur robe, a Dry-town woman's robe. Her wrists were manacled, the jeweled tight bracelets fastened together by the links of a long fine chain of silvered gilt that clashed a little, thinly, as her hands fell to her sides.

"What's wrong, Juli? Where's Rakhal?"

She shivered and now I could see that she was in a state of shock.

"Gone. He's gone, that's all I know. And—oh, Race, Race, he took Rindy with him!"

From the tone of her voice I had thought she was sobbing. Now I realized that her eyes were dry; she was long past tears. Gently I unclasped her clenched fingers and put her back in the chair. She sat like a doll, her hands falling to her sides with a thin clash of chains. When I picked them up and laid them in her lap she let them lie there motionless. I stood over her and demanded, "Who's Rindy?" She didn't move.

"My daughter, Race. Our little girl."

Magnusson broke in, his voice harsh. "Well, Cargill, should I have let you leave?"

"Don't be a damn fool!"

"I was afraid you'd tell the poor kid she had to live with her own mistakes," growled Magnusson. "You're capable of it."

For the first time Juli showed a sign of animation. "I was afraid to come to you, Mack. You never wanted me to marry Rakhal, either."

"Water under the bridge," Magnusson grunted. "And I've got lads of my own, Miss Cargill—Mrs.—" he stopped in distress, vaguely remembering that in the Dry-towns an improper form of address can be a deadly insult.

But she guessed his predicament.

"You used to call me Juli, Mack. It will do now."

"You've changed," he said quietly. "Juli, then. Tell Race what you told me. All of it."

She turned to me. "I shouldn't have come for myself—"

I knew that. Juli was proud, and she had always had the courage to live with her own mistakes. When I first saw her, I knew this wouldn't be anything so simple as the complaint of an abused wife or even an abandoned or deserted mother. I took a chair, watching her and listening.

She began. "You made a mistake when you turned Rakhal out of the Service, Mack. In his way he was the most loyal man you had on Wolf."

Magnusson had evidently not expected her to take this tack. He scowled and looked disconcerted, shifting uneasily in his big chair, but when Juli did not continue, obviously awaiting his answer, he said, "Juli, he left me no choice. I never knew how his mind worked. That final deal he engineered—have you any idea how much that cost the Service? And have you taken a good look at your brother's face, Juli girl?"

Juli raised her eyes slowly, and I saw her flinch. I knew how she felt. For three years I had kept my mirror covered, growing an untidy straggle of beard because it hid the scars and saved me the ordeal of facing myself to shave.

Juli whispered, "Rakhal's is just as bad. Worse."

"That's some satisfaction," I said, and Mack stared at us, baffled. "Even now I don't know what it was all about."

"And you never will," I said for the hundredth time. "We've been over this before. Nobody could understand it unless he'd lived in the Dry-towns. Let's not talk about it. You talk, Juli. What brought you here like this? What about the kid?"

"There's no way I can tell you the end without telling you the beginning," she said reasonably. "At first Rakhal worked as a trader in Shainsa."

I wasn't surprised. The Dry-towns were the core of Terran trade on Wolf, and it was through their cooperation that Terra existed here peaceably, on a world only half human, or less.

The men of the Dry-towns existed strangely poised between two worlds. They had made dealings with the first Terran ships, and thus gave entrance to the wedge of the Terran Empire.

And yet they stood proud and apart. They alone had never yielded to the Terranizing which overtakes all Empire planets sooner or later.

There were no Trade Cities in the Dry-towns; an Earthman who went there unprotected faced a thousand deaths, each one worse than the last. There were those who said that the men of Shainsa and Daillon and Ardcarran had sold the rest of Wolf to the Terrans, to keep the Terrans from their own door.

Even Rakhal, who had worked with Terra since boyhood, had finally come to a point of decision and gone his own way. And it was not Terra's way.

That was what Juli was saying now.

"He didn't like what Terra was doing on Wolf. I'm not so sure I like it myself—"

Magnusson interrupted her again. "Do you know what Wolf was like when we came here? Have you seen the Slave Colony, the Idiot's Village? Your own brother went to Shainsa and routed out The Lisse."

"And Rakhal helped him!" Juli reminded him. "Even after he left you, he tried to keep out of things. He could have told them a good deal that would hurt you, after ten years in Intelligence, you know."

I knew. It was, although I wasn't going to tell Juli this, one reason why, at the end—during that terrible explosion of violence which no normal Terran mind could comprehend—I had done my best to kill him. We had both known that after this, the planet would not hold the two of us. We could both go on living only by dividing it unevenly. I had been given the slow death of the Terran Zone. And he had all the rest.

"But he never told them anything! I tell you, he was one of the most loyal—"

Mack grunted, "Yeah, he's an angel. Go ahead."

She didn't, not immediately. Instead she asked what sounded like an irrelevant question. "Is it true what he told me? That the Empire has a standing offer of a reward for a working model of a matter transmitter?"

"That offer's been standing for three hundred years, Terran reckoning. One million credits cash. Don't tell me he was figuring to invent one?"

"I don't think so. But I think he heard rumors about one. He said with that kind of money he could bargain the Terrans right out of Shainsa. That was where it started. He began coming and going at odd times, but he never said any more about it. He wouldn't talk to me at all."

"When was all this?"

"About four months ago."

"In other words, just about the time of the riots in Charin."

She nodded. "Yes. He was away in Charin when the Ghost Wind blew, and he came back with knife cuts in his thigh. I asked if he had been mixed-up in the anti-Terran rioting, but he wouldn't tell me. Race, I don't know anything about politics. I don't really care. But just about that time, the Great House in Shainsa changed hands. I'm sure Rakhal had something to do with that.

"And then—" Juli twisted her chained hands together in her lap—"he tried to mix Rindy up in it. It was crazy, awful! He'd brought her some sort of nonhuman toy from one of the lowland towns, Charin I think. It was a weird thing, scared me. But he'd sit Rindy down in the sunlight and have her look into it, and Rindy would gabble all sorts of nonsense about little men and birds and a toymaker."

The chains about Juli's wrists clashed as she twisted her hands together. I stared somberly at the fetters. The chain, which was long, did not really hamper her movements much. Such chains were symbolic ornaments, and most Dry-town women went all their lives with fettered hands. But even after the years I'd spent in the Dry-towns, the sight still brought an uneasiness to my throat, a vague discomfort.

"We had a terrible fight over that," Juli went on. "I was afraid, afraid of what it was doing to Rindy. I threw it out, and Rindy woke up and screamed—" Juli checked herself and caught at vanishing self-control.

"But you don't want to hear about that. It was then I threatened to leave him and take Rindy. The next day—" Suddenly the hysteria Juli had been forcing back broke free, and she rocked back and forth in her chair, shaken and strangled with sobs. "He took Rindy! Oh, Race, he's crazy, crazy. I think he hates Rindy, he—he, Race, *he smashed her toys*. He took every toy the child had and broke them one by one, smashed them into powder, every toy the child had—"

"Juli, please, please," Magnusson pleaded, shaken. "If we're dealing with a maniac—"

"I don't dare think he'd harm her! He warned me not to come here, or I'd never see her again, but if it meant war against Terra I had to come. But Mack, please, don't do anything against him, please, please. He's got my baby, he's got my little girl…" Her voice failed and she buried her face in her hands.

Mack picked up the solidopic cube of his five-year-old son, and turned it between his pudgy fingers, saying unhappily, "Juli, we'll take every precaution. But can't you see, we've got to get him? If there's a question of a matter transmitter, or anything like that, in the hands of Terra's enemies—"

I could see that, too, but Juli's agonized face came between me and the picture of disaster. I clenched my fist around the chair arm, not surprised to see the fragile plastic buckle, crack and split under my grip. *If it had been Rakhal's neck…*

"Mack, let me handle this. Juli, shall I find Rindy for you?"

A hope was born in her ravaged face, and died, while I looked. "Race, he'd kill you. Or have you killed."

"He'd try," I admitted. The moment Rakhal knew I was outside the Terran zone, I'd walk with death. I had accepted the code during my years in Shainsa. But now I was an Earthman and felt only contempt.

"Can't you see? Once he knows I'm at large, that very code of his will force him to abandon any intrigue, whatever you call it, conspiracy, and come after me first. That way we do two things: we get him out of hiding, and we get him out of the conspiracy, if there is one."

I looked at the shaking Juli and something snapped. I stooped and lifted her, not gently, my hands biting her shoulders. "And I won't kill him, do you hear? He may wish I had; by the time I get through with him—I'll beat the living hell out of him; I'll cram my fists down his throat. But I'll settle it with him like an Earthman. I won't kill him. *Hear me, Juli?* Because that's the worst thing I could do to him—catch him and let him live afterward!"

Magnusson stepped toward me and pried my crushing hands off her arms. Juli rubbed the bruises mechanically, not knowing she was doing it. Mack said, "You can't do it, Cargill. You wouldn't get as far as Daillon. You haven't been out of the zone in six years. Besides—"

His eyes rested full on my face. "I hate to say this, Race, but damn it, man, go and take a good look at yourself in a mirror. Do you think I'd ever have pulled you off the Secret Service otherwise? How in hell can you disguise yourself now?"

"There are plenty of scarred men in the Dry-towns," I said. "Rakhal will remember my scars, but I don't think anyone else would look twice."

Magnusson walked to the window. His huge form bulked against the light, perceptibly darkening the office. He looked over the faraway panorama, the neat bright Trade City below and the vast wilderness lying outside. I could almost hear the wheels grinding in his head. Finally he swung around.

"Race, I've heard these rumors before. But you're the only man I could have sent to track them down, and I wouldn't send you out in cold blood to be killed. I won't now. Spaceforce will pick him up."

I heard the harsh inward gasp of Juli's breath and said, "Damn it, no. The first move you make—" I couldn't finish. Rindy was in his hands, and when I knew Rakhal, he hadn't been given to making idle threats. We all three knew what Rakhal might do at the first hint of the long arm of Terran law reaching out for him.

I said, "For God's sake let's keep Spaceforce out of it. Let it look like a personal matter between Rakhal and me, and let us settle it on those terms. Remember he's got the kid."

Magnusson sighed.

Again he picked up one of the cubes and stared into the clear plastic, where the three-dimensional image of a nine-year-old girl looked out at him, smiling and innocent. His face was transparent as the plastic cube. Mack acts tough, but he has five kids and he is as soft as a dish of pudding where a kid is concerned.

"I know. Another thing, too. If we send out Spaceforce, after all the riots—how many Terrans are on this planet? A few thousand, no more. What chance would we have, if it turned into a full-scale rebellion? None at all, unless we wanted to order a massacre. Sure, we have bombs and dis-guns and all that.

"But would we dare to use them? And where would we be after that? We're here to keep the pot from boiling over, to keep out of planetary incidents, not push them along to a point where bluff won't work. That's why we've got to pick up Rakhal before this gets out of hand."

I said, "Give me a month. Then you can move in, if you have to. Rakhal can't do much against Terra in that time. And I might be able to keep Rindy out of it."

Magnusson stared at me, hard-eyed. "If you do this against my advice, I won't be able to step in and pull you out of a jam later on, you know. And God help you if you start up the machines and can't stop them."

I knew that. A month wasn't much. Wolf is forty thousand miles of diameter, at least half unexplored; mountain and forest swarming with nonhuman and semi-human cities where Terrans had never been.

Finding Rakhal, or any one man, would be like picking out one star in the Andromeda nebula. Not impossible. Not *quite* impossible.

Mack's eyes wandered again to his child's face, deep in the transparent cube. He turned it in his hands. "Okay, Cargill," he said slowly, "so we're all crazy. I'll be crazy too. Try it your way."

CHAPTER FOUR

By sunset I was ready to leave. I hadn't had any loose ends to tie up in the Trade City, since I'd already disposed of most of my gear before boarding the starship. I'd never been in better circumstances to take off for parts unknown.

Mack, still disapproving, had opened the files to me, and I'd spent most of the day in the back rooms of Floor 38, searching Intelligence files to refresh my memory, scanning the pages of my own old reports sent years ago from Shainsa and Daillon. He had sent out one of the nonhumans who worked for us, to buy or acquire somewhere in the Old Town a Dry-towner's outfit and the other things I would wear and carry.

I would have liked to go myself. I felt that I needed the practice. I was only now beginning to realize how much I might have forgotten in the years behind a desk. But until I was ready to make my presence known, no one must know that Race Cargill had not left Wolf on the starship.

Above all, I must not be seen in the Kharsa until I went there in the Dry-town disguise which had become, years ago, a deep second nature, almost an alternate personality.

About sunset I walked through the clean little streets of the Terran Trade City toward the Magnusson home where Juli was waiting for me.

Most of the men who go into Civil Service of the Empire come from Earth, or from the close-in planets of Proxima and Alpha Centaurus. They go out unmarried, and they stay that way, or marry women native to the planets where they are sent.

But Joanna Magnusson was one of the rare Earth women who had come out with her husband, twenty years ago. There are two kinds of Earthwomen like that. They make their quarterings a little bit of home, or a little bit of hell. Joanna had made their house look like a transported corner of Earth.

I never knew quite what to think of the Magnusson household. It seemed to me almost madness to live under a red sun, yet come inside to yellow light, to live on a world with the wild beauty of Wolf and yet live as they might have lived on their home planet. Or maybe I was the one who was out of step. I had done the reprehensible thing they called "going native." Possibly I had done just that, and in absorbing myself into the new world, had lost the ability to fit into the old.

Joanna, a chubby comfortable woman in her forties, opened the door and gave me her hand. "Come in, Race. Juli's expecting you."

"It's good of you." I broke off, unable to express my gratitude. Juli and I had come from Earth—our father had been an officer on the old starship *Landfall* when Juli was only a child. He had died in a wreck off Procyon, and Mack Magnusson had found me a place in Intelligence because I spoke four of the Wolf languages and haunted the Kharsa with Rakhal whenever I could get away.

They had also taken Juli into their own home, like a younger sister. They hadn't said much—because they had liked Rakhal—when the breakup came. But that terrible night when Rakhal and I nearly killed each other, and Rakhal came with his face bleeding and took Juli away with him, had hurt them hard. Yet it had made them all the kinder to me.

Joanna said forthrightly, "Nonsense, Race! What else could we do?" She drew me along the hall. "You can talk in here."

I delayed a minute before going through the door she indicated. "How is Juli?"

"Better, I think. I put her to bed in Meta's room, and she slept most of the day. She'll be all right. I'll leave you to talk." Joanna opened the door, and went away.

Juli was awake and dressed, and already some of the terrible frozen horror was gone from her face. She was still tense and devil-ridden, but not hysterical now.

The room, one of the children's bedrooms, wasn't a big one. Even at the top of the Secret Service, a cop doesn't live too well. Not on Terra's Civil Service pay scale. Not, with five youngsters. It looked as if all five of the kids had taken it to pieces, one at a time.

I sat down on a too-low chair and said, "Juli, we haven't much time, I've got to be out of the city before dark. I want to know about Rakhal, what he does, what he's like now. Remember, I haven't seen him for years. Tell me everything—his friends, his amusements, everything you know."

"I always thought you knew him better than I did." Juli had a fidgety little way of coiling the links of the chain around her wrists and it made me nervous.

"It's routine, Juli. Police work. Mostly I play by ear, but I try to start out by being methodical."

She answered everything I asked her, but the sum total wasn't much and it wouldn't help much. As I said, it's easy to disappear on Wolf. Juli knew he had been friendly with the new holders of the Great House on Shainsa, but she didn't even know their name.

I heard one of the Magnusson children fly to the street door and return, shouting for her mother. Joanna knocked at the door of the room and came in.

"There's a *chak* outside who wants to see you, Race."

I nodded. "Probably my fancy dress. Can I change in the back room, Joanna? Will you keep my clothes here till I get back?"

I went to the door and spoke to the furred nonhuman in the sibilant jargon of the Kharsa and he handed me what looked like a bundle of rags. There were hard lumps inside. The *chak* said softly, "I hear a rumor in the Kharsa, *Raiss*. Perhaps it will help you. Three men from Shainsa are in the city. They came here to seek a woman who has vanished, and a toymaker. They are returning at sunrise. Perhaps you can arrange to travel in their caravan."

I thanked him and carried the bundle inside. In the empty back room I stripped to the skin and unrolled the bundle. There was a pair of baggy striped breeches, a worn and shabby shirtcloak with capacious pockets, a looped belt with half the gilt rubbed away and the base metal showing through, and a scuffed pair of ankle-boots tied with frayed thongs of different colors. There was a little cluster of amulets and seals. I chose two or three of the commonest kind, and strung them around my neck.

One of the lumps in the bundle was a small jar, holding nothing but the ordinary spices sold in the market, with which the average Dry-towner flavors food. I rubbed some of the powder on my body, put a pinch in the pocket of my shirtcloak, and chewed a few of the buds, wrinkling my nose at the long-unfamiliar pungency.

The second lump was a skean, and unlike the worn and shabby garments, this was brand-new and sharp and bright, and its edge held a razor glint. I tucked it into the clasp of my shirtcloak, a reassuring weight. It was the only weapon I could dare to carry.

The last of the solid objects in the bundle was a flat wooden case, about nine by ten inches. I slid it open. It was divided carefully into sections cushioned with sponge-absorbent plastic, and in them lay tiny slips of glass, on Wolf as precious as jewels. They were lenses—camera lenses, microscope lenses, even eyeglass lenses. Packed close, there were nearly a hundred of them nested by the shock-absorbent stuff.

They were my excuse for travel to Shainsa. Over and above the necessities of trade, a few items of Terran manufacture—vacuum tubes, transistors, lenses for cameras and binoculars, liquors and finely forged small tools—are literally worth their weight in platinum.

Even in cities where Terrans have never gone, these things bring exorbitant prices, and trading in them is a Dry-town privilege. Rakhal had been a trader, so Juli told me, in fine wire and surgical instruments. Wolf is not a mechanized planet, and has never developed any indigenous industrial system; the psychology of the nonhuman seldom runs to technological advances.

I went down the hallway again to the room where Juli was waiting. Catching a glimpse in a full-length mirror, I was startled. All traces of the Terran civil servant, clumsy and uncomfortable in his ill-fitting clothes, had dropped away. A Dry-towner, rangy and scarred, looked out at me, and it seemed that the expression on his face was one of amazement.

Joanna whirled as I came into the room and visibly paled before, recovering her self-control, she gave a nervous little giggle. "Goodness, Race, I didn't know you!"

Juli whispered, "Yes, I—I remember you better like that. You're—you look so much like—"

The door flew open and Mickey Magnusson scampered into the room, a chubby little boy browned by a Terra-type sunlamp and glowing with health. In his hand he held some sparkling thing that gave off tiny flashes and glints of color.

I gave the kid a grin before I realized that I was disguised anyhow and probably a hideous sight. The little boy backed off, but Joanna put her plump hand on his shoulder, murmuring soothing things.

Mickey toddled toward Juli, holding up the shining thing in his hands as if to display something very precious and beloved. Juli bent and held out her arms, then her face contracted and she snatched at the plaything.

"Mickey, what's that?"

He thrust it protectively behind his back. "Mine!"

"Mickey, don't be naughty," Joanna chided.

"Please let me see," Juli coaxed, and he brought it out, slowly, still suspicious. It was an angled prism of crystal, star-shaped, set in a frame which could get the star spinning like a solidopic. But it displayed a new and comical face every time it was turned.

Mickey turned it round and round, charmed at being the center of attention. There seemed to be dozens of faces, shifting with each spin of the prism, human and nonhuman, all dim and slightly distorted. My own face, Juli's, Joanna's came out of the crystal surface, not a reflection but a caricature.

A choked sound from Juli made me turn in dismay. She had let herself drop to the floor and was sitting there, white as death, supporting herself with her two hands.

"Race! Find out where he got that—that *thing*!"

I bent and shook her. "What's the matter with you?" I demanded. She had lapsed into the dazed, sleepwalking horror of this morning. She whispered, "It's not a toy. Rindy had one. Joanna, *where did he get it*?" She pointed at the shining thing with an expression of horror which would have been laughable had it been less real, less filled with terror.

Joanna cocked her head to one side and wrinkled her forehead, reflectively. "Why, I don't know, now you come to ask me. I thought maybe one of the *chaks* had given it to Mickey. Bought it in the bazaar, maybe. He loves it. Do get up off the floor, Juli!"

Juli scrambled to her feet. She said, "Rindy had one. It—it terrified me. She would sit and look at it by the hour, and—I told you about it, Race. I threw it out once, and she woke up and screamed. She shrieked for hours and hours and she ran out in the dark and dug for it in the trash pile, where I'd buried it. She went out in the dark, broke all her fingernails, but she dug it out again." She checked herself, staring at Joanna, her eyes wide in appeal.

"Well, dear," said Joanna with mild, rebuking kindness, "you needn't be so upset. I don't think Mickey's so attached to it as all that, and anyhow I'm not going to throw it away." She patted Juli reassuringly on the shoulder, then gave Mickey a little shove toward the door and turned to follow him. "You'll want to talk alone before Race leaves. Good luck, wherever you're going, Race." She held out her hand forthrightly.

"And don't worry about Juli," she added in an undertone. "We'll take good care of her."

When I came back to Juli she was standing by the window, looking through the oddly filtered glass that dimmed the red sun to orange. "Joanna thinks I'm crazy, Race."

"She thinks you're upset."

"Rindy's an odd child, a real Dry-towner. But it's not my imagination, Race, it's not. There's something—" Suddenly she sobbed aloud again.

"Homesick, Juli?"

"I was, a little, the first years. But I was happy, believe me." She turned her face to me, shining with tears. "You've got to believe I never regretted it for a minute."

"I'm glad," I said dully. *That made it just fine.*

"Only that toy—"

"Who knows? It might be a clue to something." The toy had reminded me of something, too, and I tried to remember what it was. I'd seen nonhuman toys in the Kharsa, even bought them for Mack's kids. When a single man is invited frequently to a home with five youngsters, it's about the only way he can repay that hospitality, by bringing the children odd trifles and knicknacks. But I had never seen anything quite like this one, until—

—Until yesterday. The toy-seller they had hunted out of the Kharsa, the one who had fled into the shrine of Nebran and vanished. He had had half a dozen of those prism-and-star sparklers.

I tried to call up a mental picture of the little toy-seller. I didn't have much luck. I'd seen him only in that one swift glance from beneath his hood. "Juli, have you ever seen a little man, like a *chak* only smaller, twisted, hunchbacked? He sells toys—"

She looked blank. "I don't think so, although there are dwarf *chaks* in the Polar Cities. But I'm sure I've never seen one."

"It was just an idea." But it was something to think about. A toy-seller had vanished. Rakhal, before disappearing, had smashed all Rindy's toys. And the sight of a plaything of cunningly-cut crystal had sent Juli into hysterics.

"I'd better go before it's too dark," I said. I buckled the final clasp of my shirtcloak, fitted my skean another notch into it, and counted the money Mack had advanced me for expenses. "I want to get into the Kharsa and hunt up the caravan to Shainsa."

"You're going there first?"

"Where else?"

Juli turned, leaning one hand against the wall. She looked frail and ill, years older than she was. Suddenly she flung her thin arms around me, and a link of the chain on her fettered hands struck me hard, as she cried out, "Race, Race, he'll kill you! How can I live with that on my conscience too?"

"You can live with a hell of a lot on your conscience." I disengaged her arms firmly from my neck. A link of the chain caught on the clasp of my shirtcloak, and again something snapped inside me. I grasped the chain in my two hands and gave a mighty heave, bracing my foot against the wall. The links snapped asunder. A flying end struck Juli under the eye. I ripped at the seals of the jeweled cuffs, tore them from her arms, find threw the whole assembly into a corner, where it fell with a clash.

"Damn it," I roared, "that's over! You're never going to wear *those* things again!" Maybe after six years in the Dry-towns, Juli was beginning to guess what those six years behind a desk had meant to me.

"Juli, I'll find your Rindy for you, and I'll bring Rakhal in alive. But don't ask more than that. Just *alive*. And don't ask me how."

He'd be alive when I got through with him. Sure, he'd be alive.

Just.

CHAPTER FIVE

It was getting dark when I slipped through a side gate, shabby and inconspicuous, into the spaceport square. Beyond the yellow lamps, I knew that the old city was beginning to take on life with the falling night. Out of the chinked pebble-houses, men and woman, human and nonhuman, came forth into the moonlit streets.

If anyone noticed me cross the square, which I doubted, they took me for just another Dry-town vagabond, curious about the world of the strangers from beyond the stars, and who, curiosity satisfied, was drifting back where he belonged. I turned down one of the dark alleys that led away, and soon was walking in the dark.

The Kharsa was not unfamiliar to me as a Terran, but for the last six years I had seen only its daytime face. I doubted if there were a dozen Earthmen in the Old Town tonight, though I saw one in the bazaar, dirty and lurching drunk; one of those who run renegade and homeless between worlds, belonging to neither. This was what I had nearly become.

I went further up the hill with the rising streets. Once I turned, and saw below me the bright-lighted spaceport, the black many-windowed loom of the skyscraper like a patch of alien shadow in the red-violet moonlight. I turned my back on them and walked on.

At the fringe of the thieves market I paused outside a wineshop where Dry-towners were made welcome. A golden nonhuman child murmured something as she pattered by me in the street, and I stopped, gripped by a spasm of stagefright. Had the dialect of Shainsa grown rusty on my tongue? Spies were given short shrift on Wolf, and a mile from the spaceport, I might as well have been on one of those moons. There were no spaceport shockers at my back now. And someone might remember the tale of an Earthman with a scarred face who had gone to Shainsa in disguise…

I shrugged the shirtcloak around my shoulders, pushed the door and went in. I had remembered that Rakhal was waiting for me. Not beyond this door, but at the end of the trail, behind some other door, somewhere. And we have a byword in Shainsa: *A trail without beginning has no end.*

Right there I stopped thinking about Juli, Rindy, the Terran Empire, or what Rakhal, who knew too many of Terra's secrets, might do if he had turned renegade. My fingers went up and stroked, musingly, the ridge of scar tissue along my mouth. At that moment I was thinking only of Rakhal, of an unsettled blood-feud, and of my revenge.

Red lamps were burning inside the wineshop, where men reclined on frowsy couches. I stumbled over one of them, found an empty place and let myself sink down on it, arranging myself automatically in the sprawl of Dry-towners indoors. In public they stood, rigid and formal, even to eat and drink. Among themselves, anything less than a loose-limbed sprawl betrayed insulting watchfulness; only a man who fears secret murder keeps himself on guard.

A girl with a tangled rope of hair down her back came toward me. Her hands were unchained, meaning she was a woman of the lowest class, not worth safeguarding. Her fur smock was shabby and matted with filth. I sent her for wine. When it came it was surprisingly good, the sweet and treacherous wine of Ardcarran. I sipped it slowly, looking round.

If a caravan for Shainsa were leaving tomorrow, it would be known here. A word dropped that I was returning there would bring me, by ironbound custom, an invitation to travel in their company.

When I sent the woman for wine a second time, a man on a nearby couch got up, and walked over to me.

He was tall even for a Dry-towner, and there was something vaguely familiar about him. He was no riffraff of the Kharsa, either, for his shirtcloak was of rich silk interwoven with metallic threads, and crusted with heavy embroideries. The hilt of his skean was carved from a single green gem. He stood looking down at me for some time before he spoke.

"I never forget a voice, although I cannot bring your face to mind. Have I a duty toward you?"

I had spoken a jargon to the girl, but he addressed me in the lilting, sing-song speech of Shainsa. I made no answer, gesturing him to be seated. On Wolf, formal courtesy requires a series of polite *non sequiturs*, and while a direct question merely borders on rudeness, a direct answer is the mark of a simpleton.

"A drink?"

"I joined you unasked," he retorted, and summoned the tangle-headed girl. "Bring us better wine than this swill!"

With that word and gesture I recognized him and my teeth clamped hard on my lip. This was the loudmouth who had shown fight in the spaceport cafe, and run away before the dark girl with the sign of Nebran sprawled on her breast.

But in this poor light he had not recognized me. I moved deliberately into the full red glow. If he did not know me for the Terran he had challenged last night in the spaceport cafe, it was unlikely that anyone else would. He stared at me for some minutes, but in the end he only shrugged and poured wine from the bottle he had ordered.

Three drinks later I knew that his name was Kyral and that he was a trader in wire and fine steel tools through the nonhuman towns. And I had given him the name I had chosen, Rascar.

He asked, "Are you thinking of returning to Shainsa?"

Wary of a trap, I hesitated, but the question seemed harmless, so I only countered, "Have you been long in the Kharsa?"

"Several weeks."

"Trading?"

"No." He applied himself to the wine again. "I was searching for a member of my family."

142

"Did you find him?"

"Her," said Kyral, and ceremoniously spat. "No, I didn't find her. What is your business in Shainsa?"

I chuckled briefly. "As a matter of fact, I am searching for a member of my family."

He narrowed his eyelids as if he suspected me of mocking him, but personal privacy is the most rigid convention of the Dry-towns and such mockery showed a sensible disregard for prying questions if I did not choose to answer them. He questioned no further.

"I can use an extra man to handle the loads. Are you good with pack animals? If so, you are welcome to travel under the protection of my caravan."

I agreed. Then, reflecting that Juli and Rakhal must, after all, be known in Shainsa, I asked, "Do you know a trader who calls himself Sensar?"

He started slightly; I saw his eyes move along my scars. Then reserve, like a lowered curtain, shut itself over his face, concealing a brief satisfied glimmer. "No," he lied, and stood up.

"We leave at first daylight. Have your gear ready." He flipped something at me, and I caught it in midair. It was a stone incised with Kyral's name in the ideographs of Shainsa. "You can sleep with the caravan if you care to. Show that token to Cuinn."

Kyral's caravan was encamped in a barred field past the furthest gates of the Kharsa. About a dozen men were busy loading the pack animals—horses shipped in from Darkover, mostly. I asked the first man I met for Cuinn. He pointed out a burly fellow in a shiny red shirtcloak, who was busy at chewing out one of the young men for the way he'd put a packsaddle on his beast.

Shainsa is a good language for cursing, but Cuinn had a special talent at it. I blinked in admiration while I waited for him to get his breath so I could hand him Kyral's token.

In the light of the fire I saw what I'd half expected: he was the second of the Dry-towners who'd tried to rough me up in the spaceport cafe. Cuinn barely glanced at the cut stone and tossed it back, pointing out one of the packhorses. "Load your personal gear on that one, then get busy and show this mush-headed wearer of sandals"—an insult carrying particularly filthy implications in Shainsa—"how to fasten a packstrap."

He drew breath and began to swear at the luckless youngster again, and I relaxed. He evidently hadn't recognized me, either. I took the strap in my hand, guiding it through the saddle loop. "Like that," I told the kid, and Cuinn stopped swearing long enough to give me a curt nod of acknowledgment and point out a heap of boxed and crated objects.

"Help him load up. We want to get clear of the city by daybreak," he ordered, and went off to swear at someone else.

Kyral turned up at dawn, and a few minutes later the camp had vanished into a small scattering of litter and we were on our way.

Kyral's caravan, in spite of Cuinn's cursing, was well-managed and well-handled. The men were Dry-towners, eleven of them, silent and capable and most of them very young. They were cheerful on the trail, handled the pack animals competently, during the day, and spent most of the nights grouped around the fire, gambling silently on the fall of the cut-crystal prisms they used for dice.

Three days out of the Kharsa I began to worry about Cuinn.

It was of course a spectacular piece of bad luck to find all three of the men from the spaceport cafe in Kyral's caravan. Kyral had obviously not known me, and even by daylight he paid no attention to me except to give an occasional order. The second of the three was a gangling kid who probably never gave me a second look, let alone a third.

But Cuinn was another matter. He was a man my own age, and his fierce eyes had a shrewdness in them that I did not trust. More than once I caught him watching me, and on the two or three occasions when he drew me into conversation, I found his questions more direct than Dry-town good manners allowed. I weighed the possibility that I might have to kill him before we reached Shainsa.

We crossed the foothills and began to climb upward toward the mountains. The first few days I found myself short of breath as we worked upward into thinner air, then my acclimatization returned and I began to fall into the pattern of the days and nights on the trail. The Trade City was still a beacon in the night, but its glow on the horizon grew dimmer with each day's march.

Higher we climbed, along dangerous trails where men had to dismount and let the pack animals pick their way, foot by foot. Here in these altitudes the sun at noonday blazed redder and brighter, and the Dry-towners, who come from the parched lands in the sea-bottoms, were burned and blistered by the fierce light. I had grown up under the blazing sun of Terra, and a red sun like Wolf, even at its hottest, caused me no discomfort. This alone would have made me suspect. Once again I found Cuinn's fierce eyes watching me.

As we crossed the passes and began to descend the long trail through the thick forests, we got into nonhuman country. Racing against the Ghost Wind, we skirted the country around Charin, and the woods inhabited by the terrible Ya-men, birdlike creatures who turn cannibal when the Ghost Wind blows.

Later the trail wound through thicker forests of indigo trees and grayish-purple brushwood, and at night we heard the howls of the catmen of these latitudes. At night we set guards about the caravan, and the dark spaces and shadows were filled with noises and queer smells and rustlings.

Nevertheless, the day's marches and the night watches passed without event until the night I shared guard with Cuinn. I had posted myself at the edge of the camp, the fire behind me. The men were sleeping rolls of snores, huddled close around the fire. The animals, hobbled with double ropes, front feet to hind feet, shifted uneasily and let out long uncanny whines.

I heard Cuinn pacing behind me. I heard a rustle at the edge of the forest, a stir and whisper beyond the trees, and turned to speak to him, then saw him slipping away toward the outskirts of the clearing.

For a moment I thought nothing of it, thinking that he was taking a few steps toward the gap in the trees where he had disappeared. I suppose I had the idea that he had slipped away to investigate some noise or shadow, and that I should be at hand.

Then I saw the flicker of lights beyond the trees—light from the lantern Cuinn had been carrying in his hand! He was signaling!

I slipped the safety clasp from the hilt of my skean and went after him. In the dimming glow of the fire I fancied I saw luminous eyes watching me, and the skin on my back crawled. I crept up behind him and leaped. We went down in a tangle of flailing legs and arms, and in less than a second he had his skean out and I was gripping his wrist, trying desperately to force the blade away from my throat.

I gasped, "Don't be a fool! One yell and the whole camp will be awake! Who were you signaling?"

In the light of the fallen lantern, lips drawn back in a snarl, he looked almost inhuman. He strained at the knife for a moment, then dropped it. "Let me up," he said.

I got up and kicked the fallen skean toward him. "Put that away. What in hell were you doing, trying to bring the catmen down on us?"

For a moment he looked taken aback, then his fierce face closed down again and he said wrathfully, "Can't a man walk away from the camp without being half strangled?"

I glared at him, but realized I really had nothing to go by. He might have been answering a call of nature, and the movement of the lantern accidental. And if someone had jumped me from behind, I might have pulled a knife on him myself. So I only said, "Don't do it again. We're all too jumpy."

There were no other incidents that night, or the next. The night after, while I lay huddled in my shirtcloak and blanket by the fire, I saw Cuinn slip out of his bedroll and steal away. A moment later there was a gleam in the darkness, but before I could summon the resolve to get up and face it out with him, he returned, looked cautiously at the snoring men, and crawled back into his blankets.

While we were unpacking at the next camp, Kyral halted beside me. "Heard anything queer lately? I've got the notion we're being trailed. We'll be out of these forests tomorrow, and after that it's clear road all the way to Shainsa. If anything's going to happen, it will happen tonight."

I debated speaking to him about Cuinn's signals. No, I had my own business waiting for me in Shainsa. Why mix myself up in some other, private intrigue?

He said, "I'm putting you and Cuinn on watch again. The old men doze off, and the young fellows get to daydreaming or fooling around. That's all right most of the time, but I want someone who'll keep his eyes open tonight. Did you ever know Cuinn before this?"

"Never set eyes on him."

"Funny, I had the notion—" He shrugged, turned away, then stopped.

"Don't think twice about rousing the camp if there's any disturbance. Better a false alarm than an ambush that catches us all in our blankets. If it came to a fight, we might be in a bad way. We all carry skeans, but I don't think there's a shocker in the whole camp, let alone a gun. You don't have one by any chance?"

After the men had turned in, Cuinn patrolling the camp, halted a minute beside me and cocked his head toward the rustling forest.

"What's going on in there?"

"Who knows? Catmen on the prowl, probably, thinking the horses would make a good meal, or maybe that we would."

"Think it will come to a fight?"

"I wouldn't know."

He surveyed me for a moment without speaking. "And if it did?"

"We'd fight." Then I sucked in my breath, for Cuinn had spoken Terran Standard, and I, without thinking had answered in the same language. He grinned, showing white teeth filed to a point.

"I thought so!"

I seized his shoulder and demanded roughly, "And what are you going to do about it?"

"That depends on you," he answered, "and what you want in Shainsa. Tell me the truth. What were you doing in the Terran Zone?" He gave me no chance to answer. "You know who Kyral is, don't you?"

"A trader," I said, "who pays my wages and minds his own affairs." I moved backward, hand on my skean, braced for a sudden rush. He made no aggressive motion, however.

"Kyral told me you'd been asking questions about Rakhal Sensar," he said. "Clever. Now I, for one, could have told you he'd never set eyes on Rakhal. I—"

He broke off, hearing a noise in the forest, a long eerie howl. I muttered, "If you've brought them down on us—"

He shook his head urgently. "I had to take that chance, to get word to the others. It won't work. Where's the girl?"

I hardly heard him. I was hearing twigs snap, and silent sneaking feet. I turned for a yell that would rouse the camp and Cuinn grabbed me hard, saying insistently, "Quick! Where's the girl! Go back and tell her it won't work! If Kyral suspected—"

He never finished the sentence. Just behind us came another of the long eerie howls. I knocked Cuinn away, and suddenly the night was filled with crouching forms that came down on us like a whirlwind.

I shouted madly as the camp came alive with men struggling out of blankets, fighting for life itself. I ran hard, still shouting, for the enclosure where we had tied the horses. A catman, slim and black-furred, was crouched and cutting the hobble-strings of the nearest animal. I hurled myself on him. He exploded, clawing, raking my shoulder with talons that ripped the rough cloth like paper. I whipped out my skean and slashed upward. The talons contracted in my shoulder and I gasped with pain. Then the thing howled and fell away, clawing at the air. It twitched and lay still.

Four shots in rapid succession cracked in the clearing. Kyral to the contrary, someone must have had a pistol. I heard one of the cat-things wail, a hoarse dying rattle. Something dark clawed my arm and I slashed with the knife, going down as another set of talons fastened in my back, rolling and clutching.

I managed to get the thing's forelimbs wedged under my elbow, my knee in its spine. I heaved, bent it backward, backward till it screamed, a high wail.

Then I felt the spine snap and the dead thing mewled once, just air escaping from collapsing lungs, and slid limp from my thigh. Erect it had not been over four feet tall and in the light of the dying fire it might have been a dead lynx.

"Rascar…" I heard a gasp, a groan. I whirled and saw Kyral go down, struggling, drowning in half a dozen or more of the fierce half-humans. I leaped at the smother of bodies, ripped one away with a stranglehold, slashed at its throat.

They were easy to kill.

I heard a high, urgent scream in their mewing tongue. Then the furred black things seemed to melt into the forest as silently as they had come. Kyral, dazed, his forehead running blood, his arm slashed to the bone, was sitting on the ground, still stunned.

Somebody had to take charge. I bellowed, "Lights! Get lights. They won't come back if we have enough light, they can only see well in the dark."

Someone stirred the fire. It blazed up as they piled on dead branches, and I roughly commanded one of the kids to fill every lantern he could find, and get them burning. Four of the dead things were lying in the clearing. The youngster I'd helped loading horses, the first day, gazed down at one of the catmen, half-disemboweled by somebody's skean, and suddenly bolted for the bushes, where I heard him retching.

I set the others with stronger stomachs to dragging the bodies away from the clearing, and went back to see how badly Kyral was hurt. He had the rip in his arm and his face was covered with blood from a shallow scalp wound, but he insisted on getting up to inspect the hurts of the others.

There was no one without a claw-wound in leg or back or shoulder, but none were serious, and we were all feeling fairly cheerful when someone demanded, "Where's Cuinn?"

He didn't seem to be anywhere. Kyral, staggering slightly, insisted on searching, but I felt we wouldn't find him. "He probably went off with his friends," I snorted, and told about the signaling. Kyral looked grave.

"You should have told me," he began, but shouts from the far end of the clearing sent us racing there. We nearly stumbled over a single, solitary, motionless form, outstretched and lifeless, blind eyes staring upward at the moons.

It was Cuinn. And his throat had been torn completely out.

CHAPTER SIX

Once we were free of the forest, the road to the Dry-towns lay straight before us, with no hidden dangers. Some of us limped for a day or two, or favored an arm or leg clawed by the catmen, but I knew that what Kyral said was true; it was a lucky caravan which had to fight off only one attack.

Cuinn haunted me. A night or two of turning over his cryptic words in my mind had convinced me that whoever, or whatever he'd been signaling, it wasn't the catmen. And his urgent question "Where's the girl?" swam endlessly in my brain, making no more sense than when I had first heard it. Who had he mistaken me for? What did he think I was mixed up in? And who, above all, were the "others" who had to be signaled, at the risk of an attack by catmen which had meant his own death?

With Cuinn dead, and Kyral thinking I'd saved his life, a large part of the responsibility for the caravan now fell on me. And strangely I enjoyed it, making the most of this interval when I was separated from the thought of blood-feud or revenge, the need of spying or the threat of exposure. During those days and nights on the trail I grew back slowly into the Dry-towner I once had been. I knew I would be sorry when the walls of Shainsa rose on the horizon, bringing me back inescapably to my own quest.

We swung wide, leaving the straight trail to Shainsa, and Kyral announced his intention of stopping for half a day at Canarsa, one of the walled nonhuman cities which lay well off the traveled road. To my inadvertent show of surprise, he returned that he had trading connections there.

"We all need a day's rest, and the Silent Ones will buy from me, though they have few dealings with men. Look here, I owe you something. You have lenses? You can get a better price in Canarsa than you'd get in Ardcarran or Shainsa. Come along with me, and I'll vouch for you."

Kyral had been most friendly since the night I had dug him out from under the catmen, and I knew no way to refuse without exposing myself for the sham trader I was. But I was deathly apprehensive. Even with Rakhal I had never entered any of the nonhuman towns.

On Wolf, human and nonhuman have lived side by side for centuries. And the human is not always the superior being. I might pass, among the Dry-towners and the relatively stupid humanoid *chaks*, for another Dry-towner. But Rakhal had cautioned me I could not pass among nonhumans for native Wolfan, and warned me against trying.

Nevertheless, I accompanied Kyral, carrying the box which had cost about a week's pay in the Terran Zone and was worth a small fortune in the Dry-towns.

Canarsa seemed, inside the gates, like any other town. The houses were round, beehive fashion, and the streets totally empty. Just inside the gates a hooded figure greeted us, and gestured us by signs to follow him. He was covered from head to foot with some coarse and shiny fiber woven into stuff that looked like sacking.

But under the thick hooding was horror. It slithered and it had nothing like a recognizable human shape or walk, and I felt the primeval ape in me cowering and gibbering in a corner of my brain. Kyral muttered, close to my ear, "No outsider is ever allowed to look on the Silent Ones in their real form. I think they're deaf and dumb, but be damn careful."

"You bet," I whispered, and was glad the streets were empty. I walked along, trying not to look at the gliding motion of that shrouded thing up ahead.

The trading was done in an open hut of reeds which looked as if it had been built in a hurry, and was not square, round, hexagonal or any other recognizable geometrical shape. It formed a pattern of its own, presumably, but my human eyes couldn't see it. Kyral said in a breath of a whisper, "They'll tear it down and burn it after we leave. We're supposed to have contaminated it too greatly for any of the Silent Ones ever to enter again. My family has traded with them for centuries, and we're almost the only ones who have ever entered the city."

Then two of the Silent Ones of Canarsa, also covered with that coarse shiny stuff, slithered into the hut, and Kyral choked off his words as if he had swallowed them.

It was the strangest trading I had ever done. Kyral laid out the small forged-steel tools and the coils of thin fine wire, and I unpacked my lenses and laid them out in neat rows. The Silent Ones neither spoke nor moved, but through a thin place in the gray veiling I saw a speck which might have been a phosphorescent eye, moving back and forth as if scanning the things laid out for their inspection.

Then I smothered a gasp, for suddenly blank spaces appeared in the rows of merchandise. Certain small tools— wirecutters, calipers, surgical scissors—had vanished, and all the coils of wire had disappeared. Blanks equally had appeared in the rows of lenses; all of my tiny, powerful microscope lenses had vanished. I cast a quick glance at Kyral, but he seemed unsurprised. I recalled vague rumors of the Silent Ones, and concluded that, eerie though it seemed, this was merely their way of doing business.

Kyral pointed at one of the tools, at an exceptionally fine pair of binocular lenses, at the last of the coils of wire. The shrouded ones did not move, but the lenses and the wire vanished. The small tool remained, and after a moment Kyral dropped his hand.

I took my cue from Kyral and remained motionless, awaiting whatever surprise was coming. I had halfway expected what happened next. In the blank spaces, little points of light began to glimmer, and after a moment, blue and red and green gemstones appeared there. To me the substitution appeared roughly equitable and fair, though I am no judge of the fine points of gems.

Kyral scowled slightly and pointed to one of the green gems, and after a moment it whisked away and a blue one took its place. In another spot where a fine set of surgical instruments had lain, Kyral pointed at the blue gem which now lay there, shook his head and held out three fingers. After a moment, a second blue stone lay winking beside the first.

Kyral did not move, but inexorably held out the three fingers. There was a little swirling in the air, and then both gems vanished, and the case of surgical instruments lay in their place.

Still Kyral did not move, but held the three fingers out for a full minute. Finally he dropped them and bent to pick up the case instruments. Again the little swirl in the air, and the instruments vanished. In their place lay three of the blue gems. My mouth twitched in the first amusement I had felt since we entered this uncanny place. Evidently bargaining with the Silent Ones was not a great deal different than bargaining with anyone anywhere. Nevertheless, under the eyes of those shrouded but horrible forms—if they had eyes, which I doubted—I had no impulse to protest their offered prices.

I gathered up the rejected lenses, repacked them neatly, and helped Kyral recrate the tools and instruments the Silent Ones had not wanted. I noticed that in addition to the microscope lenses and surgical instruments, they had taken all the fine wire. I couldn't imagine, and didn't particularly want to imagine, what they intended to do with it.

On our way back through the streets, unshepherded this time, Kyral's tongue was loosened as if with a great release from tension. "They're psychokinetics," he told me. "Quite a few of the nonhuman races are. I guess they have to be, having no eyes and no hands. But sometimes I wonder if we of the Dry-towns ought to deal with them at all."

"What do you mean?" I asked, not really listening. I was thinking mostly about the way the small objects had melted away and reappeared. The sight had stirred some uncomfortable memory, a vague sense of danger. It was not tangible enough for me to know why I feared it, but just a subliminal uneasiness that kept prodding at me, like a tooth that isn't quite aching yet.

Kyral said, "We of Shainsa live between fire and flood. Terra on the one hand, and on the other maybe something worse, who knows? We know so little about the Silent Ones, and those like them. Who knows, maybe we're giving them the weapons to destroy us—" He broke off, with a gasp, and stood staring down one of the streets.

It lay open and bare between two rows of round houses, and Kyral was staring fixedly at a doorway which had opened there. I followed his paralyzed gaze, and saw the girl.

Hair like spun black glass fell in hard waves around her shoulders, and the red eyes smiled with alien malice, alien mischief, beneath the dark crown of little stars. And the Toad God sprawled in hideous embroideries across the white folds of her breast.

Kyral gulped hoarsely. His hand flew up as he clutched the charms strung about his neck. I imitated the gesture mechanically, watching Kyral, wondering if he would turn and run again. But he stood frozen for a minute. Then the spell broke and he took one step toward the girl, arms outstretched.

"Miellyn!" he cried, and there was heartbreak in his voice. And again, the cry making ringing echoes in the strange street:

"Miellyn! *Miellyn!*"

This time it was the girl who whirled and fled. Her white robes fluttered and I saw the twinkle of her flying feet as she vanished into a space between the houses and was gone.

Kyral took one blind step down the street, then another. But before he could burst into a run I had him by the arm, dragging him back to sanity.

"Man, you've gone mad! Chase, in a nonhuman town?"

He struggled for a minute, then, with a harsh sigh, he said, "It's all right, I won't—" and shook loose from my arm.

He did not speak again until we reached the gates of Canarsa and they closed, silently and untouched, behind us. I had forgotten the place already. I had space only to think of the girl, whose face I had not forgotten since the moment when she saved me and disappeared. Now she had appeared again to Kyral. What did it all mean?

I asked, as we walked toward the camp, "Do you know that girl?" But I knew the question was futile. Kyral's face was closed, conceding nothing, and his friendliness had vanished completely.

He said, "Now I know you. You saved me from the catmen, and again in Canarsa, so my hands are bound from harming you. But it is evil to have dealings with those who have been touched by the Toad God." He spat noisily on the ground, looked at me with loathing, and said, "We will reach Shainsa in three days. Stay away from me."

CHAPTER SEVEN

Shainsa, first in the chain of Dry-towns that lie in the bed of a long-dried ocean, is set at the center of a great alkali plain; a dusty, parched city bleached by a million years of sun. The houses are high, spreading buildings with many rooms and wide windows. The poorer sort were made of sun-dried brick, the more imposing being cut from the bleached salt stone of the cliffs that rise behind the city.

News travels fast in the Dry-towns. If Rakhal were in the city, he'd soon know that I was here, and guess who I was or why I'd come. I might disguise myself so that my own sister, or the mother who bore me, would not know me. But I had no illusions about my ability to disguise myself from Rakhal. He had created the disguise that was me.

When the second sun set, red and burning, behind the salt cliffs, I knew he was not in Shainsa, but I stayed on, waiting for something to happen. At night I slept in a cubbyhole behind a wineshop, paying an inordinate price for that very dubious privilege. And every day in the sleepy silence of the blood-red noon I paced the public square of Shainsa.

This went on for four days. No one took the slightest notice of another nameless man in a shabby shirtcloak, without name or identity or known business. No one appeared to see me except the dusty children, with pale fleecy hair, who played their patient games on the windswept curbing of the square. They surveyed my scarred face with neither curiosity or fear, and it occurred to me that Rindy might be such another as these.

If I had still been thinking like an Earthman, I might have tried to question one of the children, or win their confidence. But I had a deeper game in hand.

On the fifth day I was so much a fixture that my pacing went unnoticed even by the children. On the gray moss of the square, a few dried-looking old men, their faces as faded as their shirtcloaks and bearing the knife scars of a hundred forgotten fights, drowsed on the stone benches. And along the flagged walk at the edge of the square, as suddenly as an autumn storm in the salt flats, a woman came walking.

She was tall, with a proud swinging walk, and a metallic clashing kept rhythm to her swift steps. Her arms were fettered, each wrist bound with a jeweled bracelet and the bracelets linked together by a long, silver-gilt chain passed through a silken loop at her waist. From the loop swung a tiny golden padlock, but in the lock stood an even tinier key, signifying that she was a higher caste than her husband or consort, that her fettering was by choice and not command.

She stopped directly before me and raised her arm in formal greeting like a man. The chain made a tinkling sound in the hushed square as her other hand was pulled up tight against the silken loop at her waist. She stood surveying me for some moments, and finally I raised my head and returned her gaze. I don't know why I had expected her to have hair like spun black glass and eyes that burned with a red reflection of the burning star.

This woman's eyes were darker than the poison-berries of the salt cliffs, and her mouth was a cut berry that looked just as dangerous. She was young, the slimness of her shoulders and the narrow steel-chained wrists told me how very young she was, but her face had seen weather and storms, and her dark eyes had weathered worse psychic storms than that. She did not flinch at the sight of my scars, and met my gaze without dropping her eyes.

"You are a stranger. What is your business in Shainsa?"

I met the direct question with the insolence it demanded, hardly moving my lips. "I have come to buy women for the brothels of Ardcarran. Perhaps when washed you might be suitable. Who could arrange for your sale?"

She took the rebuke impassively, though the bitter crimson of her mouth twitched a little in mischief or rage. But she made no sign. The battle was joined between us, and I knew already that it would be fought to the end.

From somewhere in her draperies, something fell to the ground with a little tinkle. But I knew that trick too and I did not move. Finally she went away without bending to retrieve it and when I looked around I saw that all the fleece-haired children had stolen away, leaving their playthings lying on the curbing. But one or two of the gaffers on the stone benches, who were old enough to show curiosity without losing face, were watching me with impassive eyes.

I could have asked the woman's name then, but I held back, knowing it could only lessen the prestige I had gained from the encounter. I glanced down, without seeming to do so, at the tiny mirror which had fallen from the recesses of the fur robe. Her name might have been inscribed on the reverse.

But I left it lying there to be picked up by the children when they returned, and went back to the wineshop. I had accomplished my first objective; if you can't be inconspicuous, be so damned conspicuous that nobody can miss you. And that in itself is a fair concealment. How many people can accurately describe a street riot?

I was finishing off a bad meal with a stone bottle of worse wine when the *chak* came in, disregarding the proprietor, and made straight for me. He was furred immaculately white. His velvet muzzle was contracted as if the very smells might soil it, and he kept a dainty paw outstretched to ward off accidental contact with greasy counters or tables or tapestries. His fur was scented, and his throat circled with a collar of embroidered silk. This pampered minion surveyed me with the innocent malice of an uninvolved nonhuman for merely human intrigues.

"You are wanted in the Great House of Shanitha, thcarred man." He spoke the Shainsa dialect with an affected lisp. "Will it pleathe you, come wis' me?"

I came, with no more than polite protest, but was startled. I had not expected the encounter to reach the Great House so soon. Shainsa's Great House had changed hands four times since I had last been in Shainsa. I wasn't overly anxious to appear there.

The white *chak*, as out of place in the rough Dry-town as a jewel in the streets or a raindrop in the desert, led me along a winding boulevard to an outlying district. He made no attempt to engage me in conversation, and indeed I got the distinct impression that this cockscomb of a nonhuman considered me well beneath his notice. He seemed much more aware of the blowing dust in the street, which ruffled and smudged his carefully combed fur.

The Great House was carved from blocks of rough pink basalt, the entry guarded by two great caryatids enwrapped in chains of carved metal, set somehow into the surface of the basalt. The gilt had long ago worn away from the chains so that it alternately gleamed gold or smudged base metal. The caryatids were patient and blind, their jewel-eyes long vanished under a hotter sun than today's.

The entrance hall was enormous. A Terran starship could have stood upright inside it, was my first impression, but I dismissed that thought quickly; any Terran thought was apt to betray me. But the main hall was built on a scale even more huge, and it was even colder than the legendary hell of the *chaks*. It was far too big for the people in it.

There was a little solar heater in the ceiling, but it didn't help much. A dim glow came from a metal brazier but that didn't help much either. The *chak* melted into the shadows, and I went down the steps into the hall by myself, feeling carefully for each step with my feet and trying not to seem to be doing so. My comparative night-blindness is the only significant way in which I really differ from a native Wolfan.

There were three men, two women and a child in the room. They were all Dry-towners and had an obscure family likeness, and they all wore rich garments of fur dyed in many colors. One of the men, old and stooped and withered, was doing something to the brazier. A slim boy of fourteen was sitting cross-legged on a pile of cushions in the corner. There was something wrong with his legs.

A girl of ten in a too-short smock that showed long spider-thin legs above her low leather boots was playing with some sort of shimmery crystals, spilling them out into patterns and scooping them up again from the uneven stones of the floor. One of the women was a fat, creased slattern, whose jewels and dyed furs did not disguise her greasy slovenliness.

Her hands were unchained, and she was biting into a fruit which dripped red juice down the rich blue fur of her robe. The old man gave her a look like murder as I came in, and she straightened slightly but did not discard the fruit. The whole room had a curious look of austere, dignified poverty, to which the fat woman was the only discordant note.

But it was the remaining man and woman who drew my attention, so that I noticed the others only peripherally, in their outermost orbit. One was Kyral, standing at the foot of the dais and glowering at me.

The other was the dark-eyed woman I had rebuked today in the public square.

Kyral said, "So it's you." And his voice held nothing. Not rebuke, not friendliness or a lack of it, not even hatred.

Nothing.

There was only one way to meet it. I faced the girl—she was sitting on a thronelike chair next to the fat woman, and looked like a doe next to a pig—and said boldly, "I assume this summons to mean that you informed your kinsmen of my offer."

She flushed, and that was triumph enough. I held back the triumph, however, wary of overconfidence. The gaffer laughed the high cackle of age, and Kyral broke in with a sharp, angry monosyllable by which I knew that my remark had indeed been repeated, and had lost nothing in the telling. But only the line of his jaw betrayed the anger as he said calmly, "Be quiet, Dallisa. Where did you pick this up?"

I said boldly, "The Great House has changed rulers since last I smelled the salt cliffs. Newcomers do not know my name and theirs is unknown to me."

The old gaffer said thinly to Kyral, "Our name has lost *kihar*. One daughter is lured away by the Toymaker and another babbles with strangers in the square, and a homeless no-good of the streets does not know our name."

My eyes, growing accustomed to the dark blaze of the brazier, saw that Kyral was biting his lip and scowling. Then he gestured to a table where an array of glassware was set, and at the gesture, the white *chak* came on noiseless feet and poured wine.

"If you have no blood-feud with my family, will you drink with me?"

"I will," I said, relaxing. Even if he had associated the trader with the scarred Earthman of the spaceport, he seemed to have decided to drop the matter. He seemed startled, but he waited until I had lifted the glass and taken a sip. Then, with a movement like lightning, he leaped from the dais and struck the glass from my lips.

I staggered back, wiping my cut mouth, in a split-second juggling possibilities. The insult was terrible and deadly. I could do nothing now but fight. Men had been murdered in Shainsa for far less. I had come to settle one feud, not involve myself in another, but even while these lightning thoughts flickered in my mind, I had whipped out my skean and I was surprised at the shrillness of my own voice.

"You contrive offense beneath your own roof—"

"Spy and renegade!" Kyral thundered. He did not touch his skean. From the table he caught a long four-thonged whip, making it whistle through the air. The long-legged child scuttled backward. I stepped back one pace, trying to conceal my desperate puzzlement. I could not guess what had prompted Kyral's attack, but whatever it was, I must have made some bad mistake and could count myself lucky to get out of there alive.

Kyral's voice perceptibly trembled with rage. "You dare to come into my own home after I have tracked you to the Kharsa and back, blind fool that I was! But now you shall pay."

The whip sang through the air, hissing past my shoulders. I dodged to one side, retreating step by step as Kyral swung the powerful thongs. It cracked again, and a pain like the burning of red-hot irons seared my upper arm. My skean rattled down from numb fingers.

The whip whacked the floor.

"Pick up your skean," said Kyral. "Pick it up if you dare." He poised the lash again.

The fat woman screamed.

I stood rigid, gauging my chances of disarming him with a sudden leap. Suddenly the girl Dallisa leaped from her seat with a harsh musical chiming of chains.

"Kyral, no! No, Kyral!"

He moved slightly, but did not take his eyes from me. "Get back, Dallisa."

"No! Wait!" She ran to him and caught his whip-arm, dragging it down, and spoke to him hurriedly and urgently. Kyral's face changed as she spoke; he drew a long breath and threw the whip down beside my skean on the floor.

"Answer straight, on your life. What are you doing in Shainsa?"

I could hardly take it in that for the moment I was reprieved from sudden death, from being beaten into bloody death there at Kyral's feet. The girl went back to her thronelike chair. Now I must either tell the truth or a convincing lie, and I was lost in a game where I didn't know the rules. The explanation I thought might get me out alive might be the very one which would bring down instant and painful death. Suddenly, with a poignancy that was almost pain, I wished Rakhal were standing here at my side.

But I had to bluff it out alone.

If they had recognized me for Race Cargill, the Terran spy who had often been in Shainsa, they might release me—it was possible, I supposed, that they were Terran sympathizers. On the other hand, Kyral's shouts of "Spy, renegade!" seemed to suggest the opposite.

I stood trying to ignore the searing pain in my lashed arm, but I knew that blood was running hot down my shoulder. Finally I said, "I came to settle blood-feud."

Kyral's lips thinned in what might have been meant for a smile. "You shall, assuredly. But with whom, remains to be seen."

Knowing I had nothing more to lose, I said, "With a renegade called Rakhal Sensar."

Only the old man echoed my words dully, "Rakhal Sensar?"

I felt heartened, seeing I wasn't dead yet.

"I have sworn to kill him."

Kyral suddenly clapped his hands and shouted to the white *chak* to clean up the broken glass on the floor. He said huskily, "You are not yourself Rakhal Sensar?"

"I *told* you he wasn't," said Dallisa, high and hysterically. "I *told* you he wasn't."

"A scarred man, tall—what was I to think?" Kyral sounded and looked badly shaken. He filled a glass himself and handed it to me, saying hoarsely, "I did not believe even the renegade Rakhal would break the code so far as to drink with me."

"He would not." I could be positive about this. The codes of Terra had made some superficial impress on Rakhal, but down deep his own world held sway. If these men were at blood-feud with Rakhal and he stood here where I stood, he would have let himself be beaten into bloody rags before tasting their wine.

I took the glass, raised it and drained it. Then, holding it out before me, I said, "Rakhal's life is mine. But I swear by the red star and by the unmoving mountains, by the black snow and by the Ghost Wind, I have no quarrel with any beneath this roof." I cast the glass to the floor, where it shattered on the stones.

Kyral hesitated, but under the blazing eyes of the girl he quickly poured himself a glass of the wine and drank a few sips, then flung down the glass. He stepped forward and laid his hands on my shoulders. I winced as he touched the welt of the lash and could not raise my own arm to complete the ceremonial toast.

Kyral stepped away and shrugged. "Shall I have one of the women see to your hurt?" He looked at Dallisa, but she twisted her mouth. "Do it yourself!"

"It is nothing," I said, not truthfully. "But I demand in requital that since we are bound by spilled blood under your roof, that you give me what news you have of Rakhal, the spy and renegade."

Kyral said fiercely, "If I knew, would I be under my own roof?"

The old gaffer on the dais broke into shrill whining laughter. "You have drunk wi' him, Kyral, now he's bound you not to do him harm! I know the story of Rakhal! He was spy for Terra twelve years. Twelve years, and then he fought and flung their filthy money in their faces and left 'em. But his partner was some Dry-town halfbreed or Terran spy and they fought wi' clawed gloves, and near killed one another except the Terrans, who have no honor, stopped 'em. See the marks of the *kifirgh* on his face!"

"By Sharra the golden-chained," said Kyral, gazing at me with something like a grin. "You are, if nothing else, a very clever man. What are you, spy, or half-caste of some Ardcarran slut?"

"What I am doesn't matter to you," I said. "You have blood-feud with Rakhal, but mine is older than yours and his life is mine. As you are bound in honor to kill"—the formal phrases came easily now to my tongue; the Earthman had slipped away—"so you are bound in honor to help me kill. If anyone beneath your roof knows anything of Rakhal—"

Kyral's smile bared his teeth.

"Rakhal works against the Son of the Ape," he said, using the insulting Wolf term for the Terrans. "If we help you to kill him, we remove a goad from their flanks. I prefer to let the filthy *Terranan* spend their strength trying to remove it themselves. Moreover, I believe you are yourself an Earthman.

"You have no right to the courtesy I extend to we, the People of the Sky. Yet you have drunk wine with me and I have no quarrel with you." He raised his hand in dismissal, outfencing me. "Leave my roof in safety and my city with honor."

I could not protest or plead. A man's *kihar*, his personal dignity, is a precious thing in Shainsa, and he had placed me so I could not compromise mine further in words. Yet I lost *kihar* equally if I left at his bidding, like an inferior dismissed.

One desperate gamble remained.

"A word," I said, raising my hand, and while he half turned, startled, believing I was indeed about to compromise my dignity by a further plea, I flung it at him:

"I will bet *shegri* with you."

His iron composure looked shaken. I had delivered a blow to his belief that I was an Earthman, for it is doubtful if there are six Earthmen on Wolf who know about *shegri*, the dangerous game of the Dry-towns.

It is no ordinary gamble, for what the bettor stakes is his life, possibly his reason. Rarely indeed will a man bet *shegri* unless he has nothing further to lose.

It is a cruel, possibly decadent game, which has no parallel anywhere in the known universe.

But I had no choice. I had struck a cold trail in Shainsa. Rakhal might be anywhere on the planet and half of Magnusson's month was already up. Unless I could force Kyral to tell what he knew, I might as well quit.

So I repeated: "I will bet *shegri* with you."

And Kyral stood unmoving.

For what the *shegrin* wagers is his courage and endurance in the face of torture and an unknown fate. On his side, the stakes are clearly determined beforehand. But if he loses, his punishment or penalty is at the whim of the one who has accepted him, and he may be put to whatever doom the winner determines.

And this is the contest:

The *shegrin* permits himself to be tortured from sunrise to sunset. If he endures he wins. It is as simple as that. He can stop the torture at any moment by a word, but to do so is a concession of defeat.

This is not as dangerous as it might, at first, seem. The other party to the bet is bound by the ironclad codes of Wolf to inflict no permanent physical damage (no injury that will not heal with three suncourses). But from sunrise to sunset, any torment or painful ingenuity which the half-human mentality of Wolf can devise must be endured.

The man who can outthink the torture of the moment, the man who can hold in his mind the single thought of his goal—that man can claim the stakes he has set, as well as other concessions made traditional.

The silence grew in the hall. Dallisa had straightened and was watching me intently, her lips parted and the tip of a little red tongue visible between her teeth. The only sound was the tiny crunching as the fat woman nibbled at nuts and cast their shells into the brazier. Even the child on the steps had abandoned her game with the crystal dice, and sat looking up at me with her mouth open. Finally Kyral demanded, "Your stakes?"

"Tell me all you know of Rakhal Sensar and keep silence about me in Shainsa."

"By the red shadow," Kyral burst out, "you have courage, Rascar!"

"Say only yes or no!" I retorted.

Rebuked, he fell silent. Dallisa leaned forward and again, for some unknown reason, I thought of a girl with hair like spun black glass.

Kyral raised his hand. "I say no. I have blood-feud with Rakhal and I will not sell his death to another. Further, I believe you are Terran and I will not deal with you. And finally, you have twice saved my life and I would find small pleasure in torturing you. I say no. Drink again with me and we part without a quarrel."

Beaten, I turned to go.

"Wait," said Dallisa.

She stood up and came down from the dais, slowly this time, walking with dignity to the rhythm of her musically clashing chains. "I have a quarrel with this man."

I started to say that I did not quarrel with women, and stopped myself. The Terran concept of chivalry has no equivalent on Wolf.

She looked at me with her dark poison-berry eyes, icy and level and amused, and said, "I will bet *shegri* with you, unless you fear me, Rascar."

And I knew suddenly that if I lost, I might better have trusted myself to Kyral and his whip, or to the wild beast-things of the mountains.

CHAPTER EIGHT

I slept little that night.

There is a tale told in Daillon of a *shegri* where the challenger was left in a room alone, where he was blindfolded and told to await the beginning of the torment.

Somewhere in those dark hours of waiting, between the unknown and the unexpected, the hours of telling over to himself the horrors of past *shegri*, the torture of anticipation alone became the unbearable. A little past noon he collapsed in screams of horror and died raving, unmarred, untouched.

Daybreak came slowly, and with the first streamers of light came Dallisa and the white *chak*, maliciously uninvolved, sniffing his way through the shabby poverty of the great hall. They took me to a lower dungeon where the slant of the sunlight was less visible. Dallisa said, "The sun has risen."

I said nothing. Any word may be interpreted as a confession of defeat. I resolved to give them no excuse. But my skin crawled and I had that peculiar prickling sensation where the hair on my forearms was bristling erect with tension and fear.

Dallisa said to the *chak*, "His gear was not searched. See that he has swallowed no anesthetic drugs."

Briefly I gave her credit for thoroughness, even while I wondered in a split second why I had not thought of this. Drugs could blur consciousness, at least, or suspend reality. The white nonhuman sprang forward and pinioned my arms with one strong, spring-steel forearm. With his other hand he forced my jaws open. I felt the furred fingers at the back of my throat, gagged, struggled briefly and doubled up in uncontrollable retching.

Dallisa's poison-berry-eyes regarded me levelly as I struggled upright, fighting off the dizzy sickness of disgust. Something about her impassive face stopped me cold. I had been, momentarily, raging with fury and humiliation. Now I realized that this had been a calculated, careful gesture to make me lose my temper and thus sap my resistance.

If she could set me to fighting, if she could make me spend my strength in rage, my own imagination would fight on her side to make me lose control before the end. Swimming in the glare of her eyes, I realized she had never thought for a moment that I had taken any drug. Acting on Kyral's hint that I was a Terran, she was taking advantage of the well-known Terran revulsion for the nonhuman.

"Blindfold him," Dallisa commanded, then instantly countermanded that: "No, strip him first."

The *chak* ripped off shirtcloak, shirt, shoes, breeches, and I had my first triumph when the wealed clawmarks on my shoulders—worse, if possible, than those which disfigured my face—were laid bare. The *chak* screwed up his muzzle in fastidious horror, and Dallisa looked shaken. I could almost read her thoughts:

If he endured this, what hope have I to make him cry mercy?

Briefly I remembered the months I lay feverish and half dead, waiting for the wounds Rakhal had inflicted to heal, those months when I had believed that nothing would ever hurt me again, that I had known the worst of all suffering. But I had been younger then.

Dallisa had picked up two small sharp knives. She weighed them, briefly, gesturing to the *chak*. Without resisting, I let myself be manhandled backward, spreadeagled against the wall.

Dallisa commanded, "Drive the knives through his palms to the wall!"

My hands twitched convulsively, anticipating the slash of steel, and my throat closed in spasmodic dread. This was breaking the compact, bound as they were not to inflict physical damage. I opened my lips to protest this breaking of the bond of honor and met her dark blazing stare, and suddenly the sweat broke out on my forehead. I had placed myself wholly in their hands, and as Kyral had said, they were in no way bound by honor to respect a pledge to a Terran!

Then, as my hands clenched into fists, I forced myself to relax. This was a bluff, a mental trick to needle me into breaking the pact and pleading for mercy. I set my lips, spread my palms wide against the wall and waited impassively.

She said in her lilting voice, "Take care not to sever the tendons, or his hands would be paralyzed and he may claim we have broken our compact."

The points of the steel, razor-sharp, touched my palms, and I felt blood run down my hand before the pain. With an effort that turned my face white, I did not pull away from the point. The knives drove deeper.

Dallisa gestured to the *chak*. The knives dropped. Two pinpricks, a quarter of an inch deep, stung in my palm. I had outbluffed her. Had I?

If I had expected her to betray disappointment—and I had—I was disappointed. Abruptly, as if the game had wearied her already, she gestured, and I could not hold back a gasp as my arms were hauled up over my head, twisted violently around one another and trussed with thin cords that bit deep into the flesh. Then the rough upward pull almost jerked my shoulders from their sockets and I heard the giant *chak* grunt with effort as I was hauled upward until my feet barely, on tiptoe, touched the floor.

"Blindfold him," said Dallisa languidly, "so that he cannot watch the ascent of the sun or its descent or know what is to come."

A dark softness muffled my eyes. After a little I heard her steps retreating. My arms, wrenched overhead and numbed with the bite of the cords, were beginning to hurt badly now. But it wasn't too bad. Surely she did not mean that this should be all...

Sternly I controlled my imagination, taking a tight rein on my thoughts. There was only one way to meet this—hanging blind and racked in space, my toes barely scrabbling at the floor—and that was to take each thing as it came and not look ahead for an instant. First of all I tried to get my feet under me, and discovered that by arching upwards to my fullest height I could bear my weight on tiptoe and ease, a little, the dislocating ache in my armpits by slackening the overhead rope.

But after a little, a cramping pain began to flare through the arches of my feet, and it became impossible to support my weight on tiptoe. I jarred down with violent strain on my wrists and wrenched shoulders again, and for a moment the shooting agony was so intense that I nearly screamed. I thought I heard a soft breath near me.

After a little it subsided to a sharp ache, then to a dull ache, and then to the violent cramping pain again, and once more I struggled to get my toes under me. I realized that by allowing my toes barely to touch the floor they had doubled and tripled the pain by the tantalizing hope of, if not momentary relief, at least the alteration of one pain for another.

I haven't the faintest idea, even now, how long I repeated that agonizing cycle: struggle for a toehold on rough stone, scraping my bare feet raw; arch upward with all my strength to release for a few moments the strain on my wrenched shoulders; the momentary illusion of relief as I found my balance and the pressure lightened on my wrists.

Then the slow creeping, first of an ache, then of a pain, then of a violent agony in the arches of feet and calves. And, delayed to the last endurable moment, that final terrible anguish when the drop of my full weight pulled shoulder and wrist and elbow joints with that bone-shattering jerk.

I started once to estimate how much time had passed, how many hours had crawled by, then checked myself, for that was imminent madness. But once the process had begun my brain would not abandon and I found myself, with compulsive precision, counting off the seconds and the minutes in each cycle: stretch upward, release the pressure on the arms; the beginning of pain in calves and arches and toes; the creeping of pain up ribs and loins and shoulders; the sudden jarring drop on the arms again.

My throat was intolerably dry. Under other circumstances I might have estimated the time by the growth of hunger and thirst, but the rough treatment I had received made this impossible. There were other, unmentionable, humiliating pains.

After a time, to bolster my flagging courage, I found myself thinking of all the ways it might have been worse. I had heard of a *shegrin* exposed to the bite of poisonous—not fatal, but painfully poisonous—insects, and to the worrying of the small gnawing rodents which can be trained to bite and tear. Or I might have been branded…

I banished the memory with the powerful exorcism; the man in Daillon whose anticipation, alone, of a torture which never came, had broken his mind. There was only one way to conquer this, and that was to act as if the present moment was the only one, and never for a moment to forget that the strongest of compacts bound them not to harm me, that the end of this was fixed by sunset.

Gradually, however, all such rational thoughts blurred in a semidelirium of thirst and pain, narrowing to a red blaze of agony across my shoulder blades. I eased up on my toes again.

White-hot pain blazed through my feet. The rough stone on which my toes sank had been covered with metal and I smelled scorching flesh, jerking up my feet with a wordless snarl of rage and fury, hanging in agony by my shoulders alone.

And then I lost consciousness, at least for several moments, for when I became aware again, through the nightmare of pain, my toes were resting lightly and securely on cold stone. The smell of burned flesh remained, and the painful stinging in my toes. Mingled with that smell was a drift of perfume close by.

Dallisa murmured, "I do not wish to break our bargain by damaging your feet. It's only a little touch of fire to keep you from too much security in resting them."

I felt the taste of blood mingle in my mouth with the sour taste of vomit. I felt delirious, lightheaded. After another eternity I wondered if I had really heard Dallisa's lilting croon or whether it was a nightmare born of feverish pain:

Plead with me. A word, only a word and I will release you, strong man, scarred man. Perhaps I shall demand only a little space in your arms. Would not such doom be light upon you? Perhaps I shall set you free to seek Rakhal if only to plague Kyral. A word, only a word from you. A word, only a word from you...

It died into an endlessly echoing whisper. Swaying, blinded, I wondered why I endured. I drew a dry tongue over lips, salty and bloody, and nightmarishly considered yielding, winning my way somehow around Dallisa. Or knocking her suddenly senseless and escaping—I, who need not be bound by Wolf's codes either. I fumbled with a stiff shape of words.

And a breath saved me, a soft, released breath of anticipation. It was another trick. I swayed, limp and racked. I was not Race Cargill now. I was a dead man hanging in chains, swinging, filthy vultures pecking at my dangling feet. I was...

The sound of boots rang on the stone and Kyral's voice, low and bitter, demanded somewhere behind me, "What have you done with him?"

She did not answer, but I heard her chains clash lightly and imagined her gesture. Kyral muttered, "Women have no genius at any torture except..." His voice faded out into great distances. Their words came to me over a sort of windy ringing, like the howling of lost men, dying in the snowfast passes of the mountains.

"Speak up, you fool, he can't hear you now."

"If you have let him faint, you are clumsy!"

"*You* talk of clumsiness!" Dallisa's voice, even thinned by the nightmare ringing in my head, held concentrated scorn. "Perhaps I shall release him, to find Rakhal when you failed! The Terrans have a price on Rakhal's head, too. And at least this man will not confuse himself with his prey!"

"If you think I would let you bargain with a *Terranan*—"

Dallisa cried passionately, "You trade with the Terrans! How would you stop me, then?"

"I trade with them because I must. But for a matter involving the honor of the Great House—"

"The Great House whose steps you would never have climbed, except for Rakhal!" Dallisa sounded as if she were chewing her words in little pieces and spitting them at Kyral. "Oh, you were clever to take us both as your consorts! You did not know it was Rakhal's doing, did you? Hate the Terrans, then!" She spat an obscenity at him. "Enjoy your hate, wallow in hating, and in the end all Shainsa will fall prey to the Toymaker, like Miellyn."

"If you speak that name again," said Kyral very low, "I will kill you."

"Like Miellyn, Miellyn, Miellyn," Dallisa repeated deliberately. "You fool, Rakhal knew nothing of Miellyn!"

"He was seen—"

"With *me*, you fool! With *me*! You cannot yet tell twin from twin? Rakhal came to *me* to ask news of her!"

Kyral cried out hoarsely, like a man in anguish, "Why didn't you tell me?"

"You don't really have to ask, do you, Kyral?"

"You bitch!" said Kyral. "You filthy bitch!" I heard the sound of a blow. The next moment Kyral ripped the blindfold from my eyes and I blinked in the blaze of light. My arms were wholly numb now, twisted above my head, but the jar of his touch sent fresh pain racing through me. Kyral's face swam out of the blaze of hell. "If that is true, then this is a damnable farce, Dallisa. You have lost our chance of learning what he knows of Miellyn."

"What *he* knows?" Dallisa lowered her hand from her face, where a bruise was already darkening.

"Miellyn has twice appeared when I was with him. Loose him, Dallisa, and bargain with him. What we know of Rakhal for what he knows of Miellyn."

"If you think I would let you bargain with *Terranan*," she mocked. "Weakling, this quarrel is *mine*! You fool, the others in the caravan will give me news, if you will not! *Where is Cuinn?*"

From a million miles away Kyral laughed. "You've slipped the wrong hawk, Dallisa. The catmen killed him." His skean flicked loose. He climbed to a perch near the rope at my wrists. "Bargain with me, Rascar!"

I coughed, unable to speak, and Kyral insisted, "Will you bargain? End this damned woman's farce which makes a mock of *shegri?*"

The slant of sun told me there was light left. I found a shred of voice, not knowing what I was going to say until I had said it, irrevocably. "This is between Dallisa and me."

Kyral glared at me in mounting rage. With four strides he was out of the room, flinging back a harsh, furious "I hope you kill each other!" and the door slammed.

Dallisa's face swam red, and again as before, I knew the battle which was joined between us would be fought to a dreadful end. She touched my chest lightly, but the touch jolted excruciating pain through my shoulders.

"Did you kill Cuinn?"

I wondered, wearily, what this presaged.

"Did you?" In a passion, she cried, "Answer! Did you kill him?" She struck me hard, and where the touch had been pain, the blow was a blaze of white agony. I fainted.

"Answer!" She struck me again and the white blaze jolted me back to consciousness. "Answer me! Answer!" Each cry bought a blow until I gasped finally, "He signaled...set catmen on us..."

"No!" She stood staring at me and her white face was a death mask in which the eyes lived. She screamed wildly and the huge *chak* came running.

"Cut him down! Cut him down! Cut him down!"

A knife slashed the rope and I slumped, falling in a bone-breaking huddle to the floor. My arms were still twisted over my head. The *chak* cut the ropes apart, pulled my arms roughly back into place, and I gagged with the pain as the blood began flowing painfully through the chafed and swollen hands.

And then I lost consciousness. More or less permanently, this time.

CHAPTER NINE

When I came to again I was lying with my head in Dallisa's lap, and the reddish color of sunset was in the room. Her thighs were soft under my head, and for an instant I wondered if, in delirium, I had conceded to her. I muttered, "Sun...not down..."

She bent her face to mine, whispering, "Hush. Hush."

It was heaven, and I drifted off again. After a moment I felt a cup against my lips.

"Can you swallow this?"

I could and did. I couldn't taste it yet, but it was cold and wet and felt heavenly trickling down my throat. She bent and looked into my eyes, and I felt as if I were falling into those reddish and stormy depths. She touched my scarred mouth with a light finger. Suddenly my head cleared and I sat upright.

"Is this a trick to force me into calling my bet?"

She recoiled as if I had struck her, then the trace of a smile flitted around her red mouth. Yes, between us it was battle. "You are right to be suspicious, I suppose. But if I tell you what I know of Rakhal, will you trust me then?"

I looked straight at her and said, "No."

Surprisingly, she threw back her head and laughed. I flexed my freed wrists cautiously. The skin was torn away and chafed, and my arms ached to the bone. When I moved harsh lances of pain drove through my chest.

"Well, until sunset I have no right to ask you to trust me," said Dallisa when she had done laughing. "And since you are bound by my command until the last ray has fallen, I command that you lay your head upon my knees."

I blazed, "You are making a game of me!"

"Is that my privilege? Do you refuse?"

"Refuse?" It was not yet sunset. This might be a torture more complex than any which had yet greeted me. From the scarlet glint in her eyes I felt she was playing with me, as the cat-things of the forest play with their helpless victims. My mouth twitched in a grimace of humiliation as I lowered myself obediently until my head rested on her fur-clad knees.

She murmured, smiling, "Is this so unbearable, then?"

I said nothing. Never, never for an instant could I forget that—all human, all woman as she seemed—Dallisa's race was worn and old when the Terran Empire had not left their home star. The mind of Wolf, which has mingled with the nonhuman since before the beginnings of recorded time, is unfathomable to an outsider. I was better equipped than most Earthmen to keep pace with its surface acts, but I could never pretend to understand its deeper motivations.

It works on complex and irrational logic. Mischief is an integral part of it. Even the deadly blood-feud with Rakhal had begun with an overelaborate practical joke—which had lost the Service, incidentally, several thousand credits worth of spaceship.

And so I could not trust Dallisa for an instant. Yet it was wonderful to lie here with my head resting against the perfumed softness of her body.

Then suddenly her arms were gripping me, frantic and hungry; the subdued thing in her voice, her eyes, flamed out hot and wild. She was pressing the whole length of her body to mine, breasts and thighs and long legs, and her voice was hoarse.

"Is this torture too?"

Beneath the fur robe she was soft and white, and the subtle scent of her hair seemed a deeper entrapment than any. Frail as she seemed, her arms had the strength of steel, and pain blazed down my wrenched shoulders, seared through the twisted wrists. Then I forgot the pain.

Over her shoulder the last dropping redness of the sun vanished and plunged the room into orchid twilight.

I caught her wrists in my hands, prizing them backward, twisting them upward over her head. I said thickly, "The sun's down." And then I stopped her wild mouth with mine.

And I knew that the battle between us had reached climax and victory simultaneously, and any question about who had won it was purely academic.

During the night sometime, while her dark head lay motionless on my shoulder, I found myself staring into the darkness, wakeful. The throbbing of my bruises had little to do with my sleeplessness; I was remembering other chained girls from the old days in the Dry-towns, and the honey and poison of them distilled into Dallisa's kisses. Her head was very light on my shoulders, and she felt curiously insubstantial, like a woman of feathers.

One of the tiny moons was visible through the slitted windows. I thought of my rooms in the Terran Trade City, clean and bright and warm, and all the nights when I had paced the floor, hating, filled to the teeth with bitterness, longing for the windswept stars of the Dry-towns, the salt smell of the winds and the musical clashing of the walk of the chained women.

With a sting of guilt, I realized that I had half forgotten Juli and my pledge to her and her misfortune which had freed me again, for this.

Yet I had won, and what they knew had narrowed my planet-wide search to a pinpoint. Rakhal was in Charin.

I wasn't altogether surprised. Charin is the only city on Wolf, except the Kharsa, where the Terran Empire has put down deep roots into the planet, built a Trade City, a smaller spaceport. Like the Kharsa, it lies within the circle of Terran law—and a million miles outside it.

A nonhuman town, inhabited largely by *chaks*, it is the core and center of the resistance movement, a noisy town in a perpetual ferment. It was the logical place for a renegade. I settled myself so that the ache in my racked shoulders was less violent, and muttered, "Why Charin?"

Slight as the movement was, it roused Dallisa. She rolled over and propped herself on her elbows, quoting drowsily, "The prey walks safest at the hunter's door."

I stared at the square of violet moonlight, trying to fit together all the pieces of the puzzle, and asked half aloud, "What prey and what hunters?"

Dallisa didn't answer. I hadn't expected her to answer. I asked the real question in my mind: "Why does Kyral hate Rakhal Sensar, when he doesn't even know him by sight?"

"There are reasons," she said somberly. "One of them is Miellyn, my twin sister. Kyral climbed the steps of the Great House by claiming us both as his consorts. He is our father's son by another wife."

That explained much. Brother-and-sister marriages, not uncommon in the Dry-towns, are based on expediency and suspicion, and are frequently, though not always loveless. It explained Dallisa's taunts, and it partly explained, only partly, why I found her in my arms. It did not explain Rakhal's part in this mysterious intrigue, nor why Kyral had taken me for Rakhal, (but only after he remembered seeing me in Terran clothing).

I wondered why it had never occurred to me before that I might be mistaken for Rakhal. There was no close resemblance between us, but a casual description would apply equally well to me or to Rakhal. My height is unusual for a Terran—within an inch of Rakhal's own—and we had roughly the same build, the same coloring. I had copied his walk, imitated his mannerisms, since we were boys together.

And, blurring minor facial characteristics, there were the scars of the *kifirgh* on my mouth, cheeks, and shoulders. Anyone who did not know us by sight, anyone who had known us by reputation from the days when we had worked together in the Dry-towns, might easily take one of us for the other. Even Juli had blurted, "You're so much like—" before thinking better of it.

Other odd bits of the puzzle floated in my mind, stubbornly refusing to take on recognizable patterns, the disappearance of a toy-seller; Juli's hysterical babbling; the way the girl—Miellyn?— had vanished into a shrine of Nebran; and the taunts of Dallisa and the old man about a mysterious "Toymaker." And something, some random joggling of a memory, in that eerie trading in the city of the Silent Ones. I knew all these things fitted together somehow, but I had no real hope that Dallisa could complete their pattern for me.

She said, with a vehemence that startled me, "Miellyn is only the excuse! Kyral hates Rakhal because Rakhal will compromise and because he'll fight!"

She rolled over and pressed herself against me in the darkness. Her voice trembled. "Race, our world is dying. We can't stand against Terra. And there are other things, worse things."

I sat up, surprised to find myself defending Terra to this girl. After all these years I was back in my own world. And yet I heard myself say quietly, "The Terrans aren't exploiting Wolf. We haven't abolished the rule of Shainsa. We've changed nothing."

It was true. Terra held Wolf by compact, not conquest. They paid, and paid generously, for the lease of the lands where their Trade Cities would rise, and stepped beyond them only when invited to do so.

"We let any city or state that wants to keep its independence govern itself until it collapses, Dallisa. And they do collapse after a generation or so. Very few primitive planets can hold out against us. The people themselves get tired of living under feudal or theocratic systems, and they beg to be taken into the Empire. That's all."

"But that's just it," Dallisa argued. "You give the people all those things we used to give them, and you do it better. Just by being here, you are killing the Dry-towns. They're turning to you and leaving us, and you let them do it."

I shook my head. "We've kept the Terran Peace for centuries. What do you expect? Should we give you arms, planes, bombs, weapons to hold your slaves down?"

"Yes!" she flared at me. "The Dry-towns have ruled Wolf since—since—you, you can't even imagine how long! And we made compact with you to trade here—"

"And we have rewarded you by leaving you untouched," I said quietly. "But we have not forbidden the Dry-towns to come into the Empire and work with Terra."

She said bitterly, "Men like Kyral will die first," and pressed her face helplessly against me. "And I will die with them. Miellyn broke away, but I cannot! Courage is what I lack. Our world is rotten, Race, rotten all through, and I'm as rotten as the core of it. I could have killed you today, and I'm here in your arms. Our world is rotten, but I've no confidence that the new world will be better!"

I put my hand under her chin, and looked down gravely into her face, only a pale oval in the darkness. There was nothing I could say; she had said it all, and truthfully. I had hated and yearned and starved for this, and when I found it, it turned salty and bloody on my lips, like Dallisa's despairing kisses. She ran her fingers over the scars on my face, then gripped her small thin hands around my wrists so fiercely that I grunted protest.

"You will not forget me," she said in her strangely lilting voice. "You will not forget me, although you were victorious." She twisted and lay looking up at me, her eyes glowing faintly luminous in darkness. I knew that she could see me as clearly as if it were day. "I think it was my victory, not yours, Race Cargill."

Gently, on an impulse I could not explain, I picked up one delicate wrist, then the other, unclasping the heavy jeweled bracelets. She let out a stifled cry of dismay. And then I tossed the chains into a corner before I drew her savagely into my arms again and forced her head back under my mouth.

I said good-bye to her alone, in the reddish, windswept space before the Great House. She pressed her head against my shoulder and whispered, "Race, take me with you!"

For answer I only picked up her narrow wrists and turned them over on my palm. The jeweled bracelets were clasped again around the thinly boned joints, and on some self-punishing impulse she had shortened the chains so that she could not even put her arms around me. I lifted the punished wrists to my mouth and kissed them gently.

"You don't want to leave, Dallisa."

I was desperately sorry for her. She would go down with her dying world, proud and cold and with no place in the new one. She kissed me and I tasted blood, her thin fettered body straining wildly against me, shaken with tearing, convulsive sobs. Then she turned and fled back into the shadow of the great dark house.

I never saw her again.

CHAPTER TEN

A few days later I found myself nearing the end of the trail.

It was twilight in Charin, hot and reeking with the gypsy glare of fires which burned, smoking, at the far end of the Street of the Six Shepherds. I crouched in the shadow of a wall, waiting.

My skin itched from the dirty shirtcloak I hadn't changed in days. Shabbiness is wise in nonhuman parts, and Dry-towners think too much of water to waste much of it in superfluous washing anyhow. I scratched unobtrusively and glanced cautiously down the street.

It seemed empty, except for a few sodden derelicts sprawled in doorways—the Street of the Six Shepherds is a filthy slum—but I made sure my skean was loose. Charin is not a particularly safe town, even for Dry-towners, and especially not for Earthmen, at any time.

Even with what Dallisa had told me, the search had been difficult. Charin is not Shainsa. In Charin, where human and nonhuman live closer together than anywhere else on the planet, information about such men as Rakhal can be bought, but the policy is to let the buyer beware. That's fair enough, because the life of the seller has a way of not being worth much afterward, either.

A dirty, dust-laden wind was blowing up along the street, heavy with strange smells. The pungent reek of incense from a street-shrine was in the smells. The heavy, acrid odor that made my skin crawl. In the hills behind Charin, the Ghost Wind was rising.

Borne on this wind, the Ya-men would sweep down from the mountains, and everything human or nearly human would scatter in their path. They would range through the quarter all night, and in the morning they would melt away, until the Ghost Wind blew again. At any other time, I would already have taken cover. I fancied that I could hear, borne on the wind, the faraway yelping, and envision the plumed, taloned figures which would come leaping down the street.

In that moment, the quiet of the street split asunder.

From somewhere a girl's voice screamed in shrill pain or panic. Then I saw her, dodging between two of the chinked pebble-houses. She was a child, thin and barefoot, a long tangle of black hair flying loose as she darted and twisted to elude the lumbering fellow at her heels. His outstretched paw jerked cruelly at her slim wrist.

The little girl screamed and wrenched herself free and threw herself straight on me, wrapping herself around my neck with the violence of a storm wind. Her hair got in my mouth and her small hands gripped at my back like a cat's flexed claws.

"Oh, help me," she gasped between sobs. "Don't let him get me, don't." And even in that broken plea I took it in that the little ragamuffin did not speak the jargon of that slum, but the pure speech of Shainsa.

What I did then was as automatic as if it had been Juli. I pulled the kid loose, shoved her behind me, and scowled at the brute who lurched toward us.

"Make yourself scarce," I advised. "We don't chase little girls where I come from. Haul off, now."

The man reeled. I smelled the rankness of his rags as he thrust one grimy paw at the girl. I never was the hero type, but I'd started something which I had to carry through. I thrust myself between them and put my hand on the skean again.

"You—you Dry-towner." The man set up a tipsy howl, and I sucked in my breath. Now I was in for it. Unless I got out of there damned fast, I'd lose what I'd come all the way to Charin to find.

I felt like handing the girl over. For all I knew, the bully could be her father and she was properly in line for a spanking. This wasn't any of my business. My business lay at the end of the street, where Rakhal was waiting at the fires. He wouldn't be there long. Already the smell of the Ghost Wind was heavy and harsh, and little flurries of sand went racing along the street, lifting the flaps of the doorways.

But I did nothing so sensible. The big lunk made a grab at the girl, and I whipped out my skean and pantomimed.

"Get going!"

"Dry-towner!" He spat out the word like filth, his pig-eyes narrowing to slits. "Son of the Ape! *Earthman!*"

"*Terranan!*" Someone took up the howl. There was a stir, a rustle, all along the street that had seemed empty, and from nowhere, it seemed, the space in front of me was crowded with shadowy forms, human and otherwise.

"Earthman!"

I felt the muscles across my belly knotting into a band of ice. I didn't believe I'd given myself away as an Earthman. The bully was using the time-dishonored tactic of stirring up a riot in a hurry, but just the same I looked quickly round, hunting a path of escape.

"Put your skean in his guts, Spilkar! Grab him!"

"Hai-ai! Earthman! *Hai-ai!*"

It was the last cry that made me panic. Through the sultry glare at the end of the street, I could see the plumed, taloned figures of the Ya-men, gliding through the banners of smoke. The crowd melted open.

I didn't stop to reflect on the fact—suddenly very obvious— that Rakhal couldn't have been at the fires at all, and that my informant had led me into an open trap, a nest of Ya-men already inside Charin. The crowd edged back and muttered, and suddenly I made my choice. I whirled, snatched up the girl in my arms and ran straight toward the advancing figures of the Ya-men.

Nobody followed me. I even heard a choked shout that sounded like a warning. I heard the yelping shrieks of the Ya-men grow to a wild howl, and at the last minute, when their stiff rustling plumes loomed only a few yards away, I dived sidewise into an alley, stumbled on some rubbish and spilled the girl down.

"Run, kid!"

She shook herself like a puppy climbing out of water. Her small fingers closed like a steel trap on my wrist. "This way," she urged in a hasty whisper, and I found myself plunging out the far end of the alley and into the shelter of a street-shrine. The sour stink of incense smarted in my nostrils, and I could hear the yelping of the Ya-men as they leaped and rustled down the alley, their cold and poisonous eyes searching out the recess where I crouched with the girl.

"Here," she panted, "stand close to me on the stone—" I drew back, startled.

"Oh, don't stop to argue," she whimpered. "Come *here*!"

"*Hai-ai!* Earthman! There he is!"

The girl's arms flung round me again. I felt her slight, hard body pressing on mine and she literally hauled me toward the pattern of stones at the center of the shrine. I wouldn't have been human if I hadn't caught her closer yet.

The world reeled. The street disappeared in a cone of spinning lights, stars danced crazily, and I plunged down through a widening gulf of empty space, locked in the girl's arms. I fell, spun, plunged head over heels through tilting lights and shadows that flung us through eternities of freefall. The yelping of the Ya-men whirled away in unimaginable distances, and for a second I felt the unmerciful blackout of a power dive, with blood breaking from my nostrils and filling my mouth.

CHAPTER ELEVEN

Lights flared in my eyes.

I was standing solidly on my feet in the street-shrine, but the street was gone. Coils of incense still smudged the air. The God squatted toadlike in his recess. The girl was hanging limp, locked in my clenched arms. As the floor straightened under my feet I staggered, thrown off balance by the sudden return of the girl's weight, and grabbed blindly for support.

"Give her to me," said a voice, and the girl's sagging body was lifted from my arms. A strong hand grasped my elbow. I found a chair beneath my knees and sank gratefully into it.

"The transmission isn't smooth yet between such distant terminals," the voice remarked. "I see Miellyn has fainted again. A weakling, the girl, but useful."

I spat blood, trying to get the room in focus. For I was inside a room, a room of some translucent substance, windowless, a skylight high above me, through which pink daylight streamed. Daylight—and it had been midnight in Charin! I'd come halfway around the planet in a few seconds!

From somewhere I heard the sound of hammering, tiny, bell-like hammering, the chiming of a fairy anvil. I looked up and saw a man—a man?—watching me.

On Wolf you see all kinds of human, half-human and nonhuman life, and I consider myself something of an expert on all three. But I had never seen anyone, or anything, who so closely resembled the human and so obviously wasn't. He, or it, was tall and lean, man-shaped but oddly muscled, a vague suggestion of something less than human in the lean hunch of his posture.

Manlike, he wore green tight-fitting trunks and a shirt of green fur that revealed bulging biceps where they shouldn't be, and angular planes where there should have been swelling muscles. The shoulders were high, the neck unpleasantly sinuous, and the face, a little narrower than human, was handsomely arrogant, with a kind of wary alert mischief that was the least human thing about him.

He bent, tilted the girl's inert body on to a divan of some sort, and turned his back on her, lifting his hand in an impatient, and unpleasantly reminiscent, gesture.

The tinkling of the little hammers stopped as if a switch had been disconnected.

"Now," said the nonhuman, "we can talk."

Like the waif, he spoke Shainsan, and spoke it with a better accent than any nonhuman I had ever known—so well that I looked again to be certain. I wasn't too dazed to answer in the same tongue, but I couldn't keep back a spate of questions:

"What happened? Who are you? What is this place?"

The nonhuman waited, crossing his hands—quite passable hands, if you didn't look too closely at what should have been nails—and bent forward in a sketchy gesture.

"Do not blame Miellyn. She acted under orders. It was imperative you be brought here tonight, and we had reason to believe you might ignore an ordinary summons. You were clever at evading our surveillance, for a time. But there would not be two Dry-towners in Charin tonight who would dare the Ghost Wind. Your reputation does you justice, Rakhal Sensar."

Rakhal Sensar! Once again Rakhal!

Shaken, I pulled a rag from my pocket and wiped blood from my mouth. I'd figured out, in Shainsa, why the mistake was logical. And here in Charin I'd been hanging around in Rakhal's old haunts, covering his old trails. Once again, mistaken identity was natural.

Natural or not, I wasn't going to deny it. If these were Rakhal's enemies, my real identity should be kept as an ace in reserve which might—just might—get me out alive again. If they were his friends...well, I could only hope that no one who knew him well by sight would walk in on me.

"We knew," the nonhuman continued, "that if you remained where you were, the *Terranan* Cargill would have made his arrest. We know about your quarrel with Cargill, among other things, but we did not consider it necessary that you should fall into his hands at present."

I was puzzled. "I still don't understand. Exactly where am I?"

"This is the mastershrine of Nebran."

Nebran!

The stray pieces of the puzzle suddenly jolted into place. Kyral had warned me, not knowing he was doing it. I hastily imitated the gesture Kyral had made, gabbling a few words of an archaic charm.

Like every Earthman who's lived on Wolf more than a tourist season, I'd seen faces go blank and impassive at mention of the Toad God. Rumor made his spies omnipresent, his priests omniscient, his anger all powerful. I had believed about a tenth of what I had heard, or less.

The Terran Empire has little to say to planetary religions, and Nebran's cult is a remarkably obscure one, despite the street-shrines on every corner. Now I was in his mastershrine, and the device which had brought me here was beyond doubt a working model of a matter transmitter.

A matter transmitter, a working model—the words triggered memory. Rakhal was after it.

"And who," I asked slowly, "are you, Lord?"

The green-clad creature hunched thin shoulders again in a ceremonious gesture. "I am called Evarin. Humble servant of Nebran and yourself," he added, but there was no humility in his manner. "I am called the Toymaker."

Evarin. That was another name given weight by rumor. A breath of gossip in a thieves market. A scrawled word on smudged paper. A blank folder in Terran Intelligence. Another puzzle-piece snapped into place—*Toymaker!*

The girl on the divan sat up suddenly passing slim hands over her disheveled hair. "Did I faint, Evarin? I had to fight to get him into the stone, and the patterns were not set straight in that terminal. You must send one of the Little Ones to set them to rights. Toymaker, you are not listening to me."

"Stop chattering, Miellyn," said Evarin indifferently. "You brought him here, and that is all that matters. You aren't hurt?"

Miellyn pouted and looked ruefully at her bare bruised feet, patted the wrinkles in her ragged frock with fastidious fingers. "My poor feet," she mourned, "they are black and blue with the cobbles and my hair is filled with sand and tangles! Toymaker, what way was this to send me to entice a man? Any man would have come quickly, quickly, if he had seen me looking lovely, but you—you send me in rags!"

She stamped a small bare foot. She was not merely as young as she had looked in the street. Though immature and underdeveloped by Terran standards, she had a fair figure for a Dry-town woman. Her rags fell now in graceful folds. Her hair was spun black glass, and I—I saw what the rags and the confusion in the filthy street had kept me from seeing before.

It was the girl of the spaceport cafe, the girl who had appeared and vanished in the eerie streets of Canarsa.

Evarin was regarding her with what, in a human, might have been rueful impatience. He said, "You know you enjoyed yourself, as always, Miellyn. Run along and make yourself beautiful again, little nuisance."

The girl danced out of the room, and I was just as glad to see her go. The Toymaker motioned to me.

"This way," he directed, and led me through a different door. The offstage hammering I had heard, tiny bell tones like a fairy xylophone, began again as the door opened, and we passed into a workroom which made me remember nursery tales from a half-forgotten childhood on Terra. For the workers were tiny, gnarled *trolls*!

They were *chaks*. *Chaks* from the polar mountains, dwarfed and furred and half-human, with witchlike faces and great golden eyes, and I had the curious feeling that if I looked hard enough I would see the little toy-seller they had hunted out of the Kharsa. I didn't look. I figured I was in enough trouble already.

Tiny hammers pattered on miniature anvils in a tinkling, jingling chorus of musical clinks and taps. Golden eyes focused like lenses over winking jewels and gimcracks. Busy elves. Makers of toys!

Evarin jerked his shoulders with an imperative gesture. I followed him through a fairy workroom, but could not refrain from casting a lingering look at the worktables. A withered leprechaun set eyes into the head of a minikin hound. Furred fingers worked precious metals into invisible filigree for the collarpiece of a dancing doll. Metallic feathers were thrust with clockwork precision into the wings of a skeleton bird no longer than my fingernail. The nose of the hound wabbled and sniffed, the bird's wings quivered, the eyes of the little dancer followed my footsteps.

Toys?

"This way," Evarin rapped, and a door slid shut behind us. The clinks and taps grew faint, fainter, but never ceased.

My face must have betrayed more than conventional impassivity, for Evarin smiled. "Now you know, Rakhal, why I am called Toymaker. Is it not strange—the masterpriest of

Nebran, a maker of Toys, and the shrine of the Toad God a workshop for children's playthings?"

Evarin paused suggestively. They were obviously not children's playthings and this was my cue to say so, but I avoided the trap. Evarin opened a sliding panel and took out a doll.

She was perhaps the length of my longest finger, molded to the precise proportions of a woman, and costumed after the bizarre fashion of the Ardcarran dancing girls. Evarin touched no button or key that I could see, but when he set the figure on its feet, it executed a whirling, armtossing dance in a fast, tricky tempo.

"I am, in a sense, benevolent," Evarin murmured. He snapped his fingers and the doll sank to her knees and poised there, silent. "Moreover, I have the means and, let us say, the ability to indulge my small fantasies.

"The little daughter of the President of the Federation of Trade Cities on Samarra was sent such a doll recently. What a pity that Paolo Arimengo was so suddenly impeached and banished!" The Toymaker clucked his teeth commiseratingly. "Perhaps this small companion will compensate the little Carmela for her adjustment to her new...position."

He replaced the dancer and pulled down something like a whirligig. "This might interest you," he mused, and set it spinning. I stared at the pattern of lights that flowed and disappeared, melting in and out of visible shadows. Suddenly I realized what the thing was doing. I wrested my eyes away with an effort. Had there been a lapse of seconds or minutes? Had Evarin spoken?

Evarin arrested the compelling motion with one finger. "Several of these pretty playthings are available to the children of important men," he said absently. "An import of value for our exploited and impoverished world. Unfortunately they are, perhaps, a little...ah, obvious. The incidence of nervous breakdowns is, ah, interfering with their sale. The children, of course, are unaffected, and love them." Evarin set the hypnotic wheel moving again, glanced sidewise at me, then set it carefully back.

"Now"—Evarin's voice, hard with the silkiness of a cat's snarl, clawed the silence—"we'll talk business."

I turned, composing my face. Evarin had something concealed in one hand, but I didn't think it was a weapon. And if I'd known, I'd have had to ignore it anyway.

"Perhaps you wonder how we recognized and found you?" A panel cleared in the wall and became translucent. Confused flickers moved, dropped into focus and I realized that the panel was an ordinary television screen and I was looking into the well-known interior of the Cafe of Three Rainbows in the Trade City of Charin.

By this time I was running low on curiosity and didn't wonder till much, much later how televised pictures were transmitted around the curve of a planet. Evarin sharpened the focus down on the long Earth-type bar where a tall man in Terran clothes was talking to a pale-haired girl. Evarin said, "By now, Race Cargill has decided, no doubt, that you fell into his trap and into the hands of the Ya-men. He is off-guard now."

And suddenly the whole thing seemed so unbearably, illogically funny that my shoulders shook with the effort to keep back dangerous laughter. Since I'd landed in Charin, I'd taken great pains to avoid the Trade City, or anyone who might have associated me with it. And Rakhal, somehow aware of this, had conveniently filled up the gap. By posing as me.

It wasn't nearly as difficult as it sounded. I had found that out in Shainsa. Charin is a long, long way from the major Trade City near the Kharsa. I hadn't a single intimate friend there, or within hundreds of miles, to see through the imposture. At most, there were half a dozen of the staff that I'd once met, or had a drink with, eight or ten years ago.

Rakhal could speak perfect Standard when he chose; if he lapsed into Dry-town idiom, that too was in my known character. I had no doubt he was making a great success of it all, probably doing much better with my identity than I could ever have done with his.

Evarin rasped, "Cargill meant to leave the planet. What stopped him? You could be of use to us, Rakhal. But not with this blood-feud unsettled."

That needed no elucidation. No Wolfan in his right mind will bargain with a Dry-towner carrying an unresolved blood-feud. By law and custom, declared blood-feud takes precedence over any other business, public or private, and is sufficient excuse for broken promises, neglected duties, theft, even murder.

"We want it settled once and for all." Evarin's voice was low and unhurried. "And we aren't above weighting the scales. This Cargill can, and has, posed as a Dry-towner, undetected. We don't like Earthmen who can do that. In settling your feud, you will be aiding us, and removing a danger. We would be…grateful."

He opened his closed hand, displaying something small, curled, inert.

"Every living thing emits a characteristic pattern of electrical nerve impulses. We have ways of recording those impulses, and we have had you and Cargill under observation for a long time. We've had plenty of opportunity to key this Toy to Cargill's pattern."

On his palm the curled thing stirred, spread wings. A fledgling bird lay there, small soft body throbbing slightly. Half-hidden in a ruff of metallic feathers I glimpsed a grimly elongated beak. The pinions were feathered with delicate down less than a quarter of an inch long. They beat with delicate insistence against the Toymaker's prisoning fingers.

"This is not dangerous to you. Press here"—he showed me—"and if Race Cargill is within a certain distance—and it is up to you to be *within* that distance—it will find him, and kill him. Unerringly, inescapably, untraceably. We will not tell you the critical distance. And we will give you three days."

He checked my startled exclamation with a gesture. "Of course this is a test. Within the hour Cargill will receive a warning. We want no incompetents who must be helped too much! Nor do we want cowards! If you fail, or release the bird at a distance too great, or evade the test"—the green inhuman malice in his eyes made me sweat—"we have made another bird."

By now my brain was swimming, but I thought I understood the complex inhuman logic involved. "The other bird is keyed to me?"

With slow contempt Evarin shook his head. "You? You are used to danger and fond of a gamble. Nothing so simple! We have given you three days. If, within that time, the bird you carry has not killed, the other bird will fly. And it will kill. Rakhal, you have a wife."

Yes, Rakhal had a wife. They could threaten Rakhal's wife. And his wife was my sister Juli.

Everything after that was anticlimax. Of course I had to drink with Evarin, the elaborate formal ritual without which no bargain on Wolf is concluded. He entertained me with gory and technical descriptions of the way in which the birds, and other of his hellish Toys, did their killing, and worse tasks.

Miellyn danced into the room and upset the exquisite solemnity of the wine-ritual by perching on my knee, stealing a sip from my cup, and pouting prettily when I paid her less attention than she thought she merited. I didn't dare pay much attention, even when she whispered, with the deliberate and thorough wantonness of a Dry-town woman of high-caste who has flung aside her fetters, something about a rendezvous at the Three Rainbows.

But eventually it was over and I stepped through a door that twisted with a giddy blankness, and found myself outside a bare windowless wall in Charin again, the night sky starred and cold. The acrid smell of the Ghost Wind was thinning in the streets, but I had to crouch in a cranny of the wall when a final rustling horde of Ya-men, the last of their receding tide, rustled down the street. I found my way to my lodging in a filthy *chak* hostel, and threw myself down on the verminous bed.

Believe it or not, I slept.

CHAPTER TWELVE

An hour before dawn there was a noise in my room. I roused, my hand on my skean. Someone or something was fumbling under the mattress where I had thrust Evarin's bird. I struck out, encountered something warm and breathing, and grappled with it in the darkness. A foul-smelling something gripped over my mouth. I tore it away and struck hard with the skean. There was a high shrilling. The gripping filth loosened and fell away and something died on the floor.

I struck a light, retching in revulsion. It hadn't been human. There wouldn't have been that much blood from a human. Not that color, either.

The *chak* who ran the place came and gibbered at me. *Chaks* have a horror of blood and this one gave me to understand that my lease was up then and there, no arguments, no refunds. He wouldn't even let me go into his stone outbuilding to wash the foul stuff from my shirtcloak. I gave up and fished under the mattress for Evarin's Toy.

The *chak* got a glimpse of the embroideries on the silk in which it was wrapped, and stood back, his loose furry lips hanging open, while I gathered my few belongings together and strode out of the room. He would not touch the coins I offered; I laid them on a chest and he let them lie there, and as I went into the reddening morning they came flying after me into the street.

I pulled the silk from the Toy and tried to make some sense from my predicament. The little thing lay innocent and silent in my palm. It wouldn't tell me whether it had been keyed to me, the real Cargill, some time in the past, or to Rakhal, using my name and reputation in the Terran Colony here at Charin.

If I pressed the stud it might play out this comedy of errors by hunting down Rakhal, and all my troubles would be over. For a while, at least, until Evarin found out what had happened. I didn't deceive myself that I could carry the impersonation through another meeting.

On the other hand, if I pressed the stud, the bird might turn on me. And then all my troubles would be over for good.

If I delayed past Evarin's deadline, and did nothing, the other bird in his keeping would hunt down Juli and give her a swift and not too painless death.

I spent most of the day in a *chak* dive, juggling plans. Toys, innocent and sinister. Spies, messengers. Toys which killed horribly. Toys which could be controlled, perhaps, by the pliant mind of a child, and every child hates its parents now and again!

Even in the Terran colony, who was safe? In Mack's very home, one of the Magnusson youngsters had a shiny thing which might, or might not, be one of Evarin's hellish Toys. Or was I beginning to think like a superstitious Dry-towner?

Damn it, Evarin couldn't be infallible; he hadn't even recognized me as Race Cargill! Or—suddenly the sweat broke out, again, on my forehead—*or had he?* Had the whole thing been one of those sinister, deadly and incomprehensible nonhuman jokes?

I kept coming to the same conclusion. Juli was in danger, but she was half a world away. Rakhal was here in Charin. There was a child involved—Juli's child. The first step was to get inside the Terran colony and see how the land lay.

Charin is a city shaped like a crescent moon, encircling the small Trade City: a miniature spaceport, a miniature skyscraper HQ, the clustered dwellings of the Terrans who worked there, and those who lived with them and supplied them with necessities, services and luxuries.

Entry from one to the other is through a guarded gateway, since this is hostile territory, and Charin lies far beyond the impress of ordinary Terran law. But the gate stood wide-open, and the guards looked lax and bored. They had shockers, but they didn't look as if they'd used them lately.

One raised an eyebrow at his companion as I shambled up. I could pretty well guess the impression I made, dirty, unkempt and stained with nonhuman blood. I asked permission to go into the Terran Zone.

They asked my name and business, and I toyed with the notion of giving the name of the man I was inadvertently impersonating. Then I decided that if Rakhal had passed himself off as Race Cargill, he'd expect exactly that. And he was also capable of the masterstroke of impudence—putting out a pickup order, through Spaceforce, for his own name!

So I gave the name we'd used from Shainsa to Charin, and tacked one of the Secret Service passwords on the end of it. They looked at each other again and one said, "Rascar, eh? This is the guy, all right." He took me into the little booth by the gate while the other used an intercom device. Presently they took me along into the HQ building, and into an office that said "Legate."

I tried not to panic, but it wasn't easy! Evidently I'd walked square into another trap. One guard asked me, "All right, now, what exactly is your business in the Trade City?"

I'd hoped to locate Rakhal first. Now I knew I'd have no chance and at all costs I must straighten out this matter of identity before it went any further.

"Put me straight through to Magnusson's office, Level 38 at Central HQ, by visi," I demanded. I was trying to remember if Mack had ever even heard the name we used in Shainsa. I decided I couldn't risk it. "Name of Race Cargill."

The guard grinned without moving. He said to his partner, "That's the one, all right." He put a hand on my shoulder, spinning me around.

"Haul off, man. Shake your boots."

There were two of them, and Spaceforce guards aren't picked for their good looks. Just the same, I gave a pretty good account of myself until the inner door opened and a man came storming out.

"What the devil is all this racket?"

One guard got a hammerlock on me. "This Dry-towner bum tried to talk us into making a priority call to Magnusson, the Chief at Central. He knew a couple of the S.S. passwords. That's what got him through the gate. Remember, Cargill passed the word that somebody would turn up trying to impersonate him."

"I remember." The strange man's eyes were wary and cold.

"You damned fools," I snarled. "Magnusson will identify me! Can't you realize you're dealing with an impostor?"

One of the guards said to the legate in an undertone, "Maybe we ought to hold him as a suspicious character." But the legate shook his head. "Not worth the trouble. Cargill said it was a private affair. You might search him, make sure he's not concealing contraband weapons," he added, and talked softly to the wide-eyed clerk in the background while the guards went through my shirtcloak and pockets.

When they started to unwrap the silk-shrouded Toy I yelled—if the thing got set off accidentally, there'd be trouble. The legate turned and rebuked, "Can't you see it's embroidered with the Toad God? It's a religious amulet of some sort, let it alone."

They grumbled, but gave it back to me, and the legate commanded, "Don't mess him up any more. Give him back his knife and take him to the gates. But make sure he doesn't come back."

I found myself seized and frog-marched to the gate. One guard pushed my skean back into its clasp. The other shoved me hard, and I stumbled, fell sprawling in the dust of the cobbled street, to the accompaniment of a profane statement about what I could expect if I came back. A chorus of jeers from a cluster of *chak* children and veiled women broke across me.

I picked myself up, glowered so fiercely at the giggling spectators that the laughter drained away into silence, and clenched my fists, half inclined to turn back and bull my way through. Then I subsided. First round to Rakhal. He had sprung the trap on me, very neatly.

The street was narrow and crooked, winding between doubled rows of pebble-houses, and full of dark shadows even in the crimson noon. I walked aimlessly, favoring the arm the guard had crushed. I was no closer to settling things with Rakhal, and I had slammed at least one gate behind me.

Why hadn't I had sense enough to walk up and demand to *see* Race Cargill? Why hadn't I insisted on a fingerprint check? I could prove my identity, and Rakhal, using my name in my absence, to those who didn't know me by sight, couldn't. I could at least have made him try. But he had maneuvered it very cleverly, so I never had a chance to insist on proofs.

I turned into a wineshop and ordered a dram of greenish mountainberry liquor, sipping it slowly and fingering the few bills and coins in my pockets. I'd better forget about warning Juli. I couldn't 'vise her from Charin, except in the Terran zone. I had neither the money nor the time to make the trip in person, even if I could get passage on a Terran-dominated airline after today.

Miellyn. She had flirted with me, and like Dallisa, she might prove vulnerable. It might be another trap, but I'd take the chance. At least I could get hints about Evarin. And I needed information. I wasn't used to this kind of intrigue any more. The smell of danger was foreign to me now, and I found it unpleasant.

The small lump of the bird in my pocket tantalized me. I took it out again. It was a temptation to press the stud and let it settle things, or at least start them going, then and there.

After a while I noticed the proprietors of the shop staring at the silk of the wrappings. They backed off, apprehensive. I held out a coin and they shook their heads. "You are welcome to the drink," one of them said. "All we have is at your service. Only please go. Go quickly."

They would not touch the coins I offered. I thrust the bird in my pocket, swore and went. It was my second experience with being somehow tabu, and I didn't like it.

It was dusk when I realized I was being followed.

At first it was a glimpse out of the corner of my eye, a head seen too frequently for coincidence. It developed into a too-persistent footstep in uneven rhythm.

Tap-*tap*-tap. Tap-*tap*-tap.

I had my skean handy, but I had a hunch this wasn't anything I could settle with a skean. I ducked into a side street and waited.

Nothing.

I went on, laughing at my imagined fears.

Then, after a time, the soft, persistent footfall thudded behind me again.

I cut across a thieves market, dodging from stall to stall, cursed by old women selling hot fried goldfish, women in striped veils railing at me in their chiming talk when I brushed their rolled rugs with hasty feet. Far behind I heard the familiar uneven hurry: tap-*tap*-tap, tap-*tap*-tap.

I fled down a street where women sat on flower-decked balconies, their open lanterns flowing with fountains and rivulets of gold and orange fire. I raced through quiet streets where furred children crept to doors and watched me pass with great golden eyes that shone in the dark.

I dodged into an alley and lay there, breathing hard. Someone not two inches away said, "Are you one of us, brother?"

I muttered something surly, in his dialect, and a hand, reassuringly human, closed on my elbow. "This way."

Out of breath with long running, I let him lead me, meaning to break away after a few steps, apologize for mistaken identity and vanish, when a sound at the end of the street made me jerk stiff and listen.

Tap-*tap*-tap. Tap-*tap*-tap.

I let my arm relax in the hand that guided me, flung a fold of my shirtcloak over my face, and went along with my unknown guide.

CHAPTER THIRTEEN

I stumbled over steps, took a jolting stride downward, and found myself in a dim room jammed with dark figures, human and nonhuman.

The figures swayed in the darkness, chanting in a dialect not altogether familiar to me, a monotonous wailing chant, with a single recurrent phrase: "Kamaina! Kama-aina!" It began on a high note, descending in weird chromatics to the lowest tone the human ear could resolve.

The sound made me draw back. Even the Dry-towners shunned the orgiastic rituals of Kamaina. Earthmen have a reputation for getting rid of the more objectionable customs—by human standards—on any planet where they live. But they don't touch religions, and Kamaina, on the surface anyhow, was a religion.

I started to turn round and leave, as if I had inadvertently walked through the wrong door, but my conductor hauled on my arm, and I was wedged in too tight by now to risk a roughhouse. Trying to force my way out would only have called attention to me, and the first of the Secret Service maxims is; when in doubt, go along, keep quiet, and watch the other guy.

As my eyes adapted to the dim light, I saw that most of the crowd were Charin plainsmen or *chaks*. One or two wore Dry-town shirtcloaks, and I even thought I saw an Earthman in the crowd, though I was never sure and I fervently hope not. They were squatting around small crescent-shaped tables, and all intently gazing at a flickery spot of light at the front of the cellar. I saw an empty place at one table and dropped there, finding the floor soft, as if cushioned.

On each table, small smudging pastilles were burning, and from these cones of ash-tipped fire came the steamy, swimmy smoke that filled the darkness with strange colors. Beside me an immature *chak* girl was kneeling, her fettered hands strained tightly back at her sides, her naked breasts pierced for jeweled rings.

Beneath the pallid fur around her pointed ears, the exquisite animal face was quite mad. She whispered to me, but her dialect was so thick that I could follow only a few words, and would just as soon not have heard those few. An older *chak* grunted for silence and she subsided, swaying and crooning.

There were cups and decanters on all the tables, and a woman tilted pale, phosphorescent fluid into a cup and offered it to me. I took one sip, then another. It was cold and pleasantly tart, and not until the second swallow turned sweet on my tongue did I know what I tasted. I pretended to swallow while the woman's eyes were fixed on me, then somehow contrived to spill the filthy stuff down my shirt.

I was wary even of the fumes, but there was nothing else I could do. The stuff was *shallavan*, outlawed on every planet in the Terran Empire and every halfway decent planet outside it.

More and more figures, men and creatures, kept crowding into the cellar, which was not very large. The place looked like the worst nightmare of a drug-dreamer, ablaze with the colors of the smoking incense, the swaying crowd, and their monotonous cries. Quite suddenly there was a blaze of purple light and someone screamed in raving ecstasy: "*Na ki na Nebran n'hai Kamaina!*"

"Kamayeeeeeeeeeeeeeeeeena!" shrilled the tranced mob.

An old man jumped up and started haranguing the crowd. I could just follow his dialect. He was talking about Terra. He was talking about riots. He was jabbering mystical gibberish which I couldn't understand and didn't want to understand, and rabble-rousing anti-Terran propaganda which I understood much too well.

Another blaze of lights and another long scream in chorus: "Kamayeeeeeeeeeeeeeeeeeeena!"

Evarin stood in the blaze of the many-colored light.

The Toymaker, as I had seen him last, cat-smooth, gracefully alien, shrouded in a ripple of giddy crimsons. Behind him was a blackness. I waited till the painful blaze of lights abated, then, straining my eyes to see past him, I got my worst shock.

A woman stood there, naked to the waist, her hands ritually fettered with little chains that stirred and clashed musically as she moved stiff-legged in a frozen dream. Hair like black grass banded her brow and naked shoulders, and her eyes were crimson.

And the eyes lived in the dead dreaming face. They lived, and they were mad with terror although the lips curved in a gently tranced smile.

Miellyn.

Evarin was speaking in that dialect I barely understood. His arms were flung high and his cloak went spilling away from them, rippling like something alive. The jammed humans and nonhumans swayed and chanted and he swayed above them like an iridescent bug, weaving arms rippling back and forth, back and forth. I strained to catch his words.

"Our world...an old world."

"Kamayeeeeena," whimpered the shrill chorus.

"...humans, humans, all humans would make slaves of us all, all save the Children of the Ape..."

I lost the thread for a moment. True. The Terran Empire has one small blind spot in otherwise sane policy, ignoring that nonhuman and human have lived placidly here for millennia: they placidly assumed that humans were everywhere the dominant race, as on Earth itself.

The Toymaker's weaving arms went on spinning, spinning. I rubbed my eyes to clear them of *shallavan* and incense. I hoped that what I saw was an illusion of the drug—something, something huge and dark, was hovering over the girl. She stood placidly, hands clasped on her chains, but her eyes writhed in the frozen calm of her face.

Then something—I can only call it a sixth sense—bore it on me that there was *someone* outside the door. I was perhaps the only creature there, except for Evarin, not drugged with *shallavan*, and perhaps that's all it was. But during the days in the Secret Service I'd had to develop some extra senses. Five just weren't enough for survival.

I *knew* somebody was fixing to break down that door, and I had a good idea why. I'd been followed, by the legate's orders, and, tracking me here, they'd gone away and brought back reinforcements.

Someone struck a blow on the door and a stentorian voice bawled, "Open up there, in the name of the Empire!"

The chanting broke in ragged quavers. Evarin stopped. Somewhere a woman screamed. The lights abruptly went out and a stampede started in the room. Women struck me with chains, men kicked, there were shrieks and howls. I thrust my way forward, butting with elbows and knees and shoulders.

A dusky emptiness yawned and I got a glimpse of sunlight and open sky and knew that Evarin had stepped through into *somewhere* and was gone. The banging on the door sounded like a whole regiment of Spaceforce out there. I dived toward the shimmer of little stars which marked Miellyn's tiara in the darkness, braving the black horror hovering over her, and touched rigid girl-flesh, cold as death.

I grabbed her and ducked sideways. This time it wasn't intuition—nine times out of ten, anyway, intuition is just a mental shortcut which adds up all the things which your subconscious has noticed while you were busy thinking about something else. Every native building on Wolf had concealed entrances and exits and I know where to look for them. This one was exactly where I expected. I pushed at it and found myself in a long, dim corridor.

The head of a woman peered from an opening door. She saw Miellyn's limp body hanging on my arm and her mouth widened in a silent scream. Then the head popped back out of sight and a door slammed. I heard the bolt slide. I ran for the end of the hall, the girl in my arms, thinking that this was where I came in, as far as Miellyn was concerned, and wondering why I bothered.

The door opened on a dark, peaceful street. One lonely moon was setting beyond the rooftops. I set Miellyn on her feet, but she moaned and crumpled against me. I put my shirtcloak around her bare shoulders. Judging by the noises and yells, we'd gotten out just in time. No one came out the exit behind us. Either the Spaceforce had plugged it or, more likely, everyone else in the cellar had been too muddled by drugs to know what was going on.

But it was only a few minutes, I knew, before Spaceforce would check the whole building for concealed escape holes. Suddenly, and irrelevantly, I found myself thinking of a day not too long ago, when I'd stood up in front of a unit-in-training of Spaceforce, introduced to them as an Intelligence expert on native towns, and solemnly warned them about concealed exits and entrances. I wondered, for half a minute, if it might not be simpler just to wait here and let them pick me up.

Then I hoisted Miellyn across my shoulders. She was heavier than she looked, and after a minute, half conscious, she began to struggle and moan. There was a *chak*-run cookshop down the street, a place I'd once known well, with an evil reputation and worse food, but it was quiet and stayed open all night. I turned in at the door, bending at the low lintel.

The place was smoke-filled and foul-smelling. I dumped Miellyn on a couch and sent the frowsy waiter for two bowls of noodles and coffee, handed him a few extra coins, and told him to leave us alone. He probably drew the worst possible inference—I saw his muzzle twitch at the smell of *shallavan*—but it was that kind of place anyhow. He drew down the shutters and went.

I stared at the unconscious girl, then shrugged and started on the noodles. My own head was still swimmy with the fumes, incense and drug, and I wanted it clear. I wasn't quite sure what I was going to do, but I had Evarin's right-hand girl, and I was going to use her.

The noodles were greasy and had a curious taste, but they were hot, and I ate all of one bowl before Miellyn stirred and whimpered and put up one hand, with a little clinking of chains, to her hair. The gesture was indefinably reminiscent of Dallisa, and for the first time I saw the likeness between them. It made me wary and yet curiously softened.

Finding she could not move freely, she rolled over, sat up and stared around in growing bewilderment and dismay.

"There was a sort of riot," I said. "I got you out. Evarin ditched you. And you can quit thinking what you're thinking, I put my shirtcloak on you because you were bare to the waist and it didn't look so good." I stopped to think that over, and amended: "I mean I couldn't haul you around the streets that way. It looked good enough."

To my surprise, she gave a shaky little giggle, and held out her fettered hands. "Will you?"

I broke her links and freed her. She rubbed her wrists as if they hurt her, then drew up her draperies, pinned them so that she was decently covered, and tossed back my shirtcloak. Her eyes were wide and soft in the light of the flickering stub of candle.

"O, Rakhal," she sighed. "When I saw you there—" She sat up, clasping her hands hard together, and when she continued her voice was curiously cold and controlled for anyone so childish. It was almost as cold as Dallisa's.

"If you've come from Kyral, I'm not going back. I'll never go back, and you may as well know it."

"I don't come from Kyral, and I don't care where you go. I don't care what you do." I suddenly realized that the last statement was wholly untrue, and to cover my confusion I shoved the remaining bowl of noodles at her.

"Eat."

She wrinkled her nose in fastidious disgust. "I'm not hungry."

"Eat it anyway. You're still half doped, and the food will clear your head." I picked up one mug of the coffee and drained it at a single swallow. "What were you doing in that disgusting den?"

Without warning she flung herself across the table at me, throwing her arms round my neck. Startled, I let her cling a moment, then reached up and firmly unfastened her hands.

"None of that now. I fell for it once, and it landed me in the middle of the mudpie."

But her fingers bit my shoulder.

"Rakhal, Rakhal, I tried to get away and find you. Have you still got the bird? You haven't set it off yet? Oh, don't, don't, don't, Rakhal, you don't know what Evarin is, you don't know what he's doing." The words spilled out of her like floodwaters. "He's won so many of you, don't let him have you too, Rakhal. They call you an honest man, you worked once for Terra, the Terrans would believe you if you went to them and told them what he—Rakhal, take me to the Terran Zone, take me there, take me there where they'll protect me from Evarin."

At first I tried to stop her, question her, then waited and let the torrent of entreaty run on and on. At last, exhausted and breathless, she lay quietly against my shoulder, her head fallen forward. The musty reek of *shallavan* mingled with the flower scent of her hair.

"Kid," I said heavily at last, "you and your Toymaker have both got me wrong. I'm not Rakhal Sensar."

"You're not?" She drew back, regarding me in dismay. Her eyes searched every inch of me, from the gray streak across my forehead to the scar running down into my collar. "Then who—"

"Race Cargill. Terran Intelligence."

She stared, her mouth wide like a child's.

Then she laughed. She *laughed!* At first I thought she was hysterical. I stared at her in consternation. Then, as her wide eyes met mine, with all the mischief of the nonhuman which has mingled into the human here, all the circular complexities of Wolf illogic behind the woman in them, I started to laugh too.

I threw back my head and roared, until we were clinging together and gasping with mirth like a pair of raving fools. The *chak* waiter came to the door and stared at us, and I roared "Get the hell out," between spasms of crazy laughter.

Then she was wiping her face, tears of mirth still dripping down her cheeks, and I was frowning bleakly into the empty bowls.

"Cargill," she said hesitantly, "you can take me to the Terrans where Rakhal—"

"Hell's bells," I exploded. "I can't take you anywhere, girl. I've got to find Rakhal—" I stopped in midsentence and looked at her clearly for the first time.

"Child, I'll see that you're protected, if I can. But I'm afraid you've walked from the trap to the cookpot. There isn't a house in Charin that will hold me. I've been thrown out twice today."

She nodded. "I don't know how the word spreads, but it happens, in nonhuman parts. I think they can see trouble written in a human face, or smell it on the wind." She fell silent, her face propped sleepily between her hands, her hair falling in tangles. I took one of her hands in mine and turned it over.

It was a fine hand, with birdlike bones and soft rose-tinted nails; but the lines and hardened places around the knuckles reminded me that she, too, came from the cold austerity of the salt Dry-towns. After a moment she flushed and drew her hand from mine.

"What are you thinking, Cargill?" she asked, and for the first time I heard her voice sobered, without the coquetry, which must after all have been a very thin veneer.

I answered her simply and literally. "I am thinking of Dallisa. I thought you were very different, and yet, I see that you are very like her."

I thought she would question what I knew of her sister, but she let it pass in silence. After a time she said, "Yes, we were twins." Then, after a long silence, she added, "But she was always much the older."

And that was all I ever knew of whatever obscure pressures had shaped Dallisa into an austere and tragic Clytemnestra, and Miellyn into a pixie runaway.

Outside the drawn shutters, dawn was brightening. Miellyn shivered, drawing her thin draperies around her bare throat. I glanced at the little rim of jewels that starred her hair and said, "You'd better take those off and hide them. They alone would be enough to have you hauled into an alley and strangled, in this part of Charin." I hauled the bird Toy from my pocket and slapped it on the greasy table, still wrapped in its silk. "I don't suppose you know which of us this thing is set to kill?"

"I know nothing about the Toys."

"You seem to know plenty about the Toymaker."

"I thought so. Until last night." I looked at the rigid, clamped mouth and thought that if she were really as soft and delicate as she looked, she would have wept. Then she struck her small hand on the tabletop and burst out, "It's not a religion. It isn't even an honest movement for freedom! Its a—a front for smuggling, and drugs, and—and every other filthy thing!

"Believe it or not, when I left Shainsa, I thought Nebran was the answer to the way the Terrans were strangling us! Now I know there are worse things on Wolf than the Terran Empire! I've heard of Rakhal Sensar, and whatever you may think of Rakhal, he's too decent to be mixed up in anything like this!"

"Suppose you tell me what's really going on," I suggested. She couldn't add much to what I knew already, but the last fragments of the pattern were beginning to settle into place. Rakhal, seeking the matter transmitter and some key to the nonhuman sciences of Wolf—I knew now what the city of Silent Ones had reminded me of!—had somehow crossed the path of the Toymaker.

Evarin's words now made sense: "*You were clever at evading our surveillance—for a while.*" Possibly, though I'd never know, Cuinn had been keeping one foot in each camp, working for Kyral and

THE DOOR THROUGH SPACE

for Evarin. The Toymaker, knowing of Rakhal's anti-Terran activities, had believed he would make a valuable ally and had taken steps to secure his help.

Juli herself had given me the clue: *"He smashed Rindy's Toys."* Out of the context it sounded like the work of a madman. Now, having encountered Evarin's workshop, it made plain good sense.

And I think I had known all along that Rakhal could not have been playing Evarin's game. He might have turned against Terra—though now I was beginning even to doubt that—and certainly he'd have killed me if he found me. But he would have done it himself, and without malice. *Killed without malice*—that doesn't make sense in any of the languages of Terra. But it made sense to me.

Miellyn had finished her brief recitation and was drowsing, her head pillowed on the table. The reddish light was growing, and I realized that I was waiting for dawn as, days ago, I had waited for sunset in Shainsa, with every nerve stretched to the breaking point. It was dawn of the third morning, and this bird lying on the table before me must fly or, far away in the Kharsa, another would fly at Juli.

I said, "There's some distance limitation on this one, I understand, since I have to be fairly near its object. If I lock it in a steel box and drop it in the desert, I'll guarantee it won't bother anybody. I don't suppose you'd have a shot at stealing the other one for me?"

She raised her head, eyes flashing. "Why should you worry about Rakhal's wife?" she flared, and for no good reason it occurred to me that she was jealous. "I might have known Evarin wouldn't shoot in the dark! Rakhal's wife, that Earthwoman, what do you care for her?"

It seemed important to set her straight. I explained that Juli was my sister, and saw a little of the tension fade from her face, but not all. Remembering the custom of the Dry-towns, I was not wholly surprised when she added, jealously, "When I heard of your feud, I guessed it was over that woman!"

"But not in the way you think," I said. Juli had been part of it, certainly. Even then I had not wanted her to turn her back on her world, but if Rakhal had remained with Terra, I would have accepted his marriage to Juli. Accepted it. I'd have rejoiced. God knows we had been closer than brothers, those years in the Dry-towns. And then, before Miellyn's flashing eyes, I suddenly faced my secret hate, my secret fear. No, the quarrel had not been all Rakhal's doing.

He had not turned his back, unexplained on Terra. In some unrecognized fashion, I had done my best to drive him away. And when he had gone, I had banished a part of myself as well, and thought I could end the struggle by saying it didn't exist. And now, facing what I had done to all of us, I knew that my revenge—so long sought, so dearly cherished—must be abandoned.

"We still have to deal with the bird," I said. "It's a gamble, with all the cards wild." I could dismantle it, and trust to luck that Wolf illogic didn't include a tamper mechanism. But that didn't seem worth the risk.

"First I've got to *find* Rakhal. If I set the bird free and it killed him, it wouldn't settle anything." For I could not kill Rakhal. Not, now, because I knew life would be a worse punishment than death. But because—I knew it, now—if Rakhal died, Juli would die, too. And if I killed him I'd be killing the best part of myself. Somehow Rakhal and I must strike a balance between our two worlds, and try to build a new one from them.

"And I can't sit here and talk any longer. I haven't time to take you—" I stopped, remembering the spaceport cafe at the edge of the Kharsa. There was a street-shrine, or matter transmitter, right there, across the street from the Terran HQ. *All these years...*

"You know your way in the transmitters. You can go there in a second or two." She could warn Juli, tell Magnusson. But when I suggested this, giving her a password that would take her straight to the top, she turned white. "All jumps have to be made through the Mastershrine."

I stopped and thought about that.

"Where is Evarin likely to be, right now?"

She gave a nervous shudder. "He's everywhere!"

"Rubbish! He's not omniscient! Why, you little fool, he didn't even recognize me. He thought I was Rakhal!" I wasn't too sure, myself, but Miellyn needed reassurance. "Or take *me* to the Mastershrine. I can find Rakhal in that scanning device of Evarin's." I saw refusal in her face and pushed on, "If Evarin's there, I'll prove he's fallible enough with a skean in his throat! And here"—I thrust the Toy into her hand—"hang on to this, will you?"

She put it matter-of-factly into her draperies. "I don't mind that. But to the shrine—" Her voice quivered, and I stood up and pushed at the table.

"Let's get going. Where's the nearest street-shrine?"

"No, no! Oh, I don't dare!"

"You've got to." I saw the *chak* who owned the place edging round the door again and said, "There's no use arguing, Miellyn." When she had readjusted her robes a little while ago, she had pinned them so that the flat sprawl of the Nebran embroideries was over her breasts. I put a finger against them, not in a sensuous gesture, and said, "The minute they see these, they'll throw us out of here, too."

"If you knew what I know of Nebran, you wouldn't *want* me to go near the Mastershrine again!" There was that faint coquettishness in her sidewise smile.

And suddenly I realized that I didn't want her to. But she was not Dallisa and she could not sit in cold dignity while her world fell into ruin. Miellyn must fight for the one she wanted.

And then some of that primitive male hostility which lives in every man came to the surface, and I gripped her arm until she whimpered. Then I said, in the Shainsan which still comes to my tongue when moved or angry, "Damn it, you're *going*. Have

211

you forgotten that if it weren't for me you'd have been torn to pieces by that raving mob, or something worse?"

That did it. She pulled away and I saw again, beneath the veneer of petulant coquetry, that fierce and untamable insolence of the Dry-towner. The more fierce and arrogant, in this girl, because she had burst her fettered hands free and shaken off the ruin of the past.

I was seized with a wildly inappropriate desire to seize her, crush her in my arms, taste the red honey of that teasing mouth. The effort of mastering the impulse made me rough.

I shoved at her and said, "Come on. Let's get there before Evarin does."

CHAPTER FOURTEEN

Outside in the streets it was full day, and the color and life of Charin had subsided into listlessness again, a dim morning dullness and silence. Only a few men lounged wearily in the streets, as if the sun had sapped their energy. And always the pale fleecy-haired children, human and furred nonhuman, played their mysterious games on the curbs and gutters and staring at us with neither curiosity nor malice.

Miellyn was shaking when she set her feet into the patterned stones of the street-shrine.

"Scared, Miellyn?"

"I know Evarin. You don't. But"—her mouth twitched in a pitiful attempt at the old mischief—"when I am with a great and valorous Earthman…"

"Cut it out," I growled, and she giggled. "You'll have to stand closer to me. The transmitters are meant only for one person."

I stooped and put my arms round her. "Like this?"

"Like this," she whispered, pressing herself against me. A staggering whirl of dizzy darkness swung round my head. The street vanished. After an instant the floor steadied and we stepped into the terminal room in the Mastershrine, under a skylight dim with the last red slant of sunset. Distant hammering noises rang in my ears.

Miellyn whispered, "Evarin's not here, but he might jump through at any second." I wasn't listening.

"Where is this place, Miellyn? Where on the planet?"

"No one knows but Evarin, I think. There are no doors. Anyone who goes in or out, jumps through the transmitter." She pointed. "The scanning device is in there, we'll have to go through the workroom."

She was patting her crushed robes into place, smoothing her hair with fastidious fingers. "I don't suppose you have a comb? I've no time to go to my own—"

I'd known she was a vain and pampered brat, but this passed all reason, and I said so, exploding at her. She looked at me as if I wasn't quite intelligent. "The Little Ones, my friend, notice things. You are quite enough of a roughneck, but if I, Nebran's priestess, walk through their workroom all blown about and looking like the tag end of an orgy in Ardcarran..."

Abashed, I fished in a pocket and offered her a somewhat battered pocket comb. She looked at it distastefully but used it to good purpose, smoothing her hair swiftly, rearranging her loose-pinned robe so that the worst of the tears and stains were covered, and giving me, meanwhile, an artless and rather tempting view of some delicious curvature. She replaced the starred tiara on her ringlets and finally opened the door of the workroom and we walked through.

Not for years had I known that particular sensation— thousands of eyes, boring holes in the center of my back somewhere. There *were* eyes; the round inhuman orbs of the dwarf *chaks*, the faceted stare of the prism eyes of the Toys. The workroom wasn't a hundred feet long, but it felt longer than a good many miles I've walked. Here and there the dwarfs murmured an obsequious greeting to Miellyn, and she made some lighthearted answer.

She had warned me to walk as if I had every right to be there, and I strode after her as if we were simply going to an agreed-on meeting in the next room. But I was drenched with cold sweat before the farther door finally closed, safe and blessedly opaque, behind us. Miellyn, too, was shaking with fright, and I put a hand on her arm.

"Steady, kid. Where's the scanner?"

She touched the panel I'd seen. "I'm not sure I can focus it accurately. Evarin never let me touch it."

This was a fine time to tell me that. "How does it work?"

"It's an adaptation of the transmitter principle. It lets you see anywhere, but without jumping. It uses a tracer mechanism like the one in the Toys. If Rakhal's electrical-impulse pattern were on file—just a minute." She fished out the bird Toy and unwrapped it. "Here's how we find out which of you this is keyed to."

I looked at the fledgling bird, lying innocently in her palm, as she pushed aside the feathers, exposing a tiny crystal. "If it's keyed to you, you'll see yourself in this, as if the screen were a mirror. If it's keyed to Rakhal…"

She touched the crystal to the surface of the screen. Little flickers of snow wavered and danced. Then, abruptly, we were looking down from a height at the lean back of a man in a leather jacket. Slowly he turned. I saw the familiar set of his shoulders, saw the back of his head come into an aquiline profile, and the profile turn slowly into a scarred, seared mask more hideously claw-marked and disfigured than my own.

"Rakhal," I muttered. "Shift the focus if you can, Miellyn, get a look out the window or something. Charin's a big city. If we could get a look at a landmark—"

Rakhal was talking soundlessly, his lips moving as he spoke to someone out of sight range of the scanning device. Abruptly Miellyn said, "There." She had caught a window in the sight field of the pane. I could see a high pylon and two of three uprights that looked like a bridge, just outside. I said, "It's the Bridge of Summer Snows. I know where he is now. Turn it off, Miellyn, we can find him—" I was turning away when Miellyn screamed.

"Look!"

Rakhal had turned his back on the scanner and for the first time I could see who he was talking to. A hunched, catlike shoulder twisted; a sinuous neck, a high-held head that was not quite human.

"Evarin!" I swore. "That does it. He knows now that I'm not Rakhal, if he didn't know it all along! Come on, girl, we're getting out of here!"

This time there was no pretense of normality as we dashed through the workroom. Fingers dropped from half-completed Toys as they stared after us. *Toys!* I wanted to stop and smash them all. But if we hurried, we might find Rakhal. And, with luck, we would find Evarin with him.

And then I was going to bang their heads together. I'd reached a saturation point on adventure. I'd had all I wanted. I realized that I'd been up all night, that I was exhausted. I wanted to murder and smash, and wanted to fall down somewhere and go to sleep, all at once. We banged the workroom door shut and I took time to shove a heavy divan against it, blockading it.

Miellyn stared. "The Little Ones would not harm me," she began. "I am sacrosanct."

I wasn't sure. I had a notion her status had changed plenty, beginning when I saw her chained and drugged, and standing under the hovering horror. But I didn't say so.

"Maybe. But there's nothing sacred about *me*!"

She was already inside the recess where the Toad God squatted. "There is a street-shrine just beyond the Bridge of Summer Snows. We can jump directly there." Abruptly she froze in my arms, with a convulsive shudder.

"Evarin! Hold me, tight—he's jumping in! Quick!"

Space reeled round us, and then…

Can you split instantaneousness into fragments? It didn't make sense, but so help me, that's what happened. And everything that happened, occurred within less than a second. We landed in the street-shrine. I could see the pylon and the bridge and the rising sun of Charin. Then there was the giddy internal wrenching, a blast of icy air whistled round us, and we were gazing out at the Polar mountains, ringed in their eternal snow.

Miellyn clutched at me. "Pray! Pray to the Gods of Terra, if there are any!"

She clung so violently that it felt as if her small body was trying to push through me and come out the other side. I hung on tight. Miellyn knew what she was doing in the transmitter; I was just along for the ride and I didn't relish the thought of being dropped off somewhere in that black limbo we traversed.

We jumped again, the sickness of disorientation forcing a moan from the girl, and darkness shivered round us. I looked on an unfamiliar street of black night and dust-bleared stars. She whimpered, "Evarin knows what I'm doing. He's jumping us all over the planet. He can work the controls with his mind. Psychokinetics—I can do it a little, but I never dared—oh, hang on *tight*."

Then began one of the most amazing duels ever fought. Miellyn would make some tiny movement, and we would be falling, blind and dizzy, through blackness. Halfway through the giddiness, a new direction would wrench us and we would be thrust elsewhere, and look out into a new street.

One instant I smelled hot coffee from the spaceport cafe near the Kharsa. An instant later it was blinding noon, with crimson fronds waving above us and a dazzle of water. We flicked in and out of the salty air of Shainsa, glimpsed flowers on a Daillon street, moonlight, noon, red twilight flickered and went, shot through with the terrible giddiness of hyperspace.

Then suddenly I caught a second glimpse of the bridge and the pylon; a moment's oversight had landed us for an instant in Charin. The blackness started to reel down, but my reflexes are fast and I made one swift, scrabbling step forward. We lurched, sprawled, locked together, on the stones of the Bridge of Summer Snows. Battered, and bruised, and bloody, we were still alive, and where we wanted to be.

THE DOOR THROUGH SPACE

I lifted Miellyn to her feet. Her eyes were dazed with pain. The ground swayed and rocked under our feet as we fled along the bridge. At the far end, I looked up at the pylon. Judging from its angle, we couldn't be more than a hundred feet from the window through which I'd seen that landmark in the scanner. In this street there was a wineshop, a silk market, and a small private house. I walked up and banged on the door.

Silence. I knocked again and had time to wonder if we'd find ourselves explaining things to some uninvolved stranger. Then I heard a child's high voice, and a deep familiar voice hushing it. The door opened, just a crack, to reveal part of a scarred face.

It drew into a hideous grin, then relaxed.

"I thought it might be you, Cargill. You've taken at least three days longer than I figured, getting here. Come on in," said Rakhal Sensar.

CHAPTER FIFTEEN

He hadn't changed much in six years. His face *was* worse than mine; he hadn't had the plastic surgeons of Terran Intelligence doing their best for him. His mouth, I thought fleetingly, must hurt like hell when he drew it up into the kind of grin he was grinning now. His eyebrows, thick and fierce with gray in them, went up as he saw Miellyn; but he backed away to let us enter, and shut the door behind us.

The room was bare and didn't look as if it had been lived in much. The floor was stone, rough-laid, a single fur rug laid before a brazier. A little girl was sitting on the rug, drinking from a big double-handled mug, but she scrambled to her feet as we came in, and backed against the wall, looking at us with wide eyes.

She had pale-red hair like Juli's, cut straight in a fringe across her forehead, and she was dressed in a smock of dyed red fur that almost matched her hair. A little smear of milk like a white moustache clung to her upper lip where she had forgotten to wipe her mouth. She was about five years old, with deep-set dark eyes like Juli's, that watched me gravely without surprise or fear; she evidently knew who I was.

"Rindy," Rakhal said quietly, not taking his eyes from me. "Go into the other room."

Rindy didn't move, still staring at me. Then she moved toward Miellyn, looking up intently not at the woman, but at the pattern of embroideries across her dress. It was very quiet, until Rakhal added, in a gentle and curiously moderate voice, "Do you still carry a skean, Race?"

I shook my head. "There's an ancient proverb on Terra, about blood being thicker than water, Rakhal. That's Juli's daughter. I'm not going to kill her father right before her eyes." My rage spilled over then, and I bellowed, "To hell with your damned Dry-town feuds and your filthy Toad God and all the rest of it!"

Rakhal said harshly, "Rindy. I told you to get out."

"She needn't go." I took a step toward the little girl, a wary eye on Rakhal. "I don't know quite what you're up to, but it's nothing for a child to be mixed up in. Do what you damn please. I can settle with you any time.

"The first thing is to get Rindy out of here. She belongs with Juli and, damn it, that's where she's going." I held out my arms to the little girl and said, "It's over, Rindy, whatever he's done to you. Your mother sent me to find you. Don't you want to go to your mother?"

Rakhal made a menacing gesture and warned, "I wouldn't—"

Miellyn darted swiftly between us and caught up the child in her arms. Rindy began to struggle noiselessly, kicking and whimpering, but Miellyn took two quick steps, and flung an inner door open. Rakhal took a stride toward her. She whirled on him, fighting to control the furious little girl, and gasped, "Settle it between you, without the baby watching!"

Through the open door I briefly saw a bed, a child's small dresses hanging on a hook, before Miellyn kicked the door shut and I heard a latch being fastened. Behind the closed door

Rindy broke into angry screams, but I put my back against the door.

"She's right. We'll settle it between the two of us. What have you done to that child?"

"If you thought—" Rakhal stopped himself in midsentence and stood watching me without moving for a minute. Then he laughed.

"You're as stupid as ever, Race. Why, you fool, I knew Juli would run straight to you, if she was scared enough. I knew it would bring you out of hiding. Why, you damned fool!" He stood mocking me, but there was a strained fury, almost a frenzy of contempt behind the laughter.

"You filthy coward, Race! Six years hiding in the Terran zone. Six years, and I gave you six months! If you'd had the guts to walk out after me, after I rigged that final deal to give you the chance, we could have gone after the biggest thing on Wolf. And we could have brought it off together, instead of spending years spying and dodging and hunting! And now, when I finally get you out of hiding, all you want to do is run back where you'll be safe! I thought you had more guts!"

"Not for Evarin's dirty work!"

Rakhal swore hideously. "Evarin! Do you really believe—I might have known he'd get to you too! That girl—and you've managed to wreck all I did there, too!" Suddenly, so swiftly my eyes could hardly follow, he whipped out his skean and came at me. "Get away from that door!"

I stood my ground. "You'll have to kill me first. And I won't fight you, Rakhal. We'll settle this, but we'll do it my way for once, like Earthmen."

"*Son of the Ape!* Get your skean out, you stinking coward!"

"I won't do it, Rakhal." I stood and defied him. I had outmaneuvered Dry-towners in a *shegri* bet. I knew Rakhal, and I knew he would not knife an unarmed man. "We fought once with the *kifirgh* and it didn't settle anything. This time we'll do it my way. I threw my skean away before I came here. I won't fight."

He thrust at me. Even I could see that the blow was a feint, and I had a flashing, instantaneous memory of Dallisa's threat to drive the knife through my palms. But even while I commanded myself to stand steady, sheer reflex threw me forward, grabbing at his wrist and the knife.

Between my grappling hand he twisted and I felt the skean drive home, rip through my jacket with a tearing sound; felt the thin fine line of touch, not pain yet, as it sliced flesh. Then pain burned through my ribs and I felt hot blood, and I wanted to kill Rakhal, wanted to get my hands around his throat and kill him with them. And at the same time I was raging because I didn't want to fight the crazy fool, I wasn't even mad at him.

Miellyn flung the door open, shrieking, and suddenly the Toy, released, was darting a small whirring droning horror, straight at Rakhal's eyes. I yelled. But there was no time even to warn him. I bent and butted him in the stomach. He grunted, doubled up in agony and fell out of the path of the diving Toy. It whirred in frustration, hovered.

He writhed in agony, drawing up his knees, clawing at his shirt, while I turned on Miellyn in immense fury—and stopped. Hers had been a move of desperation, an instinctive act to restore the balance between a weaponless man and one who had a knife. Rakhal gasped, in a hoarse voice with all the breath gone from it:

"Didn't want to use. Rather fight clean—" Then he opened his closed fist and suddenly there were *two* of the little whirring droning horrors in the room and this one was diving at me, and as I threw myself headlong to the floor the last puzzle-piece fell into place: Evarin had made the same bargain with Rakhal as with me!

I rolled over, dodging. Behind me in the room there was a child's shrill scream: "Daddy! Daddy!" And abruptly the birds collapsed in midair and went limp. They fell to the floor like dropping stones and lay there quivering. Rindy dashed across the room, her small skirts flying, and grabbed up one of the terrible vicious things in either hand.

"Rindy!" I bellowed. "No!"

She stood shaking, tears pouring down her round cheeks, a Toy squeezed tight in either hand. Dark veins stood out almost black on her fair temples. "Break them, Daddy," she implored in a little thread of a voice. "Break them, *quick*. I can't hang on…"

Rakhal staggered to his feet like a drunken man and snatched one of the Toys, grinding it under his heel. He made a grab at the second, reeled and drew an anguished breath. He crumpled up, clutching at his belly where I'd butted him. The bird screamed like a living thing.

Breaking my paralysis of horror I leaped up, ran across the room, heedless of the searing pain along my side. I snatched the bird from Rindy and it screamed and shrilled and died as my foot crunched the tiny feathers. I stamped the still-moving thing into an amorphous mess and kept on stamping and smashing until it was only a heap of powder.

Rakhal finally managed to haul himself upright again. His face was so pale that the scars stood out like fresh burns.

"That was a foul blow, Race, but I—I know why you did it." He stopped and breathed for a minute. Then he muttered, "You…saved my life, you know. Did you know you were doing it, when you did it?"

Still breathing hard, I nodded. Done knowingly, it meant an end of blood-feud. However we had wronged each other, whatever the pledges. I spoke the words that confirmed it and ended it, finally and forever:

"There is a life between us. Let it stand for a death."

Miellyn was standing in the doorway, her hands pressed to her mouth, her eyes wide. She said shakily, "You're walking around with a knife in your ribs, you fool!"

Rakhal whirled and with a quick jerk he pulled the skean loose. It had simply been caught in my shirtcloak, in a fold of the rough cloth. He pulled it away, glanced at the red tip, then relaxed. "Not more than an inch deep," he said. Then, angrily, defending himself: "You did it yourself, you ape. I was trying to get rid of the knife when you jumped me."

But I knew that and he knew I knew it. He turned and scooped up Rindy, who was sobbing noisily. She dug her head into his shoulder and I made out her strangled words. "The other Toys hurt you when I was mad at you…" she sobbed, rubbing her fists against smeared cheeks. "I—I wasn't that mad at you. I wasn't that mad at anybody, not even…him."

Rakhal pressed his hand against his daughter's fleecy hair and said, looking at me over her head, "The Toys activate a child's subconscious resentments against his parents—I found out that much. That also means a child can control them for a few seconds. No adult can." A stranger would have seen no change in his expression, but I knew him, and saw.

"Juli said you threatened Rindy."

He chuckled and set the child on her feet. "What else could I say that would have scared Juli enough to send her running to you? Juli's proud, almost as proud as you are, you stiff-necked Son of the Ape." The insult did not sting me now.

"Come on, sit down and let's decide what to do, now we've finished up the old business." He looked remotely at Miellyn and said, "You must be Dallisa's sister? I don't suppose your talents include knowing how to make coffee?"

They didn't, but with Rindy's help Miellyn managed, and while they were out of the room Rakhal explained briefly. "Rindy has rudimentary ESP. I've never had it myself, but I could teach her something—not much—about how to use it. I've been on Evarin's track ever since that business of The Lisse.

"I'd have got it sooner, if you were still working with me, but I couldn't do anything as a Terran agent, and I had to be kicked out so thoroughly that the others wouldn't be afraid I was still working secretly for Terra. For a long time I was just chasing rumors, but when Rindy got big enough to look in the crystals of Nebran, I started making some progress.

"I was afraid to tell Juli; her best safety was the fact that she didn't know anything. She's always been a stranger in the Dry-towns." He paused, then said with honest self-evaluation, "Since I left the Secret Service I've been a stranger there myself."

I asked, "What about Dallisa?"

"Twins have some ESP to each other. I knew Miellyn had gone to the Toymaker. I tried to get Dallisa to find out where Miellyn had gone, learn more about it. Dallisa wouldn't risk it, but Kyral saw me with Dallisa and thought it was Miellyn. That put him on my tail, too, and I had to leave Shainsa. I was afraid of Kyral," he added soberly. "Afraid of what he'd do. I couldn't do anything without Rindy and I knew if I told Juli what I was doing, she'd take Rindy away into the Terran Zone, and I'd be as good as dead."

As he talked, I began to realize how vast a web Evarin and the underground organization of Nebran had spread for us. "Evarin was here today. What for?"

Rakhal laughed mirthlessly. "He's been trying to get us to kill each other off. That would get rid of us both. He wants to turn over Wolf to the nonhumans entirely, I think he's sincere enough, but"—he spread his hands helplessly—"I can't sit by and see it."

I asked point-blank, "Are you working for Terra? Or for the Dry-towns? Or any of the anti-Terran movements?"

"I'm working for *me*", he said with a shrug. "I don't think much of the Terran Empire, but one planet can't fight a galaxy. Race, I want just one thing. I want the Dry-towns and the rest of Wolf, to have a voice in their own government. Any planet which makes a substantial contribution to galactic science, by the laws of the Terran Empire, is automatically given the status of an independent commonwealth.

"If a man from the Dry-towns discovers something like a matter transmitter, Wolf gets dominion status. But Evarin and his gang want to keep it secret, keep it away from Terra, keep it locked up in places like Canarsa! Somebody has to get it away from them. And if I do it, I get a nice fat bonus, and an official position."

I believed that, where I would have suspected too much protestation of altruism. Rakhal tossed it aside.

"You've got Miellyn to take you through the transmitters. Go back to the Mastershrine, and tell Evarin that Race Cargill is dead. In the Trade City they think I'm Cargill, and I can get in and out as I choose—sorry if it caused you trouble, but it was the safest thing I could think of—and I'll 'vise Magnusson and have him send soldiers to guard the street-shrines. Evarin might try to escape through one of them."

I shook my head. "Terra hasn't enough men on all Wolf to cover the street-shrines in Charin alone. And I can't go back with Miellyn." I explained. Rakhal pursed his lips and whistled when I described the fight in the transmitter.

"You have all the luck, Cargill! I've never been near enough even to be sure how they work—and I'll bet you didn't begin to understand! We'll have to do it the hard way, then. It won't be the first time we've bulled our way through a tight place! We'll face Evarin in his own hideout! If Rindy's with us, we needn't worry."

I was willing to let him assume command, but I protested, "You'd take a child into that—that—"

"What else can we do? Rindy can control the Toys, and neither you nor I can do that, if Evarin should decide to throw his whole arsenal at us." He called Rindy and spoke softly to her. She looked from her father to me, and back again to her father, then smiled and stretched out her hand to me.

Before we ventured into the street, Rakhal scowled at the sprawled embroideries of Miellyn's robe. He said, "In those things you show up like a snowfall in Shainsa. If you go out in them, you could be mobbed. Hadn't you better get rid of them now?"

"I can't," she protested. "They're the keys to the transmitter!"

Rakhal looked at the conventionalized idols with curiosity, but said only, "Cover them up in the street, then. Rindy, find her something to put over her dress."

When we reached the street-shrine, Miellyn admonished: "Stand close together on the stones. I'm not sure we can all make the jump at once, but we'll have to try."

Rakhal picked up Rindy and hoisted her to his shoulder. Miellyn dropped the cloak she had draped over the pattern of the Nebran embroideries, and we crowded close together. The street swayed and vanished and I felt the now-familiar dip and swirl of blackness before the world straightened out again. Rindy was whimpering, dabbing smeary fists at her face. "Daddy, my nose is bleeding…"

Miellyn hastily bent and wiped the blood from the snubby nose. Rakhal gestured impatiently.

"The workroom. Wreck everything you see. Rindy, if anything starts to come at us, you stop it. Stop it quick. And"—he bent and took the little face between his hands—"*chiya*, remember they're not toys, no matter how pretty they are."

Her grave gray eyes blinked, and she nodded.

Rakhal flung open the door of the elves' workshop with a shout. The ringing of the anvils shattered into a thousand dissonances as I kicked over a workbench and half-finished Toys crashed in confusion to the floor.

The dwarfs scattered like rabbits before our assault of destruction. I smashed tools, filigree, jewels, stamping everything with my heavy boots. I shattered glass, caught up a hammer and smashed crystals. There was a wild exhilaration to it.

A tiny doll, proportioned like a woman, dashed toward me, shrilling in a supersonic shriek. I put my foot on her and ground the life out of her, and she screamed like a living woman as she came apart. Her blue eyes rolled from her head and lay on the floor watching me. I crushed the blue jewels under my heel.

Rakhal swung a tiny hound by the tail. Its head shattered into debris of almost-invisible gears and wheels. I caught up a chair and wrecked a glass cabinet of parts with it, swinging furiously. A berserk madness of smashing and breaking had laid hold on me.

I was drunk with crushing and shattering and ruining, when I heard Miellyn scream a warning and turned to see Evarin standing in the doorway. His green cat-eyes blazed with rage. Then he raised both hands in a sudden, sardonic gesture, and with a loping, inhuman glide, raced for the transmitter.

"Rindy," Rakhal panted, "can you block the transmitter?"

Instead Rindy shrieked. "We've got to get out! The roof is falling down! The house is going to fall down on us! The roof, look at the roof!"

I looked up, transfixed by horror. I saw a wide rift open, saw the skylight shatter and break, and daylight pouring through the cracking walls, Rakhal snatched Rindy up, protecting her from the falling debris with his head and shoulders. I grabbed Miellyn round the waist and we ran for the rift in the buckling wall.

We shoved through just before the roof caved in and the walls collapsed, and we found ourselves standing on a bare grassy hillside, looking down in shock and horror as below us, section after section of what had been apparently bare hill and rock caved in and collapsed into dusty rubble.

Miellyn screamed hoarsely. "Run. Run, hurry!"

I didn't understand, but I ran. I ran, my sides aching, blood streaming from the forgotten flesh-wound in my side. Miellyn raced beside me and Rakhal stumbled along, carrying Rindy.

Then the shock of a great explosion rocked the ground, hurling me down full length, Miellyn falling on top of me. Rakhal went down on his knees. Rindy was crying loudly. When I could see straight again, I looked down at the hillside.

There was nothing left of Evarin's hideaway or the Mastershrine of Nebran except a great, gaping hole, still oozing smoke and thick black dust. Miellyn said aloud, dazed, "So *that's* what he was going to do!"

It fitted the peculiar nonhuman logic of the Toymaker. He'd covered the traces.

"Destroyed!" Rakhal raged. "All destroyed! The workrooms, the science of the Toys, the matter transmitter—the minute we find it, it's destroyed!" He beat his fists furiously. "Our one chance to learn—"

"We were lucky to get out alive," said Miellyn quietly. "Where on the planet are we, I wonder?"

I looked down the hillside, and stared in amazement. Spread out on the hillside below us lay the Kharsa, topped by the white skyscraper of the HQ.

"I'll be damned," I said, "right here. We're home. Rakhal, you can go down and make your peace with the Terrans, and Juli. And you, Miellyn—" Before the others, I could not say what I was thinking, but I put my hand on her shoulder and kept it there. She smiled, shakily, with a hint of her old mischief. "I can't go into the Terran Zone looking like this, can I? Give me that comb again. Rakhal, give me your shirtcloak, my robes are torn."

"You vain, stupid female, worrying about a thing like that at a time like this!" Rakhal's look was like murder. I put my comb in her hand, then suddenly saw something in the symbols across her breasts. Before this I had seen only the conventionalized and intricate glyph of the Toad God. But now—

I reached out and ripped the cloth away.

"Cargill!" she protested angrily, crimsoning, covering her bare breasts with both hands. "Is this the place? And before a child, too!"

I hardly heard. "Look!" I exclaimed. "Rakhal, look at the symbols embroidered into the glyph of the God! You can read the old nonhuman glyphs. You did it in the city of The Lisse. Miellyn said they were the key to the transmitters! I'll bet the formula is written out there for anyone to read!

"Anyone, that is, who *can* read it! I can't, but I'll bet the formula equations for the transmitters are carved on every Toad God glyph on Wolf. Rakhal, it makes sense. There are two ways of hiding something. Either keep it locked away, or hide it right out in plain sight. Whoever bothers even to *look* at a conventionalized Toad God? There are so many *billions* of them…"

He bent his head over the embroideries, and when he looked up his face was flushed. "I believe—by the chains of Sharra, I believe you have it, Race! It may take years to work out the glyphs, but I'll do it, or die trying!" His scarred and hideous face looked almost handsome in exultation, and I grinned at him.

"If Juli leaves enough of you, once she finds out how you maneuvered her. Look, Rindy's fallen asleep on the grass there. Poor kid, we'd better get her down to her mother."

"Right." Rakhal thrust the precious embroidery into his shirtcloak, then cradled his sleeping daughter in his arms. I watched him with a curious emotion I could not identify. It seemed to pinpoint some great change, either in Rakhal or myself. It's not difficult to visualize one's sister with children, but there was something, some strange incongruity in the sight of Rakhal carrying the little girl, carefully tucking her up in a fold of his cloak to keep the sharp breeze off her face.

Miellyn was limping in her thin sandals, and she shivered. I asked, "Cold?"

"No, but—I don't believe Evarin is dead, I'm afraid he got away."

For a minute the thought dimmed the luster of the morning. Then I shrugged. "He's probably buried in that big hole up there." But I knew I would never be sure.

We walked abreast, my arm around the weary, stumbling woman, and Rakhal said softly at last, "Like old times."

It wasn't old times, I knew. He would know it too, once his exultation sobered. I had outgrown my love for intrigue, and I had the feeling this was Rakhal's last adventure. It was going to take him, as he said, years to work out the equations for the transmitter. And I had a feeling my own solid, ordinary desk was going to look good to me in the morning.

But I knew now that I'd never run away from Wolf again. It was my own beloved sun that was rising. My sister was waiting for me down below, and I was bringing back her child. My best friend was walking at my side. What more could a man want?

If the memory of dark, poison-berry eyes was to haunt me in nightmares, they did not come into the waking world. I looked at Miellyn, took her slender unmanacled hand in mine, and smiled as we walked through the gates of the city. Now, after all my years on Wolf, I understood the desire to keep their women under lock and key that was its ancient custom. I vowed to myself as we went that I should waste no time finding a fetter shop and having forged therein the perfect steel chains that should bind my love's wrists to my key forever.

THE END

If you've enjoyed this book, you will not want to miss these terrific titles…

ARMCHAIR SCI-FI & HORROR DOUBLE NOVELS, $12.95 each

D-101   **THE CONQUEST OF THE PLANETS** by John W. Campbell
THE MAN WHO ANNEXED THE MOON by Bob Olsen

D-102   **WEAPON FROM THE STARS** by Rog Phillips
THE EARTH WAR by Mack Reynolds

D-103   **THE ALIEN INTELLIGENCE** by Jack Williamson
INTO THE FOURTH DIMENSION by Ray Cummings

D-104   **THE CRYSTAL PLANETOIDS** by Stanton A. Coblentz
SURVIVORS FROM 9,000 B. C. by Robert Moore Williams

D-105   **THE TIME PROJECTOR** by David H. Keller, M.D. and David Lasser
STRANGE COMPULSION by Philip Jose Farmer

D-106   **WHOM THE GODS WOULD SLAY** by Paul W. Fairman
MEN IN THE WALLS by William Tenn

D-107   **LOCKED WORLDS** by Edmond Hamilton
THE LAND THAT TIME FORGOT by Edgar Rice Burroughs

D-108   **STAY OUT OF SPACE** by Dwight V. Swain
REBELS OF THE RED PLANET by Charles L. Fontenay

D-109   **THE METAMORPHS** by S. J. Byrne
MICROCOSMIC BUCCANEERS by Harl Vincent

D-110   **YOU CAN'T ESCAPE FROM MARS** by E. K. Jarvis
THE MAN WITH FIVE LIVES by David V. Reed

ARMCHAIR SCIENCE FICTION CLASSICS, $12.95 each

C-34   **30 DAY WONDER**
by Richard Wilson

C-35   **G.O.G. 666**
by John Taine

C-36   **RALPH 124C 41+**
by Hugo Gernsback

ARMCHAIR SCI-FI & HORROR GEMS SERIES, $12.95 each

G-11   **SCIENCE FICTION GEMS, Vol. Six**
Edmond Hamilton and others

G-12   **HORROR GEMS, Vol. Six**
H. P. Lovecraft and others

If you've enjoyed this book, you will not want to miss these terrific titles…

ARMCHAIR SCI-FI & HORROR DOUBLE NOVELS, $12.95 each

D-111 **THE MOON ERA** by Jack Williamson
REVENGE OF THE ROBOTS by Howard Browne

D-112 **SON OF THE BLACK CHALICE** by Milton Lesser
SENTRY OF THE SKY by Evelyn E. Smith

D-113 **OUTPOST ON THE MOON** by Joslyn Maxwell
POTENTIAL ZERO by S. J. Byrne

D-114 **OUTPOST INFINITY** by Raymond F. Jones
THE WHITE INVADERS by Ray Cummings

D-115 **TIME TRAP** by Rog Phillips
THE COSMIC DESTROYER by Alexander Blade

D-116 **THE OTHER SIDE OF THE MOON** by Edmond Hamilton
SECRET INVASION by Walter Kubilius

D-117 **DANGER MOON** by Frederik Pohl
THE HIDDEN UNIVERSE by Ralph Milne Farley

D-118 **THE WAILING ASTEROID** by Murray Leinster
THE WORLD THAT COULDN'T BE by Clifford D. Simak

D-119 **THE WHISPERING GORILLA** by Don Wilcox
RETURN OF THE WHISPERING GORILLA by David V. Reed

D-120 **SPECIAL EFFECT** by J. F. Bone
WARLORD OF KOR by Terry Carr

ARMCHAIR SCIENCE FICTION CLASSICS, $12.95 each

C-37 **THE GREEN MAN RETURNS**
by Harold M. Sherman

C-38 **THE SHAVER MYSTERY, Book Five**
by Richard S, Shaver

C-39 **MARS CHILD**
by Cyril Judd

ARMCHAIR MASTERS OF SCIENCE FICTION SERIES, $16.95 each

MS-9 **MASTERS OF SCIENCE FICTION AND FANTASY, Vol. Nine**
Poul Anderson, "The Star Beast" and other tales

MS-10 **MASTERS OF SCIENCE FICTION, Vol. Ten**
Robert Moore Williams, "Time Tolls for Toro" and other tales

If you've enjoyed this book, you will not want to miss these terrific titles…

ARMCHAIR MYSTERY & SCIENCE FICTION CLASSICS
$12.95 each

C-40   **MODEL FOR MURDER**
by Stephen Marlowe

C-41   **PRELUDE TO MURDER**
by Sterling Noel

C-42   **DEAD WEIGHT**
by Frank Kane

C-43   **A DAME CALLED MURDER**
by Milton Ozaki

C-44   **THE GREATEST ADVENTURE**
by John Taine

C-45   **THE EXILE OF TIME**
by Ray Cummings

C-46   **STORM OVER WARLOCK**
by Andre Norton

C-47   **MAN OF MANY MINDS**
by E. Everett Evans

C-48   **THE GODS OF MARS**
by Edgar Rice Burroughs

C-49   **BRIGANDS OF THE MOON**
by Ray Cummings

C-50   **SPACE HOUNDS OF IPC**
by E. E. "Doc" Smith

C-51   **THE LANI PEOPLE**
by J. F. Bone

C-52   **THE MOON POOL**
by A. Merritt

C-53   **IN THE DAYS OF THE COMET**
by H. G. Wells

C-54   **TRIPLANETARY**
E. E. Doc Smith